WATCHING
OVER YOU

Praise for *Watching Over You*

'...*ng Over You* is a tense, erotic thriller with one of the most ...ing antagonists I've ever read. The worst terrors are always th... ...at hide closest to home and Charley's experiences – ...ing her path alone – will be familiar to many. She is as ...le as any of us, stronger than she realises, and yet still in ...ger. Charley is my new best friend, and Ella a terrifying villa... outwardly ordinary and utterly unhinged. *Watching Over You* is the book you'll wish you could read from behind a cushion.'
—Eli...beth Haynes, author of *Into the Darkest Corner*.

Mel Sherratt
WATCHING OVER YOU

 THOMAS & MERCER

This is a work of fiction. Names, characters, organizations, places, events, and incidents are either products of the author's imagination or are used fictitiously.

Text copyright © 2014 Mel Sherratt
All rights reserved.

Published by Thomas & Mercer, Seattle

www.apub.com

Amazon, the Amazon logo, and Thomas & Mercer are trademarks of Amazon .com, Inc., or its affiliates.

ISBN-13: 9781477819722
ISBN-10: 147781972X

Cover design by The Book Designers

Library of Congress Control Number: 2013920517

Printed in the United States of America

To Alison, for being the best friend a girl could wish for – and nothing like Ella Patrick.

Prologue

Charley Belington stood by the side of the road, the grass verge underneath her bare feet soggy, almost squishy between her toes. Rain lashed down around her. Partly sheltered by the boughs of the oak tree, she was still soaked through, her pyjamas clinging to the goose-bumps that covered most of her skin.

It was the early hours of a Saturday. This had to be a dream – no, a nightmare. She was going to wake up one of these mornings and find that the last twelve months hadn't happened. It couldn't be true.

Raindrops dripped from her cheeks – or were they tears? She really couldn't tell anymore. Running a tongue across her upper lip, she tasted salt. But then again, there were always tears as she relived every moment.

She could see the car, its front crumpled beyond recognition. She could see Dan in the passenger seat, a gash above his right eye the only visual indication that he'd been involved in a crash. She could see the paramedics bustling around fighting to keep him alive, the fireman struggling to get him out of the vehicle; it was embedded so far into the tree. She could hear the shrill sound of the cutters as the roof came off to allow them access, the noise of an army of people trying to help. The flashing of emergency lights in the still of the night.

All these were scenes that she'd conjured up over the days, the weeks, the months since his death, because she hadn't been with Dan during his last moments. But she did know that it wasn't the accident that had killed him; he'd been on his way home from work when he'd suffered a heart attack. Only two streets away when he'd smashed into the tree head on. Just like that, she'd lost him. *Two streets away from home.* And then she'd lost their baby. Consumed by sorrow, raw with pain, she'd miscarried two weeks later. She pressed a hand to her stomach now, almost feeling the swell of her bump. A girl: she'd been due the middle of November. They were going to call her Poppy.

It wasn't the first time she'd found herself under the tree. Charley had visited the same spot quite often over the past year. Each time the grief came rushing back as if it were yesterday. Dan had been thirty-seven when he'd been taken away from her. And at thirty-four, Charley's life had paused. She was stuck, powerless to move on, unable to deal with the loss of her husband and daughter in less than a fortnight.

Yet finding herself here again, she knew what she had to do. She *had* to move on; find a new home, a smaller place than the one she'd shared with Dan. A flat maybe, not too far away, where she didn't see him in every room, or listen out for him as she went to bed. Somewhere in The Potteries; she didn't want to leave her job. Or Stoke-on-Trent. It wasn't a big city in England but she did love it, having lived there all her life.

Neither did she want to be far from the place where Dan was buried. But there were too many memories in the house. Coming home to them had been comforting at first. Now they stopped her from healing.

Charley dropped to her knees, ignoring the wetness seeping through the thin material of her pyjama bottoms. Shoulders shaking as she sobbed uncontrollably, she held a hand out in front, wanting to feel the bark, to connect with the last place Dan had been alive. Like the tree with its root, Dan had grounded her, but she didn't want to touch it either because it reminded her of what she'd lost.

How the hell was she going to live her life without him?

Chapter One

When I was seven, I remember all being well in my world. I had my mum and my dad and my baby sister. I remember day trips to Rhyl and Llandudno, seaside resorts in Wales, to play on the beach. I remember going to Alton Towers, near to where we lived, and running around the gardens, glad I was too short to go on some of the rides because they looked so scary.

I remember happy days at school, being cared for by a neighbour afterwards until Mum came to pick me and my sister up when she'd finished work. I remember fish fingers and oven chips with lots of tomato sauce. I remember cuddling up on the settee while we watched Animal Magic *if Dad was home from work in time – or falling asleep to* Cagney and Lacey *if he wasn't.*

I was such a happy child when I was seven.

When I was nine, my whole world changed as you were all taken away from me.

And that was when my life became all. Fucked. Up.

My mum and dad and little sister were killed in a car accident. I was the only one who survived. I didn't come out without a scratch, mind you. My right leg was broken, along with my right thumb and two of my ribs. I had to have pins put in my leg to hold it together but it's fine now.

How do you get over losing your family at such a young age? Answer: you don't. I was so lonely. We didn't have an extended family. I had no one to care for me. Why had I been left behind? Why didn't I die too? It wasn't fair.

I was in the children's ward for ages afterwards. I had a nurse called Angela and she looked after me all the time. I had an injury to my head, you see. I know, I know. If you're reading this, you're going to say this is what caused me to be how I am. It could have been the cause; it could have been the start – who knows, it could have happened without the head injury. It could have been inside me anyway. I could just be evil.

What makes someone evil? Something has to set it off. The accident has always been called my trigger point, in all the therapy groups I've been part of, and believe me, there have been a lot. Every professional said it made me change but I reckon not. I reckon I was an evil bitch on a path to destruction. Maybe I would have killed my parents and my sister in a fit of frenzy one night. Paths in lives are not destiny; they lead you to where you choose to go. Dreams, goals, achieving or not – that's all in the mind, right? So if I'm a bad one to start with, then nothing will make me better.

If my family hadn't been killed in the car crash, does that mean I would have turned out right, married a rich and gorgeous man, become a wonderful wife and a mother to two or three kids? Was that the path I should have taken until some mindless fucker rammed our car off the road? Who knows? WHO FUCKING KNOWS?

Ella Patrick pushed her long auburn hair away from her face as she tried to gaze seductively at the man sitting next to her. Having drunk enough for three women and far more than her small frame could manage, she hoped tonight wasn't about to turn into a disaster. Earlier she'd tried to pick up another fella but he'd refused her advances. And he'd only bought her the one drink, the tight bastard.

The man by her side was giving off 'stay away' vibes too. They were polite ones – but she would have him. He wouldn't be able to resist her. And if he did, she could always pick a fight with someone instead, get rid of her aggression another way.

She'd been in Chicago Rock in the city centre since nine thirty and it was now close to midnight. It was Friday and the place was heaving. The air was charged, the mood lively. Groups of women chattered loudly, swishy limp hair, panda eyes and remains of lipstick around the outside of their lips. Groups of men with splashes of beer down their shirts, red faces and sweat patches. Couples getting to know each other in every direction she looked.

Perched precariously on a high stool at the bar, Ella hitched her black dress up her thigh a little bit further, a platform shoe dangling from the toes of her right foot. She swirled a finger round the rim of her glass, then popped it into her mouth to suck it dry. The man glanced at her, then away just as quickly.

'Where is it you said you came from?' she asked, trying to remember their earlier conversation.

'Manchester,' he replied in a broad accent.

'So what are you doing in Stoke? Business or pleasure?'

'Coming to Stoke can hardly be called a pleasure.'

She opened her mouth to speak out.

'I'm joking,' he explained. 'I like the city – it has a good vibe to it.'

'It's a great place to live. We have,' Ella frowned. 'We have ... what do we have? Ah, a couple of football teams. We have Mr Robbie Williams of Take That fame. We have a pottery industry with some good names – Wedgwood, Moorcroft. Not so many as in the good old days but we're still making the stuff and selling it proudly. And, well, we do okay for a small city in the Midlands.'

'I suppose. It definitely seems to be up and coming.'

Ella snorted. 'I wish you were up and coming, if you catch my drift.' She placed a hand on his leg but he moved it away. 'Another drink, then?' She waved to get the attention of the bar man.

'No thanks.'

Before she could protest, a woman behind her jostled to get to the bar. Ella turned to glare at her, not at all intimidated with the way she would have towered over her had she been standing up. She was blonde, curvy to Ella's stick-thin appearance. Right now, her chest was level with Ella's mouth.

Ella smiled, licked her lips – not bad. But she turned back to the man at her side. She had more important things on her mind. She didn't want a woman tonight. She wanted *him* to screw her.

'So you're not for up and coming then?' she said.

'I don't think so.'

Ella leaned nearer to him. 'I think you're vey – vey sexy,' she slurred, reaching forward again to tap him lightly on his leg but missing in the process. He caught her arm before she slid off the stool and onto the floor.

She laughed loudly. A few heads turned her way. She tried to stop, which made her laugh even more.

'You are gorgeous,' she tried again. 'Are you sure you don't want to fuck?'

He threw her a murderous look before knocking back his drink.

'Don't you want to talk anymore?' She smiled in what she thought would be a flirtatious manner. 'Or is talking too much? Would you prefer action to talking? I like action.'

'I have to go.'

'But it's early yet!'

'It's not the time I want to leave behind.'

'What?' Ella had only heard him mutter. As he stood up, she jumped down from her stool like a clumsy five-year-old. Steadying herself on her heels, she wrapped her arms around his neck and pouted. 'You can take me back to your hotel. No one will ever find out.'

He pulled down her arms, not saying a word.

'But surely you'd like a bit of fun?'

'You don't even know my name.'

'I do!' Ella thought back to their conversation. Dave? Terry? Or was it … 'Paul!'

'My name is *not* Paul.' He moved her gently back to sitting on the stool. 'Have a good night but leave me be.'

Ella watched as he walked away; he had a nice butt, filling out the jeans he wore perfectly. And a crisp white shirt that she wanted to rip from his back, feel his skin next to hers. She pulled her watch nearer to her face. It was just after twelve. There was still time to pick up someone else; some sad soul would always shag her, even if she hadn't been so lucky yet. But she wanted *him*. No one rejected her!

A little too late, she realised he was leaving. She got down from her seat and followed him quickly.

'Wait!'

By the time she got to the door, he was a good way along Foundry Street. It had been one of the hottest days of August, hitting a temperature of 28 degrees. A rainstorm earlier had disappeared and, although there was still drizzle in the air, it was undoubtedly hot. Maybe that was why she felt so horny: removing clothes always made her feel sexy.

Dodging the people and the traffic in the narrow street, she ran down the pavement towards him. 'Paul, or whatever your name is, stop!'

He kept on walking but, reaching him at last, Ella grabbed his arm.

'Hey, don't walk off while I'm –'

He turned abruptly. 'What is wrong with you?' he hissed. 'Can't I make it any clearer? I'm not interested!'

'But I thought –'

'No. You saw me, you interrupted me, and now you have me feeling pissed off because I wanted to be alone.'

'No one wants to be alone.' Slurring again, Ella pulled him close, seeing an opportunity to hug him as another couple drawing near would need to get past on the pavement. 'Come home with me instead and you can leave in the morning.'

'What?'

She pressed a finger first to her own lips, and then to his. 'I won't tell anyone. It will be our little secret.' She cackled.

'You're unbelievable.'

In desperation, she grabbed his arm and pointed to a narrow alleyway. 'We could go down there if you fancy a quickie?'

'Go home.'

'You can't tell me what to do.'

'I don't want you!' He pushed her away. 'Can't you see that?'

Ella stared at him for a moment, not quite believing his words. Who the fuck was he to turn her down? If she looked closer, she might see more of a throw-back than a catch. He wasn't anything special, just someone to scratch an itch.

She still wanted him.

But, seeing the repulsion in his eyes, she slapped him across the face. 'How dare you!' she cried.

His arms flailed as he tried to stop her from hitting him again. 'Get off me,' she screamed.

'Will you be quiet!' Heads turned their way. A taxi beeped a horn.

'No, I will not be fucking quiet!'

He pushed her again. Stumbling backwards, she lost her balance at the kerb and fell down into a puddle.

'That's where you belong – in the gutter,' he sneered. 'People like you give decent women a bad reputation. Now, piss off and leave me alone!'

'You piss off, you bastard,' Ella shouted after him, feeling the water soaking her dress. Another couple walking past gave her a wide berth. 'What are you fucking staring at?' she snapped. 'Haven't you seen a woman on all fours before?'

As people made their way home from the city centre, Ella sat and cried. Another evening ending in disaster. Why was it so hard to get attention? He didn't want her ... Paul – or whatever his name was. No one wanted her. Why?

'What's wrong with me?' she screamed. She got up, supporting herself on the wall of a nearby building, and staggered down the street. 'What's fucking wrong with *me*?'

Chapter Two

Finding herself at the scene of her husband's fatal accident again had prompted Charley to think about moving. But it had taken another six months before she'd plucked up the courage to sell the house. Mixed reactions from family and friends had kept her undecided. Her parents wanted her to stay where she lived in Werrington, saying the property market was too much of a gamble right now. Being an only child meant she hadn't any siblings to chat to, but friends told Charley to move, start afresh, new pastures and all that. Well, what friends she had left. Since Dan's death, most of the couples they'd gone out with on a regular basis had filtered away. Things were never the same when one part of a team disappeared, through death or break-up. It hadn't helped when she'd gone into her shell, refusing invitations to go out with them. Being around couples had been too much of a reminder that someone was missing. In the end, after umpteen rejections, they'd stopped ringing.

But one weekend, on impulse, she'd put the house on the market. A couple and their young daughter had come to view it during the next week and Charley had agreed to a sale quicker than she had anticipated. Finding herself with nowhere to go, rather than rush into things, she decided to find a temporary place to tide her over. Seeing a flat for rent in Trentham, over in the south of the city, she decided to take a look.

Thirty-seven Warwick Avenue was situated in a quiet cul-de-sac full of pre-war semi-detached properties and town houses. The respectable, leafy avenue had the air of belonging in a wealthier suburb rather than Stoke-on-Trent. Less than a mile from the site of the former Hem Heath colliery, it had a mixture of old and new. Mature rambling houses, some with three floors; old sash windows, some replaced, some original. Dotted amongst them, a few newly built semi-detached properties.

Charley parked up at the end of the cul-de-sac, spotting two large bay windows to the right of the entrance of number thirty-seven and two more directly above. She looked up, trying to guess how many flats the property had been split into. She reckoned on four: two up and two down. If that was the case, they wouldn't be very big but they would be big enough for her.

The house was set at the far end of a block of four. There were no properties at the head of the road and it opened onto a large playing field. Charley could see into one of the rooms downstairs as she made her way up six white-washed stone steps to the Wedgwood-blue entrance door. The paintwork looked fresh and inviting – pale walls and a light-polished wooden floor. But there was no furniture; perhaps this was the one she'd come to view.

She rang the doorbell and waited, glancing up the avenue. Even though this was a short-term lease, the flat still needed to be satisfactory. From first impressions, it seemed acceptable. Cars parked on the road were mostly new; orderly gardens on either side, hedges on the whole trimmed and neat.

Pride, she thought. People took pride living here. She liked that.

The door opened behind her and Charley turned to see a young woman, mid-thirties at a guess. She was of small build, dramatically thin with long auburn hair and steely blue eyes – friendly eyes, Charley noted. Her smile was warm too, lips with a dash of pink rose lipstick, but her skin was ashen, a cluster of spots around her chin. She wore cropped black trousers and a long-sleeved blue shirt with a granddad collar. Barefoot, showing painted red toenails.

'Hi, there. You must be Charley.' The woman held the door open. 'Come on in.'

She was shown into a large entrance, which she assumed had originally been a grand hallway in one house. Now the doorway to what she thought could have been the sitting room had a front door lock on it, with the letter A to its left. As she stepped in farther, Charley glanced upstairs to see a door at the top with the letter B on it. Great – it looked as if there were only two flats after all.

She caught a whiff of artificial air freshener as she glanced around the clean and tidy hallway. The flooring was a mosaic effect, multi-coloured browns, whites and blues, the room edged by a large wooden skirting board. Charley was sure the tiles were original Minton, made there in the Potteries, and wondered if they were as old as the house.

'Yes,' said Ella.

Charley looked up. 'Sorry?'

'Yes, they're original. There were some in the Palace of Westminster until recently, you know. They'd been there since it was rebuilt after the Great Fire of London. These were here when I bought the property and they have never, to my knowledge, been covered up. There was an old couple in here before me. Died within a few weeks of each other – true love. Come on, I'll show you the flat.'

Charley followed Ella down the side of the stairs and along a small corridor to the door with the letter A on it, waited while it was unlocked.

'This is it.' Ella stood to one side again so that Charley could go in first.

She stepped through into a long hallway. A door to her right took her into a bright mass of space, the room she'd seen on her way in.

Light flooded in through the bay windows, almost side by side, and across polished floorboards, bouncing off walls painted a shade of cream. An Adams-style fireplace with a coal fire effect heater took over a chimney breast. Despite the empty room – Charley knew the flat came unfurnished – she could already picture herself curled up on her settee pushed up against the wall there, with a glass of wine and a book to hand.

In a line to the back of the property was first a kitchen, then a bedroom with a walk-in closet and a small bathroom. All the rooms were bright and airy; all the fittings looked untouched.

'Will I be the first tenant?' she asked as the smell of fresh paint hit her nostrils in every room.

'Oh, no,' said Ella. 'I decided to spruce the place up a bit. It does have only the one bedroom, though. Are you moving in on your own?'

'Yes.' Charley didn't offer anything more than that and she was thankful that Ella didn't ask. She wasn't sure she'd be able to hold back the tears. It was great to think of a new beginning but letting go of her past would take a lot longer than putting everything away into boxes.

Ella showed her into the bedroom, a decent-sized double with French doors that led to a tiny flagged area. She pointed out to the garden.

'The fence around the edge separates your space from mine. I can use my back door or the entry at the side of the property to get to it, but you're welcome to use my garden area if you wish. It gives you the best of both. We get the sun at the front in the morning and around here for most of the afternoon. It's great for catching a ray or two.

'And that's it,' said Ella as they moved back into the front room again. 'What do you think?'

'It's lovely,' said Charley, feeling the warmth of the house. What she had seen had been inviting and seemed a good place to settle. 'And do you have any problems with the open area at the side?'

'Not really. Sometimes kids play footie on there but it's big enough to take it.'

'No loiterers?'

'No, but that might be because we also have our own resident Neighbourhood Watch.' Ella pointed upwards to the property directly facing them. Another town house. It, too, was at the end of a block of four.

Charley followed her gaze to see a woman in an upstairs window. She seemed to be sitting down by the way she filled the bottom half of the window only. From what Charley could make out – a shot of grey hair and hunched shoulders – she assumed she was elderly.

'That's Jean; she's housebound, poor thing.' Ella waved to her. 'I only know her name because I hear the girl who comes to look after her shouting goodbye when she leaves. I've been here near on six months and I've never seen her, apart from in that window. I reckon she knows everything that goes on. Thinks we can't see her behind those blinds, though.'

'You mean she spies on you?' Charley baulked.

'Yeah, I suppose she does.' Ella frowned. 'I hadn't thought of it that way. She just seems to always be in the window. I'm sure she doesn't watch us, more gazes out at the world. She lives alone. It seems all she has left in her life. But you'll get used to her if you take the flat.'

'And no one minds?'

Ella shrugged. 'Why should they? And we're the last houses in the avenue so she can't see that much.'

Charley looked up to the window, just as the woman waved back at Ella. She found herself waving too. It would be rude not to, she supposed. Even so, she wasn't sure she wanted a neighbour seeing her every move. It seemed a little creepy.

But, as she turned back to the room and saw the sun flooding in, filling it with warmth that she knew she could settle into, she realised that, for the first time in ages, she felt relaxed walking into somewhere. It was important that she felt comfortable; she spent a lot of time at home. Her job wasn't too anti-social, hours-wise, even though she often took paperwork home, so mostly her nights were free. Maybe, if she positioned her furniture as she'd imagined when she'd first seen the room, she could spend a fair bit of time sitting in the bay window to the right, gazing down the avenue. Pretty much like Jean, she suspected.

She turned to Ella and nodded. 'I'll take it.'

'Really?' Ella grinned. 'That's great news.'

Charley smiled shyly. 'It's kind of a new beginning for me.'

'That's settled then. I'm sure we'll get along like a house on fire.'

Looking down from her upstairs window, Jean Cooper was glad to see the new woman waving back alongside her neighbour, Ella. She'd watched her approach and go into the house; clocked her arriving in her car first; written down the make, model, and registration number in her notebook. A white Ford, if her eyesight served her well, which, even with age, it usually did – although she had recently sent off for some new binoculars, lighter, more compact.

The car had a fairly new registration plate, showing Jean that the woman had money, or an ability to get money if it was on tick. She liked people to provide for themselves if they lived in Warwick Avenue; she hated scroungers who milked the system. There were plenty of them dotted around the city – lots in every city, no doubt.

Jean prided herself on having been a hard worker. Apart from working limited hours as she had raised her two sons, she'd been a full-time care assistant until retiring at the age of sixty. Even then, eight years ago, people had been more willing to work. She couldn't understand for the life of her the layabouts of today.

Tom, the tabby cat who had made his home with her some years ago, stirred at the bottom of her bed. She smiled at him, envious as he stretched out supple limbs. Jean wished she had half of Tom's grace; it wasn't easy growing old with osteoporosis but she was determined to stay in Warwick Avenue for as long as she could. She liked it here. They were all ordinary people, the slightest thing making one or the other spin out of control, their worlds crashing down in no end of different ways, good or bad.

She picked up her binoculars and looked down once more. The women had moved from the window so there was nothing more for her to see.

She had to admit to being surprised when her home help, young Ruby, told her she'd seen an advertisement in the newsagent's window. The last person had left Ella's house in such a hurry a few months ago. She'd been a woman too, although slightly younger, early twenties Jean reckoned, and had stayed for three weeks and two days before moving out as quickly as she had moved in. Jean had never found out why but she had her suspicions.

It was a few minutes before she saw them come into view again. Jean leaned forward a little. She was a beauty, the new woman, quite tall and thin, no fat on her to talk about; medium build with dark brown hair. From what she could see, her clothes looked clean and presentable. Jean remembered a time when she'd been good-looking too. She'd also had dark hair that fell below her shoulders, not the wiry-grey mess she'd been left with after her menopause. But her eyes were her best asset, closely followed by her hearing – she could hear a lot of what went on in Warwick Avenue.

Living there since she'd been married, Jean knew most of the neighbours in the houses near to her. She knew that Mr Reynolds from number thirty-three had been thrown out by his wife because he'd been 'getting his end away with that ugly floozy.' She knew before the house became empty that Mr and Mrs Morrison from number twenty-eight were doing a moonlight flit. Then there had been all the rigmarole over Diane and Terry Gregson's teenage son as he'd been caught in a stolen car, which had brought the police straight to their door and netted Matthew Gregson a custodial sentence in a youth detention centre.

They were all listed down in her notebooks. She glanced over at the pile. There were forty-eight altogether; she had begun writing things down when she'd retired and filled one every two months. Opening a new notebook was like starting at the beginning of a novel. Jean loved running a hand over the first page, anticipation of what she would write exciting her. And if there was nothing to see, she would switch to her laptop and search the internet for a while – with one eye on the avenue, of course.

With everything quiet, Jean made a note of all she could see. Then she picked up a new ball of wool and removed the paper wrapping around its middle. She'd decided to knit herself a cardigan. Snazzy purple, she smiled – might as well do something useful to while away the time.

As she started on the first row, she wondered whether Ella would be able to hide her drunken episodes from the new woman or if this tenant would leave too. They'd been regular occurrences since Ella had moved in six months ago. Jean often wondered where she'd been to when she came home in that state. She hadn't seen her with a proper boyfriend since she'd moved in, but she had seen her bring home lots of men, just for the one night. If she looked back through her notebooks, she could count how many. If she was having trouble sleeping, she could also tell you what time they left, whether that night or the next morning. But she did know without looking how many of them returned: none.

Jean wasn't quite sure if she pitied her neighbour or not, wasn't sure if she should. She'd seen her living a double life and had given up second-guessing who the real Ella was a long time ago. You never really knew people, did you? There was good and bad in everyone, Jean did know that, and terrible things put places on maps, like it or not.

Still, she was good at keeping secrets. She'd found out the hard way there was no point in telling the truth.

Chapter Three

At eight thirty that evening, Ella grabbed her handbag and almost bounced down the front steps to the pavement and into a waiting taxi. She slid into the back seat and closed the door.

'Rendezvous, Marsh Street,' she told him.

They set off for the city centre, and she gazed idly out of the car window as they drove down Trentham Road. She ran a finger up and down her leg from her knee to the hem of her short skirt. In anticipation, her hand moved to the neckline of her sheer blouse, fingertips running over the naked area of her chest. She couldn't wait to get into Hanley now. It had taken her a few hours to control her anger today but, God, she needed to be screwed.

She turned slightly to see the driver studying her through his rear-view mirror. Not taking her heavily made-up eyes from his, she ran her tongue suggestively over red-coated lips, fingers trailing across her skin. While he adjusted the mirror to get a better view, she moved her hand down inside her blouse, splaying her fingers and rubbing the palm of her hand back and forth across her nipple. Already she could feel it erect, sense the heat building up between her legs. The driver crunched his gears and she laughed silently before looking away. Who was she to give a free show? And besides, she was saving herself. It was her night tonight.

Finding the website *One Night Only* four months ago had been ecstasy for Ella. The danger of a one-night stand didn't bother

her – no one could abuse her more than she'd been abused before – but here she pulled the strings. If she wanted rough sex, she had rough sex. If she wanted to be dominated, she would be. If she wanted to be an out-of-control bitch, that was fine too. One thing was certain – after the disaster of last week's attempts in Chicago Rock where she'd gone home alone and horny, if she didn't find a release tonight, she'd crack and that wouldn't be good for her. She needed to rid herself of all the tension building up inside.

Tonight was the third time she'd used *One Night Only* that month. The first had been with a man; the second with a woman. This time it was with Alex, with no profile picture, so who knew? Not that she minded either way as long as she got what she wanted.

Minutes later they were heading towards Hanley, down Victoria Road. Ella's senses heightened and she crossed her legs to keep the feeling at bay. Erotic thoughts ran through her mind – images of men and women, women and women, groups, all with legs entwined, hands and mouths everywhere.

She found her mind wandering back to meeting Charley the week before. God, she was hot and so, so attractive, with her glossy dark hair and tall, thin physique. Her tanned legs had looked fantastic, high heels adding to their magnetism, making Ella want to reach out and touch. But she wouldn't do anything yet. She would bide her time.

One day she would have her – or rather, one day Cassandra would have her. Cassandra was the name she used for the website. But for the foreseeable future, Charley would get to know Ella. Maybe that was all she'd get; she'd have to figure her out first. And if she wasn't for turning, then she would find someone else.

Or maybe she could turn her, make her into a personal challenge.

The taxi driver pulled up outside Rendezvous. He turned his shoulder and peered at her, smiling lasciviously. Ella bristled. Did he really think she would stoop that low, the stupid prick? And he reeked too. The taxi smelt similar – she'd put a bet on it being his stale body odour. She paid her fare quickly; there was no way she'd be leaving him a tip.

As she entered the bar, excitement fizzed up inside her again as she speculated what Alex would look like. She really wanted a man. She wanted to be screwed hard tonight.

The room was half wooden panels, half floral wallpaper, a modern take on a gentleman's club, with a couple of booths and round stout stools at rectangular tables. It was busy for a mid-week evening, about two thirds of the tables to her right occupied with people socialising and a number of men standing around the bar area. Ella checked her watch. She was fifteen minutes late. Date or not, she didn't give a stuff about keeping anyone waiting; that way he or she would be eager to get going. And if she didn't like the look of her date, she would screw and go as quickly as possible.

She glanced around the room, delighting in all the eyes drawn to her as she waited to be picked up. She knew she looked good, dressed in a tight purple skirt that finished way above her knee, the cream sheer blouse showing the outline of her bra. Her hair was piled on her head in a messy but sexy manner, her skin tanned too from the unusually sunny weather they'd experienced for the past ten days.

A man at the back of the room waved for her attention. Keeping a smile in check, she walked over to him, putting on her own personal show as her hips swayed. High heels showed off bare legs to their maximum – it wasn't the only thing bare that night. Ella tingled yet again in anticipation of what was to come.

'Cassandra,' he greeted her.

She nodded and he stood up, kissing her briefly on the cheek. She felt the slight stubble on his chin, breathed in the scent of him, masculine tones of wood and jasmine intermingled with the wild fragrances of his sex that she hoped to taste and smell soon. His eyes never left hers as she blatantly gave him the once-over. Short, sharp hair style, dark skin, pricey shirt above designer jeans, expensive-looking watch – and those blue eyes, the most passionate she'd seen in a long time. She was going to enjoy this one.

She slid into the booth next to him.

'Do you come here often?' he asked.

'I come,' she said briskly. 'That's all you need to know.' She gave him a polite smile, realising there wouldn't be any requirements for small talk, either. One of the reasons she'd joined *One Night Only* was for anonymity. Ella didn't want to answer any questions about herself, nor did she want to ask any questions of her date. The less personal the conversation the better. Actually, Ella mused, the less *conversation* the better. It kept everything about the sex.

Wine was ordered and as they waited for it to arrive, almost immediately she felt his hand underneath the table, fingertips circling higher and higher, moving up under her skirt. She moaned slightly, opening her legs a little further as he moved aside her lace thong. While the waiter poured the wine, Ella tried not to gasp as Alex's fingers pushed into her, his thumb kneading her most sensitive point. She felt every nerve respond in her body, trying to keep in the urge to groan at the pleasure he was causing. They stared at each other; it made everything all the more erotic.

Ella cursed loudly. This wasn't going to plan. She felt like being in control tonight, yet in the crowded bar, while everyone chatted around them, he had her squirming in her seat. Realising she wanted more, she pressed down on his hand, urging him to stop.

'I'm going to powder my nose. Follow me in a couple of minutes,' she demanded quietly. 'I want you here.'

'Outside,' he said.

'Inside.'

'Outside.' He kissed her slowly then, lingering as his tongue ran across her top lip afterwards. 'I'll only have you outside.'

'No.'

'Do as you're told.' He stood up and downed his wine in one go. Ella looked up at him, met his eye. They stared at each other, each wondering who was going to give in first. She knew if she let him have his way too early, he might think he could do anything to her. But then again, wasn't that what she really wanted?

Ella followed suit with her drink and then picked up her bag.

Rendezvous was situated on the outskirts of the city centre, the streets around it mostly deserted apart from passing traffic. Hanley wasn't a vibrant place at night time unless it was a weekend or student evening. In the warm air, they walked along the street, pavement dusty from recent road works. Just past the pelican crossings, Alex pulled her down a walkway between two properties. Ella grinned – it was an excellent choice as both businesses either side were now closed.

Day had started to turn into night, grey clouds casting shadows as they continued around to the back of the buildings. Behind a row of industrial bins, against a filthy wall that matched her mood, he pressed himself to her. His tongue explored her mouth, while his hands roamed her body. Ella threw back her head to expose her neck and he covered it in kisses as she entwined her hands in his hair. He continued for a moment longer. Then he took hold of her wrists and placed them either side of her head.

'Do you like it rough?'

She stared at him, her breathing erratic.

'Tell me what you want.' One hand slid down her body to the hem of her skirt. He pushed his knee between her legs.

'Tell me.'

'I want you to stop talking and finish me off. Is that too much to ask?'

His brow furrowed for a moment.

Even so, up close, Ella realised he was even more striking; maybe she'd let him use her tonight. She kissed him again and he didn't pull back. Her hands went inside his shirt. She could feel him hard against her hip bone. She reached down, undid the zip to his trousers and curled her fingers around him. Letting out a light groan, he nibbled on her bottom lip. Then she stooped down and took him into her mouth.

The stench from the bins was enough to make anyone gag but the faint sounds of traffic passing on the road a few yards away turned her on. No one could see them, yet she imagined that they could.

For a while she let him relax into it, anticipating the thrusts of his pelvis as she excited him more. But then he put his hands on her shoulders, urging her to stand. They kissed again. Inside his shirt, Ella ran her fingertips up and down his back. As she felt the passion building inside her, she dug in her nails.

'Bitch.' Without warning, he turned her round, bent her over and pushed into her roughly from behind. He moved so fast, so deep, that she gasped in pain but soon the pleasure was all hers.

'Harder,' she cried after a moment, using the wall to steady herself. 'Come on! Do it.'

'You act like a whore.' Alex almost snarled, all the time pushing into her deeper and deeper.

'No!' Ella pulled away, turning to face him, anger flashing in her eyes. 'You don't ever call me that.'

'But you are a whore, the way you give out,' he challenged, the earlier twinkle in his eye replaced by a menacing look. 'Every bitch who joins *One Night Only* is a whore.'

Ella stared at him. If only he knew the images it conjured up for her. Being held down, pushed into forcefully while the word was used over and over again.

You're nothing but a filthy whore. A good-for-nothing stinking whore.

She was not a whore!

Her breathing accelerated; she glanced around. The sound of traffic came to her ears again. She reminded herself that anyone could happen upon them there. It still turned her on. But, aware her mood was turning black, she didn't want to hurt him.

'I am not a whore,' she told him, looking down at his cock. It stood erect, if a little dejected. 'But I am calling the shots tonight.' She grabbed the collar of his shirt, trying to pull him close again.

'Fuck you.'

Ella glared at him, not in the slightest worried about his turn of mood. Well aware of the darkness she could see in his eyes, she spoke again.

'What's wrong? Don't you want to look at me as you come?'

Alex tried to overpower her, turn her round to face the wall, but she wouldn't budge.

'Do as you're fucking told!'

'No.'

Relishing the challenge, she tried to break free when he grabbed her. Knowing he was too strong for her to stop turned her on more. He pushed her toward the wall with such force that she barely managed to stand up. Then he bent her over again, holding onto her shoulders so she couldn't move. But by this time she let him do as he wished. It was part of the game. She pressed back into him as he pushed hard into her, talking dirty until she came.

Afterwards, there were no words. Alex straightened out his clothes, whispered cheerio. Then he walked away and out of her life. She watched him, for a moment longer enjoying what they had shared. Post-orgasmic, her skin flushed, heart still racing, she felt alive again. *She* had made him happy.

Ella rearranged her skirt and reached for a mirror from her handbag. She flipped it open, and then snapped it shut. The all-too-familiar lurch in her stomach stopped her in her tracks. Tears filled her eyes, spilling down her cheeks, and she ran a hand through her hair, bunching it into a fist and pulling sharply. Often the high from the encounters could last hours, but more recently it had been minutes before the self-loathing began to appear. How could she degrade herself like that? Let any man have her, just to satisfy a need.

Alone in the alleyway, she cried. Repulsed by herself, she knew the only thing that would make her feel better. When she felt a little steadier, again she flicked open her mirror, this time wiping her eyes before reapplying her lipstick. Then she headed out of the alleyway and up towards Piccadilly.

The night was still young. Maybe she could pick someone else up later.

Chapter Four

Moving out of the home Charley had shared with Dan was every bit as harrowing as she had expected. With each room she emptied, memories of him came flooding into her mind: Dan spending an age cooking a meal in the kitchen, only for the plates to slide off the tray and onto the floor as he brought them through to the dining room; Dan trying to negotiate the stairs with crutches when he'd torn the ligaments in his knee, giving up and bumping up and down on his bottom; Dan ripping presents open on Christmas morning like an excited child in the living room; and the bedroom ... that made her heart ache the most.

Once her belongings had been removed, Charley took one final walk around the house, tears pouring down her face. But driving away – the removal van in front and her parents in their car behind – she felt at ease with herself. She couldn't turn the clock back, nor should she hang on to the past anymore. Even though it would be hard to let go of the old life, she had to think of the new.

Arriving in Warwick Avenue had felt just as strange. As she'd opened the door to the flat, she recalled how excited she and Dan had been to get the keys to the old house twelve years before. He'd carried her over the threshold, dumping her unceremoniously on the hall carpet complaining that she was too heavy, only to then roll around the floor with her. Tears welled in her eyes. She sniffed, blinking them away quickly.

If her dad noticed her watery eyes, he didn't say as he came through with the first of many boxes. But he did take time to smile at her. 'You'll be fine here, petal,' he said. 'Settled in no time. It's a beautiful place.'

From her vantage point behind the curtains at her window, Ella had watched Charley go up and down the front steps for most of the day. It had been fun, stopping the monotony of the long, empty hours stretching out before her. Ella didn't go to work – not that she would ever be capable of holding down a job, even if she did have one. Luckily she was able to manage on the money her parents had left her when they died in the accident. Besides, who would have her anyway, with her records for shoplifting and prostitution?

Once Charley was settled, she couldn't wait to start learning about her new neighbour, finding out where she worked and where she liked to visit. It would be great to spend some time with her. They would become firm friends, she was sure. Not like Susan Reilly, her last tenant, who had moved out as quickly as she'd moved in. Three weeks and two days, to be precise. Ella was so annoyed she'd wasted time on her. It had been obvious from the beginning that she wasn't going to be friend material.

She looked down again. Ella could see the older couple were Charley's parents. Charley was the image of her mother, as well as having the eyes of her father. Ella often wondered if she looked like either of her parents. She'd had a good childhood – loving mum and dad, enough money for her and her younger sister to be quite spoilt. Every once in a while, she'd reminisce about her younger years. A day trip out, a photograph being taken, borrowing lots of books from the library. Mum taking her to the hairdresser's for the first time. Out for a drive with Dad in his new car.

Sadly, Ella's memories of them were vague now. Often she'd embellish them, trying to bring them back to life again. She wondered if they too would have helped her to move properties if they were still alive. She hoped they would have supported her like Charley's parents were doing.

While she clocked Charley's curves, Ella wondered why there weren't more people helping her to move. Why wasn't she married with a husband and a couple of kids? Or at least if the husband had left, where were the kids? On the rent agreement she'd had drawn up, Charley had put her date of birth as August 1977, which made her just thirty-six – one year older than she was. It didn't seem right that she'd be alone all that time. She made a mental note to find out her story, and then see if she could befriend her quickly. Charley was such a beautiful woman; she deserved a friend like her.

Who are you trying to kid?

Ella covered her ears, trying to block out the voice inside her head. She'd had a quiet day; she didn't want to go out tonight. She was tired, willing to make her own entertainment if necessary.

Are you listening to me? You're pathetic. You think anyone would want to be your friend?

'Leave me alone.'

You'll always be alone, stupid. She won't want to know you either. You're a fool to think otherwise.

Ella shook her head, her left eye twitching a few times. Focussing on something else, anything to stop the taunts, she could see nosy Jean sitting in her window across the road. She'd been watching for most of the day too. Ella failed to see the fun in doing it all day, every day. Weren't things the same once you'd seen them for a week or so? Humans were creatures of habits, apart from her, of course. Ella hadn't got a set routine to learn. She did what she wanted when she wanted – or rather when Cassandra wanted. Couldn't imagine what it would be like to be tied to one place;

hoped she'd never get to the age where all she did was sit and stare into a world she was no longer part of. Even though her life was shit, she had a life.

Although she'd grown up in the city, Ella hadn't lived in one area for longer than a few years before she'd been on the move again. Often she'd been kicked out of somewhere, literally, during her earlier days. But maybe she'd settle this time. Her life was about to get better as soon as she got to know Charley anyway. She would be her new friend and they would go out for drinks together, go shopping together, to the movies. They'd have a housewarming party for the two of them, eat pizza and ice cream until they were sick, watch chick flicks and go gooey-eyed over the gorgeous men. They'd look out for one another, cry on each other's shoulders, borrow each other's clothes, go –

She won't want to do any of that with you! You're not worth spending time with.

As her belongings had been moved in, a sense of peace came over Charley. The flat was just as she remembered it, and everything fit as planned. Six hours later, once her parents and the removal men had left her to finish off, Charley took one of the few remaining boxes through from the hallway into the living room. To the sounds of Adele singing softly, she sat down to empty it.

Inside, she searched for her most treasured possession, rummaging around until she came to a parcel covered in tissue paper. She unwrapped it carefully to reveal a six-inch glass cube, with a photo of Dan on each side. He'd bought it for her because he thought it was unusual. Little did he realise how sentimental it would become.

Charley turned it around in her hands. The first photo she came to was one they'd had taken on a city break in London. Dan had been goofing about in the Tower of London, trying to make her laugh when everyone around her was quietly admiring the Crown Jewels. The one next to it was of the two of them dressed up for a friend's wedding. Another showed Dan on his back in the snow, his arms and legs wide, making a snow angel.

A lone tear dropped onto the glass. Charley wiped it away quickly before any more joined it.

<hr>

Ella came away from the window when she realised there was nothing more to see.

She won't want to know you anyway. Who would want you as a friend?

She threw herself down onto the settee and covered her head with a cushion. Why wouldn't she leave her alone? She was always going on at her. Nag, nag, nag. Never a rest.

Useless. Useless. USELESS!

'Leave me alone!'

You don't deserve a friend.

Ella sat up suddenly. She was stronger than this; no one was going to stop her from getting what she wanted.

I'm going to stop you!

'No, you're not.' She stood up tall and decided to go downstairs and check things out a little more. Charley was going to be *her* friend – and nothing at all to do with Cassandra.

When I came out of hospital, I was taken to a children's home. It wasn't near to where I lived before so I knew no one and felt so alone. I had to share a room with a girl called Billie; she was twelve. I was wary about Billie from the start. Don't you just get a feeling when someone doesn't like you? I mean, she was great when anyone else was there but when we were alone, she'd give me hell. I was the little girl who got in her way. I was the one everyone felt sorry for due to my circumstances. And Billie didn't like it, now, did she?

Billie was a bully. She was a big girl and used to thump me. I couldn't stand up to her. Billie told all the other kids at the home not to talk to me. No one wanted to be my friend. I was never allowed to join in. I never fitted in anywhere, for the rest of my life after that.

Kids used to come and go in the home. Some were fostered out; some were adopted. I missed my family so much and every night, I cried myself to sleep – no matter how many times Billie laid into me for making a noise. Funny how bruises become invisible, isn't it? Or don't people want to see them? I must have been covered in the bloody things. Surely everyone didn't think I was a walking disaster all the time?

No one really cared enough to ask questions, I suppose. I was left to rot – and be beaten on a daily basis. If I fought back, I got back twice as much. All the kids were scared of Billie. She used to make them hit me too, so that she wouldn't get into trouble. When a couple are holding your arms while another is thumping you in the stomach or pulling your hair until you're sure your neck will snap, you can't do anything about it.

When we were with other people, Billie would push me into things so that I would look clumsy. She'd thump me in the back or in the leg, deadening it when no one was looking. No one believed me when I said they weren't accidents so, after a while, I didn't tell anyone that I was being bullied. And if I did say anything, Billie accused me of lying, called me a troublemaker, and I was sent to my room until I could behave. Billie said I needed to get used to the fact that I was there to stay and that no evil little bitch was going to spoil her fun.

And all the while everyone believed her. How could they? How could the system let a child down so? I was made out to be the naughty one. I was the one who wet the bed. Did I? I can't remember that. All I can remember is her tipping cold water over me to wake me up and then accusing me of pissing myself. I never pissed myself. Billie made me cry so much I was permanently red-eyed. She was evil. And that's what she made me. Evil, like her.

And another thing, while I'm thinking about it, why didn't anyone question those bruises? We hear of the children that have slipped through the net. We see their faces splashed across the news, those who've had despicable things done to them at the hands of responsible adults. Just like me.

No one saw my bruises. Are we sure about that? No one? NO ONE? Not a fucking ONE?

Billie was responsible for making me into what I am. It's all her fault. Everything. EVERYTHING! She started it all.

When my family died, a part of me died too. Why did they all leave me? WHY DID THEY FUCKING LEAVE ME?

Chapter Five

Having made coffee, Charley stood looking out of the bay window in the living room. Late Friday afternoon, the avenue was quiet but getting busier by the minute, no doubt as people returned from their jobs to start their weekends. The weather forecast was looking good for it. The early September day had been fairly warm but overcast. A slight breeze played with a crisp packet that had been discarded on the pavement. Three doors down to her right, a man polished a mean-looking Toyota Hilux that only just fitted his driveway. The woman next to him was attacking overgrown hedges, leaves falling like confetti at a wedding before bunching together on the pavement.

From the corner of her eye, she saw a movement and looked across to the house opposite, number thirty-eight. That woman, Jean, was in the window again. Charley wondered if it was true that she never moved from the chair or if Ella was being ironic in her observations. She couldn't imagine being housebound. But if it was true, maybe she could help out by getting the odd bit of shopping in for her. It wasn't much to do, if she would accept help – she knew from her job that some people were too proud. Or perhaps she wouldn't be here long enough. Even though she had signed the lease for six months, she was planning on looking for a property to buy.

There came a knock on the door behind her and Ella appeared in the doorway.

'Hiya, I hope you don't mind me walking in. I wouldn't do it any other day and I only did it today because the front door was ajar. And well, I'm a nosy bag, too, on the quiet.' She paused. 'That's a joke, by the way.'

'I didn't realise the door had been left open, to be honest. I was taking a break from unpacking. I haven't annoyed you with all the noise, have I?'

'Oh, no.' Ella shook her head. 'I'm glad that you're here at last. This place gives me the creeps when it's empty.'

'Oh?'

'I like noise,' she explained. 'You'll always find me with a radio on or the TV turned down low. I won't be too noisy for you, though,' she added. 'I'm digging a hole for myself, aren't I? I'm noisy and nosy and everything you don't want in a neighbour.'

Charley smiled this time. Even though Ella was too thin for her liking, she noted her beauty as the smile was returned.

'Really, it's fine,' she said, then her shoulders sagged. 'I have so much to do.'

'You don't have to do it all in one go, surely?'

'I have a couple of days off from work. I'd like to get as much done as I can before I'm in again next week.'

'What do you do?'

'I'm a support worker at a domestic violence organisation,' said Charley.

Ella raised her chin in acknowledgement. 'Is it a local place?'

'Yes.' Charley didn't like to divulge too much information about her job; she had a good reputation for privacy. She delved into the box on the settee and pulled out a framed photograph. It was of her and Dan on their wedding day. She held back the sob she could feel building up.

'I can help, if you like?' Ella offered.

Charley composed herself quickly. 'Thanks, but I'll manage.' She passed the photograph to Ella. 'This was my husband, Dan. He was killed, just over eighteen months ago now.'

'Oh, shit, I'm sorry.' Ella grimaced.

'It's okay,' said Charley. 'It was one of the reasons I wanted a smaller place. The house we shared was too big for me on my own.'

'I'm divorced,' Ella told her, taking the photo from Charley. 'I stupidly got married at seventeen and he left me when I was eighteen. Been on my own ever since – I mean I haven't married again. I've been in the odd relationship every now and then. But nothing special, you know.'

'Yes. I was very lucky to have the time I had with him.' Charley smiled kindly. 'I'm sure there'll be someone out there for you, too.'

'Maybe – if I could just find him.' Ella laughed. 'It's fun looking, though. It's what makes life interesting, I suppose.'

Later that evening, Charley was so exhausted that she practically crawled into bed. She'd left it as late as she could, unpacking as much as possible just to put off this moment; hadn't wanted to stop because she knew once she did she would crumble. She knew the first night would be the worst, when she wouldn't be able to imagine Dan was maybe still downstairs watching the end of a horror movie, like she'd done every time she'd missed him previously.

The firsts, they were the worst. As soon as he'd died, people offered advice, always telling her what was to come. And they had been right. First, it was the shock and then the disbelief. Next came anger, and then the grief. Finally, the acceptance. Charley had accepted that Dan had gone a long time ago but still she hadn't moved on with her life. Part of moving out of their home in Werrington was acceptance. And she didn't miss him all of the time. That would be impossible; even she knew that. What she missed most was the warmth of being part of a couple. She missed having someone to share news with, good or bad. Of course she had her mum and dad to chat to but it was hardly the same. She hated making decisions on her own too, without anyone else's input.

The photograph of her and Dan that she'd shown to Ella earlier clinked on the frame of the bed as she climbed underneath new covers with it, eyes spilling tears when she realised she wouldn't be able to smell him anywhere. Of course his smell had gone a long time ago, but that still didn't help. She sniffed, more tears coming as she tried to focus on his image. Then she curled up with photograph on the pillow next to her and cried herself to sleep.

Across the road at number thirty-six, Jake Carter had been lying in bed watching YouTube on his iPad when he heard a car coming along Warwick Avenue. As it came to a halt outside his home, he checked his alarm clock. It was one fifty a.m. which could mean only one thing. He pulled the duvet back and raced to the window. Sure enough, he looked down onto the road to see Ella getting out of the passenger side of a taxi. He smiled to himself until he saw she was alone.

Jake had been watching Ella for some time now. It had started when he'd spotted her on a night out with his friends. They weren't supposed to be in the pubs around Hanley, but most of them looked older than eighteen, especially Jake because of his height at six foot one. He was always the one who'd be sent to buy the drinks if in doubt. It was where he'd spotted Ella in The Manhattan, recognising her as his neighbour. She'd been alone at the time, sitting on a stool at the end of the bar, not so crowded back there. He'd watched her then, too. She'd flashed him a sexy smile that he'd remembered long after.

Ella lived practically opposite him. If he was next door at number thirty-eight, where that nosy old bag Jean Cooper lived, he was sure he'd be able to see directly into her room upstairs. As it was, he could see enough.

It wasn't easy, though. She didn't have a set routine – Jake would have had to sit and watch the window all day and night to catch her every move – but he reckoned he caught a fair bit of what she got up to anyway. Besides that, she was always parading up and down in her window with hardly anything on. And he was pretty sure she could see him watching.

He'd seen her bring home seven men so far – one she'd shagged bent over the table in the window. Man, it had been such a turn-on. He couldn't wait to see her do it again. But not tonight, sadly.

He fantasised what it would be like to kiss her, to touch her breasts, for her to feel the weight of him pressing down as he shagged her. He dreamt about her too. Wet dreams, good dreams, wanting to turn those dreams into reality one day.

Would she notice him? He was only seventeen but he was all man. Too much man for Serena Cotton, though, when he'd tried to get into her knickers last month. She'd pushed him away and played the virgin card when he knew his mate Simon had shagged her twice already.

Disappointed, he trudged back to bed. He'd have to settle for a magazine of big tits and a box of tissues. But one day, he would have her. A woman like her wouldn't be able to resist a come-on.

* * *

Charley awoke with a start. She sat up abruptly. Had she heard a noise or had she been dreaming? She held her breath and sat still listening, but there was nothing. She flopped back onto the bed, hoping that it was just a clank of a heating pipe or one of the old sash windows that had a rattle. She supposed it would be some time before she'd adjust to the creaks and groans of a different property.

But there was the noise again. Something was banging – no, *someone* was banging. For a moment, she was unsure what to do. At least now she could tell the noise wasn't coming from inside the flat. She lay there, hearing the sound of her heart beating wildly, finally daring to get out of bed. Cautiously, she tiptoed across the room and hallway into the living room, the bay windows giving her access to view the street outside. She peeped around the corner of the window frame and let out a huge sigh of relief.

It was Ella, on the doorstep. And if she wasn't mistaken, she was drunk and trying to find her key in her handbag. Charley wondered whether to let her in. If she did, would it be a regular occurrence? She didn't want to set herself up to be the unofficial key holder. But then, who was she to judge Ella? She didn't know her yet, didn't know what had happened to make her drink so much. And she'd want Ella to let her in if she was so paralytic that she couldn't find her keys.

She got to the entrance door and pulled it open just as Ella was about to bang on it again. Ella fell forward onto her, knocking them both down onto the floor. Charley grunted as she took her weight – and the full impact of the tiled floor.

'Ohhhhhh,' laughed Ella. 'I'm sooooo sorry.'

Charley coughed. She tried to push Ella to the side, but even as small as she was, she seemed like a dead weight. She pushed again.

Ella rolled over and onto her back with another giggle. She peered at Charley, trying to focus. 'Sorry,' she repeated, blowing the hair from her face noisily, before brushing it away with her hand. 'I'm a little bit tipsy and I couldn't find my key.'

Charley got up from the floor and closed the door. 'Have you had a good night?' she asked.

'I can't remember.' Ella laughed again.

Ella stayed on the floor looking like an adorable puppy waiting to be picked up for a cuddle. Realising she wasn't going to move, Charley helped her to her feet.

'Will you be okay or do you want me to take you upstairs to your flat?'

Ella waved her hand. 'No, s'fine.' She hung onto the banister rail and peered down, swaying gently. 'I'm glad that you've moved in because ... because you can watch over me now.' She prodded Charley in the shoulder. 'I need a friend, someone to look after me.'

'You need to go to bed.'

'Yes, I do.' Ella turned and staggered up the stairs. 'G'night.' She put up a hand before disappearing around the corner.

Once Charley had heard Ella's front door open and close, she went back to her flat, praying that the episode had been a one-off.

Chapter Six

Charley awoke the following morning, rolled over onto her side, and gazed out of the window. The weather outside did look as promised; although there was an autumnal chill settling in, she could see fragments of blue sky through bright white clouds.

A few minutes later, she sat up and stretched, looking around her new bedroom. She liked the pale walls and the wooden floor but she would get a rug to add a dash of colour. Something to match the large green flowers on the bedding she had bought. She'd have a look this morning; she needed to go shopping today, having run down the food in her cupboards because of the move.

At half past ten, she was getting into her car to head off when she spotted Ella walking along the avenue coming back towards the house. She waved to catch her attention.

'Morning.' Ella came over to her. 'How was your first night? Did you sleep well?'

'I did, thanks. How about you? You were a little tipsy last night. How's your head this morning?'

Ella frowned.

Charley raised her eyebrows. 'Don't tell me you're one of those people who can drink until they drop and then don't have a hangover the next day?'

Ella shook her head. 'Nope, you've lost me.'

'Last night. You couldn't find your key and I let you in and you fell on top of me.'

'I didn't go out last night.'

'You did! Can't you remember?'

Ella shook her head again. 'You must have been dreaming.'

'No, I –'

Something made Charley pause. It was strange that Ella would deny what had happened; she hadn't been dreaming. Maybe Ella was embarrassed. Charley could recall a few times when she'd been drunk and didn't want to remember what a fool she'd made of herself.

She smiled, giving her the benefit of the doubt. 'I'm off to the supermarket – do you need anything?'

'No, thanks, I'm good.'

'Right, then. I'll see you later.'

———

Ella let herself into the house and pulled the key from the lock. She turned back in time to see Charley driving off. What had she been referring to? She hadn't gone out last night. Why would she make things up like that?

But as she let herself into her flat, she noticed a pair of black heels thrown across the floor in the hallway, and a purple skirt scrunched up on the floor as if she'd stepped out of it. Slowly things started coming back to her.

Darren, was that his name? Had she met him in Hanley? She must have been somewhere; there was mud on her shoes.

She sighed loudly. Christ, she'd had another blackout, hadn't she? She tried to remember, but she couldn't recall getting home or what time she'd left the bar – had she been to Rendezvous again?

But then she frowned: it was one thing to want excitement, a bit of need in her life, but if she wasn't careful she was going to get hurt – or worse, if anything could be any worse than what she had already faced.

She nibbled on her bottom lip as she bent to scoop up the skirt from the floor. It wouldn't hurt for Charley to assume she had been wrong. It might stand her in good stead if she blacked out again.

Or if she wanted to use it to her advantage sometime.

Charley spent the rest of the weekend sorting out the flat and was grateful for a break when Monday morning arrived. She was at her workplace in the city centre by quarter to nine, sifting through a pile of handwritten messages on the top of her desk. Situated in Stafford Street, which housed the Intu Potteries shopping centre at the far end of it, the base for Striking Back was upstairs above a furniture shop. Today, she could see a little blue sky again; the warm weather seemed determined to stick around.

She sat down at her desk, set in a bank of three – two support workers and an assistant who split the heavy workload amongst themselves. Their corner of the open-plan office was fairly quiet at the moment, Charley being the only one of their team who had arrived. She switched on her computer and caught up with what she'd missed over her two days off. Deep into it, she didn't notice someone walking towards her minutes later.

'Morning, Charley. How did it go?'

Charley looked up to see Aaron Campbell standing in front of her. Holding two plastic cups of coffee, he popped one down on her desk before perching on the end of it.

She smiled at him. 'It went okay, thanks.'

'No mishaps, broken mirrors, missing ornaments?'

'Nothing whatsoever. It all went really well. How was your weekend?'

'The usual. Football, beer, and ex-wife blues.'

Charley had known Aaron since she'd started to work at Striking Back. Recently divorced and in his late thirties, he stood a few inches taller than her at five foot ten, with sharp brown eyes and dark hair, greying at its roots. He didn't look lived in like a lot of men his age, keeping his medium frame fit and healthy by running several times a week. Clean-shaven, he always smelt of something delicious. What was it today? She sniffed discreetly – something by Hugo Boss, she reckoned.

Aaron worked on the floor above, and if it wasn't for him bringing her a coffee every now and then, Charley might never see him from one week to the next. Like the majority of the workers in the block, he spent a large amount of his time away from the office, meeting clients, attending court cases, dealing with complaints.

Striking Back had been set up four years ago, shortly after a local woman, Davina Gregory, had been murdered by her partner. Before that, Davina had suffered years of domestic violence. One particular day, the violence escalated and, in front of their three-year-old daughter, her partner had beaten her severely and then fatally stabbed her before heading off to the garage to gas himself with carbon monoxide. The little girl had been in the house with her dead mum for two hours before someone found them all.

Even though the death had been traumatic to deal with, Davina's mum had campaigned to raise funds to set up something to remember her by. Working closely with the local authority, she'd successfully gained lottery funding and formed the organisation, so a few more local companies had added their sponsorship. Charley had been a social worker in the city for five years when she'd seen the advertisement for senior support workers, so, wanting to specialise in helping victims of domestic abuse, she'd taken a chance and applied for a three-year secondment. They were still together as a team due to the project's success, and every month Charley prayed that, even though funding was being cut drastically by the local authority each year, Striking Back would survive.

The organisation was small but it did an enormous job. It would be a crime for it *not* to continue – literally.

'Here's to new beginnings.' Aaron raised his cup in a toast.

Charley copied. 'New beginnings.'

'So when do I get to see it, then?' Aaron leaned closer. 'You know, just you and me and a bottle or three.'

'Ooh, let me see.' Charley pretended to ponder on the question before she leaned in closer too. 'Never.'

'Wow, you really know how to hit a guy where it hurts.' Aaron clutched his chest and feigned pain. 'Straight to the heart.'

Charley laughed. Despite his continuous banter to get her to go out with him, his humour and constant reassurance that she was attractive was always good to hear. She pushed him gently off her desk.

'Haven't you got work to do?'

More people started to arrive and a few moments later, a woman in her early fifties came bustling in. She sat down at the desk to Charley's right with a big sigh.

'Christ on a bike, I've had a manic weekend. Ruth has come home again: says she's leaving the idle bastard for good this time, just like she said the last time. Michael has come down with some kind of virus. More like a bad hangover, if you ask me. Then the dog threw up all over a pile of ironing I'd sweated over and,' she batted a hand in front of her face, 'if these bloody hot flushes don't calm down soon, I'm sure I'll combust. My face is more or less as red as my hair!'

'Morning, Lynne,' Charley greeted, not at all fazed by her friend's outburst. Lynne was one of the best mothers she knew, with two children she'd raised single-handedly since their father had been sent to prison for her attempted murder. Although her roots were greying where the red dye needed re-touching, she wore her hair long to hide the damage caused to her face. A few years before they'd started to work together, Lynne had nearly lost the sight in her right eye because of an assault with a hammer, but luckily there had been no permanent damage to her brain. Her kids had been her lifeline after it happened, taking care of her while she got through the trauma. Now Lynne gave back to the community; Charley admired her so much for her strength.

'How did the move go?' Lynne wanted to know, once she had caught her breath and switched on her computer. 'Tickety-boo, I hope?'

'It went … okay. It was weird to be on my own there, you know?'

Lynne nodded at her. 'I can imagine.'

'I'll be fine though. It's another first done and dusted, I suppose. And I'm a firm believer that a part of him will be with me forever.'

Lynne scoffed. 'You don't believe in that old crap that they stay with you when they pass? That they are always in the ether?'

'God, I hope not.' Charley laughed. 'I have far too many bad habits for that. I used to drive Dan mad with some of the things I did.'

'Exactly.' Lynne picked up her mug. 'And some things are better done alone, anyway. I, for one, wouldn't want anyone seeing me doing everything!' She winked and stood up. 'Fancy a proper cup of coffee?'

———

Across the road, Ella flicked through a rail of clothes in Bon Marche. Feigning interest, she checked for sizes of a particular white jumper, all the time looking through the window behind and across the road to the doorway she'd seen Charley go into. Through a small window upstairs, she could just about make out the top of someone's head. It couldn't be Charley, as the hair she could see was a vivid shade of red. It must be that other woman she'd seen bustling in a few minutes ago.

Ella hadn't any intentions of following Charley to work but, after a restless night of insomnia, on impulse she'd grabbed her keys. She'd jumped in her car and sped down Warwick Avenue once Charley was out of sight.

Keeping close, she'd managed to work out where Charley was heading and stay a few cars behind her. Once arriving in Hanley, Ella parked up quickly on St John Street's multi-storey and followed close behind Charley as she made her way into the town. It hadn't been easy keeping up without being seen, especially once on foot.

Stoke-on-Trent was a city that couldn't make its mind up where its centre was. There was an on-going battle with some of its residents to keep most amenities near to Stoke, one of six towns that made up the city. The majority of its residents were fiercely supportive of their hometown, but with broken promises and regeneration plans that never materialised, some areas had been left to run down.

If Ella was in a bad mood, she would describe Hanley, what she referred to as the city centre, as consisting mainly of a few streets, a large Fountain Square that was now empty, the fountain having been filled in many years ago, and a shopping centre built in the late eighties that was part of plans to have a revamp soon. On her dark days, Ella thought no one in his or her right mind would want to invest money there.

If she was in a bright mood, like today, Hanley was an up-and-coming area. The city had a plan to attract big brands and more investment from outside commerce. A new civic centre was well under construction, a state-of-the-art bus station had recently been opened, and new hotels were going up nearby. The local newspaper, *The Sentinel*, had recently moved their offices closer again, having taken over a building opposite the Potteries Museum and Art Gallery. The Cultural Quarter was next to it – they even had their own Piccadilly.

Busy looking upwards at the architecture of some of the buildings above the high street shops, Ella had been just in time to dive into the shop when Charley stopped a few yards in front and disappeared through a doorway. Sad to think that she wouldn't see her until later; she was glad that she'd followed her there now. To be a true friend, she needed to understand Charley, to get close to her, see what she liked. Even though Ella hadn't had a friend for a while – well, apart from Susan Reilly – she knew that's what friends did. They took an interest in each other, and knowing where Charley worked made her feel closer to her. When Ella was wondering what she was doing while she was at work, she could now imagine Charley sitting at her desk upstairs in that office.

She looked through the window for the last time before coming out onto the pavement. Quickly, she crossed the road towards the door. The sign on it said that office hours were nine until five; there was no name or logo of any particular company. She smiled to herself. Charley would probably be home before six.

With that thought, Ella set off towards the centre. She'd had a brilliant idea. She'd invite Charley up to her flat for a drink of wine to celebrate her first day coming home to Warwick Avenue. And she'd buy cupcakes – everyone liked cupcakes.

Chapter Seven

Work finished for the day, Charley left the office shortly before five thirty. Back in Warwick Avenue just after six, she grappled with a pile of paperwork and files as she opened the entrance door.

'I thought I heard you.'

Charley glanced upwards to see Ella standing on the middle stair. 'Hi there,' she smiled.

'Hi yourself. Good day?'

'Yes, thanks. Busy, though. You?'

'So-so – I'm temping at the moment.' Ella pulled her hands from behind her back to reveal two bottles of wine. 'I have red and white. Fancy a glass to end the day?'

'My day won't end yet.' Charley indicated the files she was holding. 'Need to read through some of this before a meeting tomorrow.'

'I didn't mean right now, silly.' Ella giggled before turning to walk back upstairs again. 'Come up to my flat in half an hour.'

'But I –'

'I have cake too … a treat for your first day home from work. I promise I won't keep you long.'

Charley sighed at her disappearing form. In Werrington, she hadn't neighboured much so wasn't sure of the etiquette when sharing a house with someone – although technically, they were only sharing a hallway. She desperately wanted to relax in a long, hot bath, but with a glass of wine by herself.

But Ella was only being friendly; she supposed it wouldn't do any harm to have a small drink with her. And after that she could have her bath and chill.

Ella's front door was ajar when she knocked on it thirty minutes later.

'I'm in the living room,' she heard her shout, so she stepped inside.

It was weird going into a flat that was set out the same but was very different in décor and style. The long hallway seemed dim; along one side clear plastic boxes were piled high, full of hardback and paperback books. A collection of miniature bottles were arranged haphazardly on a shelf above them. Fading wallpaper was in need of stripping off and redoing. The beige carpeting underfoot felt tacky and thin; Charley almost tiptoed to join Ella.

She knocked lightly on a door. Stepping into the living room, she was greeted by a mis-match of colours, as if someone had thrown a few tins of paint up in the air and prayed they would come down in some sort of order. But strangely, it all worked. It felt warm, much more inviting than the hallway. Still as cluttered, though.

'Welcome to my humble abode.' Ella waved a hand around the room. 'I won't apologise for my mess as it will never get any better no matter how many times you visit.' She beamed. 'I like it this way – I know where everything is. Come and sit down, if you can find a place.'

As Ella left the room, Charley perched on the edge of a settee that was covered mostly with piles of papers and magazines. She sneaked a look at the page a woman's magazine was opened to: an article on sex addiction.

'Red or white?' Ella shouted.

Charley moved her hand away quickly, hoping that Ella hadn't seen her snooping. 'Whatever is open, thanks,' she replied.

'I bet you're wondering what's with all the books in the boxes out there?' Ella came through with two glasses of white. 'I can't bear to part with them once I've read them. Can you? I have a few collections too – bottles you've seen, notepads, old magazines. I can't walk past a charity shop without checking out what they have. I used to collect teapots – not sure why – but I had to give them away when I ran out of space. So I changed to something more easily storable. Magazines, old comics. I reckon they'll be worth a fortune one day.'

Ella disappeared again. Charley wondered if she ever took a breath as she looked around some more. In her line of work, she knew you could tell a lot from the state of a room. Too untidy and couldn't care less: a mind in turmoil. Too neat and too scared to make a mess: a controlled mind. Chaotic and clean but in some sort of order: happy in their own skin most of the time. From looking around this room, she couldn't quite tell which one symbolised Ella's state of mind. And there was always an exception to every rule.

She was watching a news report on *BBC Midlands Today* when Ella came back in again. She handed her a plate with an iced cupcake on it before sitting down at the opposite end of the settee.

'I hope you like it,' Ella smiled. 'I've already had one. I couldn't resist.'

'Actually, I'm fine, thanks.' Charley sat forward a little. 'I haven't eaten yet.'

'It won't hurt,' Ella urged.

'No, I'm …' An uncomfortable silence dropped between them and she picked up the cake to ease it.

'Have you lived here long?' Charley asked once she'd taken a bite, for want of something to say.

'No, my parents died when I was in my early twenties and left me a bit of money. They also owned a potteries firm over in

Middleport which I sold. I've always lived in Stoke – I had a terraced house in Penkhull then, near the University Hospital – but when I saw this place come up for sale, I fell in love immediately. And, pretty much like you, I guess, I wanted to start again, somewhere fresh.'

'I bet you miss your parents.' Charley gave Ella a half-smile.

'Not so much now. I wasn't close to them. I'm a bit of a free spirit.'

Another silence.

Charley noticed a pile of notepads stacked up on top of a few vinyl records. 'Are you a writer?'

Ella followed her gaze. 'Not really,' she shook her head, 'but I do like to keep a diary. I've written them for years; kept every one.'

'I wish I'd done that, in hindsight,' Charley confessed. 'I wrote my feelings out a few times after Dan died but I didn't keep any of it. I suppose I just needed to express myself.'

'Writing is great for that. I pour my heart out sometimes, especially if I've had a bad day. It's like having a therapist, in a way, unburdening it all. I often write things on the laptop, too, and then delete them, once they're out of my head; helps me sleep at times. I'm a terrible insomniac so forgive me if I wake you up or you hear me padding about. I do try to keep quiet.'

Charley didn't want to bring up the drunken episode again, still hoping it was a one-off that Ella was embarrassed about. Instead she sat there, waiting for enough time to have passed to seem sociable. She needed to eat and the wine was going to her head.

Ella began to show her some of the books in her collection.

Charley picked up a paperback from the middle of a small pile on the coffee table. '*Famous Five go to Devon.*' She smiled fondly as she flicked through it. 'I've read all of this series as a child. Used to devour anything by Enid Blyton. Where did you get this from?'

'I bid for most of them, on eBay. I'm always bidding for something or other. I can't help myself. I'm a sucker for a bargain.' Ella pointed to a desk in the corner of the room. Charley could just about make out a small laptop amongst the chaos. 'I get most things online. It's a lot easier, don't you think?'

'I agree. I don't have much time to do the shops anymore.'

Ella picked up another book and then squealed as she dropped it in favour of a diary poking out from underneath it. She shrieked and held it up to show Charley. '1997. The year I met Mark. I haven't seen him in a while, though. He went to work in Spain and we lost contact.' Ella shrugged. 'Part of life, I guess, but so sad that we leave people behind. Good job we now have Facebook and Twitter. Are you on Twitter?'

'Me? Not really. I opened an account but I couldn't see the point of it. I'm on Facebook and that could eat up my time if I let it. Besides, I'm not that interesting.'

'Everyone is interesting in some way.'

Charley reached over and picked up another book that had piqued her interest. '*Kama Sutra?*' She giggled, opening it. A few handwritten notes fell out and onto the carpet. 'Oops, sorry.' She dived forward to pick them up.

'Hey! Give those back.' Ella snatched them from her suddenly. 'You can't look at whatever you want to.'

'Sorry, I didn't see anything.'

'Some of my things are private. That's the trouble with people nowadays. Nosy, nosy.' Ella pushed the papers back into the book and closed it with a bang.

The intensity of Ella's stare made Charley's skin crawl for a moment. Then, suddenly Ella's face cleared and she smiled again. 'Sorry. More wine?'

Ten minutes later, Charley let herself into her flat and closed the door with a sigh of relief. Because she didn't know Ella very well yet, she'd been surprised with her little outburst. She was obviously a secretive person and Charley didn't have a problem with that. But had she known there were notes pushed inside the book that she wasn't meant to see, she would never have picked it up. She hadn't even seen what was written on them; at least that would have made Ella's reaction a bit more understandable.

Putting the episode out of her mind, she ran a bath, removed her clothes, and sank deep into the hot water. As her body started to relax into it, she hoped there wasn't any more to come.

Ella ran a hand through her hair, made a fist, and pulled at it sharply. She picked up what remained of the wine and poured it into her glass. Shit, she could feel the pressure building; she'd have to go out now. She began to pace the room. Why had Charley left so quickly?

As soon as she'd closed the door behind her, Ella had checked the papers, but there had been nothing there that would have given her away. Nothing that would make Charley turn against her like so many other people had. But something had definitely spooked her – even though she'd been on her best behaviour that evening.

What had gone wrong? Had she got *Weirdo* stamped across her forehead?

Sighing with disappointment, she logged on to *One Night Only* and checked to see if anyone was available.

I'd been at Ravenside Home a week the first time Billie locked me in the cupboard. It was one of those built over the box at the top of the stairs. I was sitting on my bed and she pushed me onto the floor. When I started to cry, she brought up her hand and slapped my cheek, grabbed a handful of my hair, and dragged me to the cupboard while I screamed. I was such a shy child back then, highly privileged, born to wealthy parents who had given me everything.

Billie had been living with her grandparents after her mum died of a drugs overdose and no one knew who her father was. She'd been with them for two years before they'd had enough of her; expelled from two schools by the time she was eleven. I heard Malcolm, the home manager, say that Billie was a law unto herself and a tough nut to crack.

I'd bang on the door to be let out of the cupboard, screaming until I made myself hoarse. Sobbed my heart out but did she open the door? Did she FUCK! She just turned up her radio so no one could hear me. She used to let me out when I could sob no more.

Why didn't anyone from the home hear me? Did they turn a blind eye or was Billie too clever? I don't fucking understand!

I realised after a while that no one was going to get me out, no matter how much noise I made. I screamed and kicked the door until I was sick but no one heard me. Billie saw to that. She was very clever.

Why did she lock me in there? I hated Billie.

I didn't like Ravenside Home.

I hated it there.

Chapter Eight

Ella's fingers clicked through image after image on the website, message after message.

Patrick, 36. *'When you have chemistry with someone, it's undeniable. It doesn't matter what they look like, or what they do. That's what I'm looking for.'*

Ella snorted. She didn't care what anyone looked like either as long as she could be screwed. She scrolled down further.

Phil, 43. *'I like to meet people and have a laugh. I hope to meet an interesting girl. From there who knows?'*

Who knows indeed? Ella favourited that link to return to if nothing else took her fancy.

Simone, 28. *'I'm looking for friendship really, great if it develops further, or maybe I'll be totally swept off my feet. Oh and by the way I'm one of the normalish women on here ... can be slightly mad but in a good way and definitely not moody and got a great sense of humour.'*

Ella sighed again. What was it with people – *great if it develops further?* The website name was the biggest clue – one night only! And Simone definitely didn't sound normal from *that* description.

She scrolled down further and noted three more possible dates who had shown an interest in meeting her – that was three men in total and a woman. Before jumping into the shower, she emailed the first one to see if he was available. When she came back into the room ten minutes later, there was a reply waiting for her. He wasn't free that evening but would be available tomorrow. Her shoulders sagged.

'I don't fucking think so!'

She moved on to the next guy, emailed him as she sat naked. When he still hadn't replied once she'd dried her hair, she went to the next one on the list. Quickly, she scanned his details: there was a mobile number. Using a separate phone she had bought purposely, she texted him before pulling on a chocolate-brown peep-through bra and matching crotchless knickers. She wanted to be screwed quickly this evening.

A text came back almost immediately. She read it eagerly, and then threw down her phone in despair. Unavailable at such short notice – what was wrong with these men? She emailed two more. If she didn't get a response soon she'd just have to go out and find someone. Thinking of Mark and the way he'd treated her always made her angry.

Slipping into her heels, she heard an email ping into her inbox. Clicking on it, she grinned. At last someone was available and could meet her within the hour. She checked her watch: seven forty-five. That would do. Stuff the guy she'd texted; he was too late now if he replied. She emailed her acceptance. Then she lay back on the bed to masturbate. Her date might be willing to wait an hour but she certainly wasn't. She needed to get rid of the anger. Her fingers moved over herself, inside herself, harder and faster as she aimed for quick release. It felt so good, so in control.

Forty minutes later, Ella was in a taxi and on her way back into Hanley. Once outside their meeting place, she glanced down towards Marsh Street, remembering the encounter with Alex three weeks ago in the alleyway. It was a shame she couldn't use the same place this evening; it would have been a blast to be screwed there by two different men. But it would have to keep for another time. Tonight, she was meeting a woman.

She went into the bar and strode confidently across the floor. Jayne stood waiting at the end of it. At first, Ella couldn't take her eyes off her low-cut sleeveless top, or the ample cleavage she was showing off. She licked her lips in excitement at what was to come. Then she looked up into brown eyes full of want. For once, Jayne was every bit as good as her photograph. Ella mostly preferred seeing what she got first. It was much better than a blind date – though some of the profile pictures from the website were highly misleading, dreadfully disappointing. Even Ella had her limits, despite her needs.

'Drink here first or shall we move to somewhere we can be a little more … intimate?' Jayne asked, after they'd greeted each other with a kiss. To anyone in the bar, they looked like girlfriends meeting for a gossip. The thought excited Ella even more. She hoped Jayne would stay around for a few hours. Maybe she could invite her home for a nightcap too.

Early next morning, Ella jumped at the sound of the entrance door closing. It must be Charley leaving for work. She lifted her head from the pillow slightly before putting it back again with a thud.

It had been a stroke of genius to tell Charley that she was registered with a temping agency and only called in as and when. Now she wouldn't have to pretend to work set times, even though she wasn't sure what regular hours were nowadays.

If she hadn't got such a raging headache after drinking champagne with Jayne last night, she would have leapt out of bed and over to the window to see Charley before she got into her car. Almost like Jean sitting forwards in her chair at the slightest of noises in the avenue, already she knew it was going to become her morning ritual. She liked to know what Charley was wearing, speculate where she was going if she wasn't in work wear. And, unlike nosy Jean, who just wanted to know what everyone was up to, she was only interested in this neighbour. No one else intrigued her like Charley.

She sat up and stretched, wondered what to do with her day. Sometimes time stood still and life became boring and monotonous as one hour rolled into the next. But, while Charley was out, it was a great opportunity to steal downstairs and have a good look around her flat. The more she knew about her, the more she would get to know Charley's likes and dislikes. And that could only benefit their friendship. It would show that she was in sync with her. It was a perfect plan, she congratulated herself.

***

In her back bedroom, Jean made a breakfast of porridge, one slice of wholemeal toast lightly buttered and a huge mug of tea. She put it all out on a tray and picked it up to carry through to her bedroom at the front of the house. She spent most of her time upstairs now; having no downstairs toilet, she was nearer to the bathroom that way.

She trod carefully along the passageway, hating the thought of one day losing her independence altogether. Looking through the upstairs window, watching the world go by on a daily basis, was the only thing she wanted to do now. It kept her sane; to remove that privilege would be taking away her life. She wanted to stay in this house for as long as she could – leave in a coffin if it were possible. She didn't want to go into any old folks' place, bungalow, residential home, or sheltered housing block. She'd rather die than be made to join in with bingo and coffee mornings and for everyone to know her business. *She* was the one who knew everyone else's business and she liked it that way.

She took her tray over to the window and placed it on the low table next to her chair. In a moment, she was settled. Most days, her blinds were drawn. She'd chosen vertical ones because of their versatility, but sometimes it was hard to look through them; they reminded her of bars up at the window when she felt lonely. But even when closed, they were still thin enough to see out and, although the glare of the street lamp outside often kept her from sleeping, she loved the fact that she could still see everything. Now the blinds were slanting to the right, allowing Jean direct access to number thirty-seven.

It was as she sat down in her chair ready to bite into her toast that she saw a shadow in the bay window of Charley's flat. She leaned forward for a closer look but there was nothing there. She looked down onto the road to see that Charley's car was still gone – she'd noted down when she'd left ten minutes earlier – so she hadn't come back, maybe forgetting something. She waited a moment longer. This time she did see someone in the window.

It was Ella – she might have known.

She reached for her binoculars so that she could take a closer look. Ella was wandering slowly around the living room, running her fingers along the back of the settee. Flabbergasted, Jean saw her looking at something on Charley's desk. Then she opened a drawer, searching through it with a hand before closing it again.

When Ella glanced towards her window, Jean sat back in the chair as quickly as she could. She watched the second hand on the clock go round one full rotation before daring to move forward again. But when she looked, Ella had gone. Her eyes rose upwards but that window was empty too. She looked up and down the street – no, she must still be inside.

After another minute of nothing, she did start to eat her toast, now cold. But then she spotted Ella standing in the window again. She was holding a mug, sipping from it carefully. How dare she, the cheeky madam! Jean had a good mind to go over and tell Ella that she shouldn't be snooping around in other people's possessions while they weren't in. The house might belong to her but she had no right to do that.

But she wouldn't tell her. She wouldn't tell anyone anything. Besides, there wasn't any point because no one listened if she caused a fuss anyway; she wasn't going to go through all that again. And perhaps Ella would be capable of twisting the truth regardless. She had seen her looking just then, she was sure.

Jean wondered, given her own penchant for people-watching, if she would want to snoop around her tenant's place if she were a landlady. She smiled, only then empathising with Ella. Of course she would. Even now, she wanted to know everything about Charley, too: why she was on her own and why she'd come to live in the flat. She must have some excess baggage not to be married with two point four children by now.

Jean picked up her notepad and wrote down what she had seen. She might not feel comfortable telling Charley that Ella was roaming around her flat when she wasn't there but she could still make a note of it.

She smiled sneakily. If anything happened to her, everyone's business in Warwick Avenue might be common knowledge. The police would have a field day if they ever saw her notes.

Chapter Nine

Over the next two weeks, it didn't take long for Ella to establish Charley's routine. Always between eight and half past during the week, she would leave the house for work. Most evenings, she was back around six. Twice, on different evenings during the week, she would head out again wearing sports gear and be gone for an hour and a half.

Apart from her meet ups with *One Night Only* dates, the weekends dragged for Ella as Charley mostly stayed in except for a trip to the supermarket and another trip to the gym. Ella knew now that she went to Green's Health and Fitness on the business park at Trentham Lakes; liked to stay for an hour, mainly running on the treadmill.

By now intrigued to see what kind of work she got up to in the field, Ella decided to follow her on a visit to one of her clients. Staying a few cars behind, she headed across to Meir and down Uttoxeter Road, where Charley parked halfway down. Ella pulled in to the kerb and watched as she walked up a pathway to a scruffy-looking house, saw her knock on the door. Charley's heels were low, her long hair tied away from her face. She wore a smart two-piece trouser suit that was neither too official nor too casual. In one hand, she held a soft briefcase, in the other her mobile phone.

The door was answered and she went in.

Despite hardly any sleep the night before after spending most of the evening with a man who called himself Zavier, Ella had managed to stay awake. It had been an hour and thirty-two minutes exactly before Charley had reappeared.

It was when she stood chatting on the doorstep that Ella's heart melted. The woman in the doorway burst into tears and Charley's compassion came out. A simple touch on the arm before she said goodbye, an encouraging squeeze, made the woman give her a weak smile in return. It was enough to spark an idea in Ella.

If *she* could make Charley upset, and offer her a shoulder to cry on, she would be able to touch her too. And then together they could begin to explore the idea of a relationship. After spending a pleasant night with Jayne, already Ella knew that she wanted to do the same with Charley. A ripple of desire flowed through her at the thought that it could lead to far more than a one-night stand.

After a harrowing morning talking one of her clients through her next appearance in court as a witness, Charley arrived back at the office to a mound of trivial paperwork that she couldn't face. Lynne was on the phone trying to urge someone to meet up with her, and Gavin, their assistant support worker, was logging in a client visit for her. She sat down, elbows on her desk, chin resting in her hands, listening to everything going on. It was all so dreary at times, yet she wouldn't swap what she did, and she was one of the lucky ones who didn't have to experience any of it first-hand. She knew that two people a week died through escalating domestic violence incidences; such a sad statistic.

When Lynne ended her call, Charley jumped to her feet. 'Who'd like a sandwich fetching from the shop, my treat? I'm feeling in the mood for cake too.'

'Ooh.' Lynne pushed her glasses up her nose. 'I'd like a vanilla slice, please. Are you off to Wright's Pie Shop?'

Wright's Pie Shop was in Tontine Square. Like the Staffordshire Oatcake, the family-run business was renowned locally for a quality product.

'Of course,' said Charley.

'Maybe I should have a meat and potato pie too – instead of a sandwich. It would work out far cheaper...'

'You're making me salivate at the thought!' Gavin popped his head around the side of his monitor, all blond spiky hair and baby face. 'I'd love a pie too. Is that okay?'

Charley started to write down their order.

'I'd like something with a big fat dollop of jam in it – I love a bit of sauce.'

Charley looked up to see Aaron by her side. 'Funny you should appear at the mention of cake,' she said, giving him a knowing look, but relishing the sight of his warm smile.

Fifteen minutes later, while she waited in the small queue at the shop, Charley tried to clear her mind. Helping Margaret Owen to send her partner to prison and off the streets so that she could live her life in peace, if only for a while, was taking its toll on both of them. Listening to what that bastard had done to Margaret, reliving it all, was atrocious for Charley and she hadn't been the one who had been brutally raped and left for dead. She prayed he went down for a very long time – it took so much out of the women she worked with asking them to testify and live through it all again. And there was so much prejudice involved in these types of things. Luckily for Margaret, the judge on her case was known to be sensitive and firm, and willing to listen to both sides of a story before making a decision.

Deep in thought, she didn't hear someone calling her name.

'Charley!'

A hand on her arm and she turned to see Ella.

'It *is* you. How are you? I haven't seen much of you since you moved in.'

'Oh, hi, Ella. I'm fine, thanks.' Charley smiled and moved forward as the queue did. 'How are you?'

'Good, too. So you work at Striking Back?'

'Hmm?'

'Striking Back.' Ella shuffled forward. 'It's the only organisation I know around here for domestic violence victims.'

Charley nodded in understanding. 'Yes, I'm on the sandwich run. You?'

Ella picked up a cheese and pickle baguette from an open display cabinet at the side of them. 'A temping job came up at Tesco. It's only a few hours a day for a fortnight but every little bit helps, so they say. And I can't buy my dinner from there or else there'd be no point walking in to town.'

'Right.' Charley handed her order over to the young girl behind the counter before turning back. 'How do you find temping? I'm too much of a stickler for routine to want to swap around all the time.'

Ella shrugged. 'It brings in the money, I suppose. And it suits me – I hate to be tied down to one place. Not that there's much chance of that around here. I'm lucky I've been temping long enough to continue to get some regular gigs. I like the variety too. I'm on stock-control in the warehouse at the moment.' She paused. 'Have you met any of our neighbours yet?'

'I've said hello to a few,' said Charley, 'and I've seen "neighbourhood watch Jean."'

They shared a grin before Ella moved forward to pay for her order. 'She's just a nosy old bag,' she said. 'Doesn't mean any harm. It must be lonely if you're housebound.'

Charley considered what Ella said for a moment. She'd hate to be tied down to the house, dependent on other people for everything and unable to get a bit of fresh air. Maybe she *had* jumped to conclusions quickly. Perhaps she'd get used to Jean eventually and see that she meant no harm. After all, she gave her clients the benefit of the doubt as she got to know them. Some she could see through straightaway – practiced lies that no longer worked. With others, she would take time to gain their trust. Either way, people responded to care.

It wouldn't hurt her to show a little leniency with Ella too, who was going out of her way to make her feel welcome. She'd noticed that her post had been piled up on the table in the hall each evening and that the flowers outside her window had been tended to, pots and hanging baskets watered.

Her order ready to go, Charley handed over a note and waited for her change. She turned to Ella.

'Are you free this evening? If so, do you fancy coming downstairs and I'll do something to eat?' she said on impulse.

Ella beamed. 'That would be great.'

'Although it won't be anything fancy. Spag bol and a salad do you?'

'Yes, it will indeed.'

'Great. See you about six.'

As Charley left the shop, a warm feeling engulfed her. Seeing Ella's face light up made her glad she'd made the effort now.

Ella took a long bath before getting ready to see Charley, pampering herself with lots of bubbles and a large glass of white wine. To say that she was looking forward to the evening was an understatement. It was ages since she'd been in the company of a friend. She couldn't wait to get to know Charley better.

Not wanting to seem too keen, she went downstairs ten minutes late, trying to contain her excitement as she knocked on the door.

'Sorry, the computer system I work on had a meltdown and ate my work,' she fibbed, pretending to be all of a flurry when Charley let her in. 'I only got in a few minutes before you. Ooh, thanks.' She took the glass of wine that Charley gave to her. 'I so need this.'

'I hope you're hungry,' Charley said as Ella followed her through to the kitchen. 'I don't know what it is about spaghetti but I always boil too much of it.'

'Fine by me,' said Ella.

'So your day was manic, then?'

'It was okay. How about yours?' Ella hoped she wouldn't blush and give herself away.

'About the same. Always too much to do and too many distractions. That's why I bring paperwork home with me. It's easier to concentrate.'

'But you don't get paid for that?'

Charley rinsed her hands and wiped them on a tea towel. 'No, but I don't mind. And someone has to help the women I deal with. There are never enough hours in the day.'

'Is it only females you work with?'

'Yes. I know men can be victims too, but Striking Back was set up by a woman whose daughter was murdered by her partner. She wanted us to concentrate on women only.'

'Sounds fair, if a little sexist.'

Charley paused. 'I suppose, but there are other charities in the city that cater for both sexes.'

'Do you enjoy it?' Ella wondered how many other women got to see Charley on a regular basis.

'Yes, I do. I'd go so far as to say I'm doing my perfect job.'

'That's deep. I've never loved any job I had.'

'No?'

Ella shook her head, hoping that Charley wouldn't ask her what she'd done in the past. She'd hate to lie all evening; it was so easy to slip up. She moved a little to allow Charley to get past. 'Oh, there was one job I had fun with. Me and my friend, Nina, went to work in a bar in Magaluf when I was in my early twenties.'

Charley raised her eyebrows and grinned mischievously. 'Plenty of sun, sea, sand, and what have you?'

'Precisely.' Ella moved out of her way again as Charley grabbed two dishes from the cupboard and slid them into the oven to warm.

Charley sighed. 'You're so brave.'

'I've always been a bit of a free soul.'

'I'd never be able to do that.'

'Why not?'

'I like being settled in one place, coming home to familiarity, the safeness of it.'

'I reckon you'll want your own place again soon, then?'

'I'm not sure. We'll see.' Charley pulled opened the cutlery drawer. 'I'm not going to run out on you as soon as I've moved in. I know I haven't been here long but I do like it here. It's so peaceful and –'

'Peaceful?' Ella snorted. 'I'm sorry, but I can't be quiet.'

'If you're that worried about making a noise, why didn't you have my flat?'

'And listen to people stomping across the ceiling all the time? I don't think so.'

'And I certainly stomp. I would have driven you mad.' Charley removed a garlic-buttered baguette from the oven and slid it off to put on a plate. 'Ow, ow, ow!' she cried out as the butter burnt her fingers.

'Oh, dear. First aid box?' Ella opened a cupboard. 'Thought I saw one in here – ah, yes. Ta-da!' She pulled out a small green box with a white cross on its lid.

'I don't need first aid, just a brain to know when not to pick up something hot –' Charley paused.

Ella clocked her expression, realising that she *had* slipped up now. 'Don't worry,' she reacted quickly. 'I saw it the other day when you were moving in. And it's because I have one in my drawer upstairs. It's the easiest place to keep it, right? Next to the cooker and on hand for emergencies.'

Charley smiled. 'Of course it is. Sorry, I forgot that your flat has the same layout as mine.'

'Are you sure you're okay?' Ella asked, seeing Charley wince.

'I'm fine, thanks. It only stings a little.'

'Not as much as this one, I bet.' Ella pulled her left sleeve up and held out her forearm. Still hurt by the reaction it got, she avoided Charley's eyes as she took in the large patch of mismatched skin and scar tissue running from her wrist to her elbow.

'Wow,' said Charley. 'That looks like it hurt a lot. How did you do it?'

'I tripped into a bonfire when I was ten,' Ella explained, giving a small titter. 'I'm so bloody accident-prone.'

'Makes me shudder just thinking of it. Did you have to have a skin graft?'

'Three. It took ages to repair itself.' Ella felt tears well in her eyes as she tried to shut out the memories. The hours in hospital, operation after operation to cover the open wound in new skin. It had hurt like hell and she'd had no one to soothe her, reassure her that it would be all right. No one to put their arms around her, hold her while she cried as she realised she would be disfigured for life.

Charley reached out a hand.

Instinctively, Ella moved her arm away but Charley placed it on her shoulder instead. Ella shuddered at her touch but more to do with desire than fear. She could still feel the weight of its presence as Charley moved it away.

'Oh, I'm sorry,' said Charley. 'I only meant to comfort you. I wasn't going to touch it but I can see how you would think that. I'm such a touchy-feely person. I –'

'It's fine,' Ella interrupted, looking up through watery eyes. 'It just brings back a lot of painful memories.'

They stood in silence for a moment before Charley shooed Ella from the kitchen.

'Why don't you go and sit down in the living room,' she told her. 'I'll dish out the food and bring it through.'

Ella turned quickly on her heel, heaving a sigh of relief. Luckily Charley hadn't sussed her out when she'd reached for the first aid box. Even though she hated anyone seeing her scar, it was much better to use it to avoid any further awkward questions.

She didn't want Charley to realise she'd been snooping around her place. Their friendship would be over before it started.

Chapter Ten

Charley came through with the food minutes later to see Ella sitting at the table with her back towards the window. Her eyes were clear and she was smiling again. Charley sat down across from her, handing her a large bowl.

'Help yourself to Parmesan cheese,' she said, passing a smaller dish to her after she'd poured wine. 'There's a lot more of it in the kitchen if you want extra. I mean, like a mound of the stuff. And more bolognese too. I always make too much. I might have to freeze some of it.'

'It's delicious,' said Ella after her first mouthful.

They sat in silence as they tucked in.

'So how did you meet Dan?' Ella asked after a while. Then she made a face. 'Sorry, I hope you don't mind me being so forward, but it's so lovely to see your face light up at the mention of his name.'

'I don't mind at all.' Charley shook her head. 'I – we met through work. We attended the same conference. It was one of those where you had to sit where you were told around tables, like you were at school, and mingle with strangers. Dan was sitting next to me and we were both moaning about it, having a giggle, and it went from there.' She smiled then. 'Actually, I knocked my drink of water over on the table and it soaked the crotch of his trousers. I was mortified!'

Ella laughed. 'That was a great first impression to make. Please tell me you didn't try to wipe it from his trousers.'

'No! But it was so embarrassing. He had a wet patch for hours.'

Ella snorted them.

Charley smiled, recalling more memories of years gone by. 'We were so in tune with each other.'

'So was it all perfect?' Ella probed. 'Not even the teeniest of arguments ever?'

'Of course! We rowed like every other couple. I just think that the nature of what I dealt with on a daily basis made me realise how lucky I was. Or maybe we worked harder at it, I don't know. I don't think I'll ever find anyone like him.'

'No, you won't. Nor do you need to. You'll find someone else.'

'It's not that easy.'

'Sure it is. You must meet men when you go out?'

'I haven't been out in a long while.'

'You mean you haven't been with anyone since Dan?'

Charley shook her head, her eyes dropping for a moment. Almost certain she would have forgotten the etiquette of dating, having been married for so long, the thought of finding someone suitable scared the hell out of her. For starters, trying to figure out compatibility would be an issue. She often heard about dates going wrong, men thinking the older the woman the more desperate they'd be, plus the men's excess baggage to contend with. Then there'd be that awkward moment when she'd have to explain that she was a widow, and the first time she would sleep with someone who wouldn't be Dan. Falling in love was definitely not on her radar for the foreseeable future. But still, she couldn't help but feel lonely every now and then.

'Not even a snog at a Christmas work do?' Ella probed.

'I'm not looking, if that's what you mean,' Charley tried to explain.

'Oh dear.'

'What?'

'When you're not looking, that's when love comes looking for you.'

'I doubt there'll be much left to choose from now. Divorced fathers with weekend children or the weirdos who've never married and still live at home with their parents. Neither of those are my scene.' She laughed nervously.

'Oh, don't worry about that. There'll be plenty to choose from, for an attractive woman like you.'

Charley beamed at the compliment. 'Maybe.' She held up the nearly empty wine bottle. 'I'm going to be a rebel and open another.'

Three hours later, Ella couldn't help but smile as she made herself comfortable on a settee across from Charley. She was buzzing so much just by being around her that she knew she didn't need any more to drink, but it wouldn't hurt her plans to indulge Charley a little more. Having finished off the second bottle, they were now on to a half litre of Bacardi.

Ella leaned forward to top up Charley's glass. 'One for the road?' She giggled at her own joke. Neither of them was going anywhere and she was very glad about that.

'I am such a lightweight when it comes to booze,' said Charley, raising her glass to her mouth and missing entirely. 'That bottle has been open for ages. I topped out a couple of inches and then left it. I can't believe how drunk I feel now, though.'

'Hello,' said Ella. 'We've sunk two bottles of wine before that!'

Charley laughed as she wiped the liquid from her chin with the back of her hand. 'I am so going to regret this in the morning.'

Ella sniggered but a smile never reached her lips. 'The times I've heard that said.'

'That sounds intriguing. Tell me more.'

'My last partner used to go on and on about my high sex drive.'

'No! I wish I had one at all!'

'I bet most women wish they had one at times but often it's hard for men to keep up. I mean, ask a man to screw you more than once every night and they soon get fed up.'

Charley's eyes widened.

Ella grinned sheepishly, praying that Charley wasn't put off too much by her outburst. She hoped instead that she'd want to hear more about her sex life. Then she could open up the conversation further. See where it led.

'So how many men have you slept with?' Charley asked eventually.

'God, I don't know.' Ella pretended to be flippant about it. She slipped off her shoes and curled her feet up beside her. 'Surely you don't keep score?'

'I don't have a score to keep.'

Ella studied her in amazement. 'Christ, you've never had a one-night stand, either, have you?'

Charley shook her head. 'Nope.'

'I thought everyone had had at least one.'

'Not me. I often wonder if I missed out when I was younger, though. But then I met Dan.'

'You haven't slept *just* with him?'

'No, there were a couple of others before we met. But –'

'A couple of …' Ella shook her head. 'We need to get you laid, girl. You have some serious catching up to do.'

'I wish it was that easy, Ella.' Charley burst into tears. 'I miss Dan so much at times. I miss the closeness, the way he made me feel protected. I miss the little things, like the cup of tea he'd bring me in the morning before he headed off to work; his smile as he'd come home of an evening. I even miss the arguing. I miss … I miss everything about him.'

Ella realised this was her moment to become indispensible when she saw Charley's face crumple up again. She rushed to sit next to her, wrapped an arm around her shoulders as Charley finally let go. Holding her as she cried, Ella soothed her with words of comfort, all the time enjoying the feel of her body close to hers.

It was a few minutes before Charley was calm enough to speak again.

'I'm sorry,' she smiled through her tears. 'Blame the drink. I'm fine until I have one too many.'

'Don't apologise,' said Ella. 'Dan wouldn't want you to be alone for the rest of your life, though. He'd want you to move on.'

'I – I know.'

'Everyone needs someone to call their own. I wish I had a partner.'

'I wish I had Dan,' Charley sniffed.

'You need to find someone else – in time, of course. But you have to get used to going out and standing on your own two feet.'

'I've been doing that since he died.'

Ella paused. 'I mean with another man.'

'I can't! I'd feel disloyal.'

'That's ridiculous. If Dan loved you as much as you say, he'd be pretty pissed that you were still moping after him. He sounded like he was a decent guy.'

Charley wiped at her tears. 'You're right, Ella. Maybe it would be okay to go out and have some fun.'

Ella gently wiped at Charley's tears too. 'And if anyone does come along, you could test the water.'

'It – it'll be hard.'

'Falling in love with someone new will bring back painful memories, yes, but then you'll be making new ones.'

Charley nodded.

'No one has to be alone,' Ella spoke again. 'You'll find happiness, once you stop grieving. When my parents died, it nearly destroyed me but I kept on going. Eventually you wake up one morning and you realise that there's a whole world out there that you've forgotten. And when that moment comes, you realise that it's time to step into it again.'

Charley smiled kindly. 'I never had you down as a philosopher, Ella.'

'I just believe that sometimes we have to help ourselves so that we choose the right path.'

'Has anyone ever told you that you talk a lot of sense when you're drunk?'

Ella giggled. 'I think I'll start training to be a life coach.'

'You should!'

She sat forward. 'Hey, how about we go out for a night, you and me?'

'I'm not sure. I –'

'Go on. We can go into Hanley! It will be fun. Please! Please!'

As Ella pleaded with her, Charley gave in. 'Okay.' She nodded. 'Why not?'

'Great! We can do it next Saturday.' Ella checked her watch and sighed. 'I really should be going. We both have work tomorrow and it's nearly midnight.'

'Shit!' Charley stood up with a wobble.

Ella caught hold of her arm as she stood up too. 'Whoops, better get you to bed,' she said.

Charley groaned. 'I am going to be good for nothing in the morning. I shouldn't get this drunk in the week!'

⌣‿⌣

Back in her own flat, Ella re-opened the bottle of wine she'd started earlier and poured another large glass. Unable to keep still, she couldn't stop grinning as she took it through to the living room, plonked it down on the coffee table, and flopped dramatically onto the settee.

The evening had gone far better than she'd anticipated. All that stuff with Charley! It hadn't taken long for her to open up; the poor woman was still grieving after so long. Her emotion was so raw, so animal. It had been terrible to see her suffer like that, pouring her heart out and crying.

But it had left Ella with a job to do – a purpose even. Charley was suffering and it was up to her to help. She needed Ella – she must, because she'd told her all that stuff – and she wanted her friendship.

More to the point, Ella felt worthy. She laughed to herself, stamping her feet lightly on the cushion. She had a friend at last, someone she could turn to, maybe in her darkest moments too. And arranging to go out together the following weekend had been a bonus. She could see them now. They'd be drinking and chatting and dancing. Maybe they'd even do some flirting, get some guys interested, and have a laugh.

But first would be the shopping for new clothes and getting ready for the night out. She wondered if Charley would prefer to come upstairs and get ready here or if she'd be invited to join her downstairs again. She could imagine sitting on the edge of Charley's bed, painting her nails while Charley applied her make-up. It was going to be such fun; if she could just keep Cassandra at bay, they could have a good evening. She doubted Charley would like Cassandra so much. Charley needed Ella; she didn't need Cassandra.

Ella poured more wine as she wondered where they could go. Perhaps they would be better going into Newcastle rather than Hanley, though. She'd hate to bump into anyone who might give Charley the wrong impression.

Who are you trying to kid, you stupid bitch? She doesn't need you.

The words popped into her head as quickly as the recent optimism, pummelling it down and dashing her hopes. She closed her eyes, begging to be left alone. She'd had a good night; didn't fancy going out again. She wanted to sit at home and think of Charley. Charley was her new friend; she needed her.

She put down her glass and turned on some music. If she didn't think too much, maybe she could ignore Cassandra. But the louder she turned the music up, the more Cassandra screamed in her ear.

You don't need anyone but me. All other people do is fuck you up and over. I can show you a good time. I can get rid of your tension. You'd like that, wouldn't you, Ella? Screw away your tension? You would, you dirty little bitch. YOU WOULD.

'No, no, NO!'

Yes, yes, YES. You think Charley cares about you like I do? She doesn't give a fuck. I'll make you happy, Ella. I'm the only friend you need.

Ella emptied her glass and went over to her laptop. She logged onto *One Night Only* and began to browse through her listings. If no one was around, she'd go out on the prowl. She'd lied when she'd told Charley the time – it was barely eleven o'clock when she'd put her to bed but she'd been too drunk to notice. It left her plenty of time to get laid.

Oh, Ella, you naughty girl. What do you make me do?

When I was seventeen, you found me, didn't you, Brendan Furnival? I was such a weak bitch, I suppose it was easy for you to get me back in your bed, move me into your scruffy bed-sit. I was in no fit state to do anything else. I was so consumed by alcohol and soon you were using me again for your own purposes. No, actually you abused me to satisfy your own cravings, your own sexual fantasies. I craved love; you wanted sex. There is a difference. It isn't being forced face down and held while you rammed yourself into me over and over. It isn't covering my mouth so I can't scream out in pain. It isn't throwing me to the ground and then repeatedly kicking me until you have no breath left to do it anymore.

I didn't deserve what you did to me then the same as I didn't deserve to be locked up every night in the home when I was fifteen. You didn't care that what you did was wrong. And then, when I was older, locking me up in your bathroom until I ripped my nails from my fingers trying to claw my way out? Well, that was cruel after what Billie had done. You knew all about that, didn't you? You were no better than her. You both treated me like an animal. No, actually I bet you wouldn't have treated an animal that badly. I must have been mad to stay with you for two years.

I can't believe I married you too – I was so foolish then. You knew that and you took advantage, making me think I was special. I can't even recall our wedding day, we were so wasted. But you told me every day that you loved me.

Actually you told me every day that you were the only person who could ever love me. You told me that you stayed with me because you felt sorry for me and that no one else would want me. It made me desperate to please you. I went out of my way to get you to love me. You just bought me more alcohol to get me off my head and when I was drunk, practically passed out on the bed, that was when you would screw me. Why did I go back to you?

If it wasn't for Amy, I would have put a knife through your heart, and turned it to enhance the pain. You were evil to me. And I will get you for it one day.

My darling Amy – where are you now? Do you cry for your mummy? Do you? DO YOU? I'm so sorry, baby. I'm so sorry.

Chapter Eleven

Half an hour later, Ella was sitting in a pub in Fenton, while the man behind the bar handed her a double vodka. He was a handsome lad, young, fit, and blond. Ella had purposely come back tonight because he'd seemed interested in her a few weeks ago and she wondered if he was still game. At the time, she'd been waiting for a date to turn up from *One Night Only* and, once he had, she hadn't given the blond a second thought.

Aroused by the glint in his eye, she realised he was giving her the come-on again now. It was time to find out if he was all about smouldering looks or if they indeed had unfinished business.

She stepped down from the stool carefully. 'I'm off to the ladies' and I might need your assistance if I'm not back in a few minutes,' she told him pointedly.

'Sure, whatever you say,' he winked.

Not entirely sure if that meant he would follow her or not, she walked to the toilets, staggering to the left slightly, and pushed on the door. Behind her, she heard laughter but as she turned her head she didn't see anyone she knew.

She went into a cubicle, pulled the toilet seat down, and sat with a thump. Resting her head in her hands for a moment, she realised how drunk she was now. But did she care, really? No, not at all.

Even under the influence, her thoughts kept flicking back to Charley. It had been great to spend time getting to know her that evening. She did need a friend and Ella was going to be there for her, no matter what.

Don't even think about it. She wouldn't want to know you.

'Leave me alone,' she muttered. Then she froze as she heard the door to the ladies' open, sighed loudly when someone went into the next cubicle. She rested her head on the cold tiles of the wall beside her.

The woman left about a minute later. The outside door opened again and a knock to her cubicle door followed.

'Are you okay in there?' a male voice asked.

'About time!' Ella drew back the lock.

With a wily grin, he stood with both hands on top of the door frame. 'You said you might need a hand?'

Ella pulled him into the cubicle, closing the door behind them. She kissed him, pushing him up against the wall in her hurry. His hands were all over her in an instant. She grabbed for the buckle of his belt, her lips never leaving his. He pushed up her bra and squeezed her breasts firmly. She heard him groan as she found what she was after. His hands moved lower as she pulled him out, relishing the thought of his cock inside her. She had to have him now. There was no time to waste.

The coupling was frantic, a little uncomfortable in the confined space and certainly not the best she'd had by a mile, but it was good enough for her to release the tension. As he bucked for the last time, kissed her for the last time, he grinned.

'Break over.'

'I guess so,' she replied.

'Vodka on the house?'

She nodded.

He left the cubicle and she tidied herself up in the mirror outside. Her face had the afterglow of sex but she'd been screwed so many times in so many toilets and by so many men, that she was too long in the tooth to let it show. It wasn't as exciting anymore – thinking she'd get caught had been a thrill at first. Now, she didn't care. As long as she reached orgasm, the night was good. She could keep Cassandra at bay for a little longer.

Jake had seen Ella go out in a taxi and was hoping she'd return while he worked into the night. He was revising for a test he had at college the next morning, cursing himself for leaving it until the last minute as usual. He'd already got a low mark for the previous one and wasn't going to flunk this one as well. Despite being known as one of the lads, he was at college to learn. He intended to move out of the city, head to London to up his chances of doing well. Stoke wasn't the kind of place for him to make serious money. One day, he'd be head of his own company. He wasn't going to work for anyone else.

When he heard a car approaching along Warwick Avenue, then coming to a halt outside his home, he looked down from his window to see Ella getting out of the passenger seat. He smiled to himself until he saw a man get out of the driver's side, lock the car, and head towards her as she waited for him on the pavement. Shit, she'd brought someone home to do what he wanted to do.

From his position hidden in the shadows, he could see everything. They were at the door now. He heard Ella laugh and then they were kissing. They didn't look like they wanted to go in.

He continued to watch them necking on the doorstep. Then, all of a sudden, were they ...? They were!

They were screwing up against the wall.

Jake grabbed his phone, zoomed in, and pressed record. Even if the sound wasn't good, the picture was clear enough. And it beat wanking off over a photograph. Watching the real thing – watching her! Wow, he had got to show his mates this. They wouldn't believe him otherwise.

Camera pointing directly at them, he zoomed in as much as he could without the image becoming distorted. His free hand pressed on his erection. Man, this was hot. It was even better than viewing a porno. Thank God he hadn't fallen asleep!

Charley awoke the next morning to the shrill of her alarm clock. She sat upright in a daze, the noise shocking as well as upsetting her; she was usually out of bed before it went off. She reached across to switch if off. Then, as her head began to pound, she dropped back to her pillow.

Her mind returned to the previous evening. She could remember chatting with Ella, cooking something to eat, and then opening another bottle of wine. She recalled laughing a lot too. It had been a good evening but something she didn't want to repeat on a regular basis during the week. Reluctantly, she dragged herself out of bed to face the day.

Forty-five minutes later, she winced as she closed her front door behind her a little too loudly. God, she was thirty-six – hangovers shouldn't be this bad, surely?

Since she'd woken up, more flashes of the evening had begun to come back to her. She'd even recalled a steamy conversation about sex. Embarrassment washed over her as she realised she must have been talking about Dan too. It was annoying that she'd got wrecked during the week but even more so knowing that she must have poured her heart out to a near stranger about her grief over losing him.

But then again, she knew with her job just how effortless it was to unburden everything on to another's shoulders if they were willing to listen. It was so much easier talking to someone you didn't know. Trouble was, she knew from experience that it was fine to do it with someone you didn't see on a regular basis but a person you might see a lot? A definite no-no. God, what would Ella think of her?

She heard a door opening upstairs.

'Hey there,' Ella shouted down to her. 'How are you this morning?'

Shit. Charley froze a moment before turning to her. 'Hi!' She smiled, voice all bright and breezy. 'I'm a bit delicate but not too bad. You?'

'Lousy.' Ella came down a few steps to her level. Resting a hand on the banister, she grinned. 'We did have a bit to drink. Sorry.'

'It wasn't your fault.'

'I know, but I don't have to be at work as early as you. I shouldn't have kept you talking. We just got carried away and one drink led to another. I –'

'Hey, no one held the glass to my lips.' Charley paused. 'Look, I'm sorry if I went on a bit about Dan. Sometimes, especially after a drink, I loosen up and all the old feelings come back. I'm fine, really.'

'I don't mind listening. I was hoping that I didn't go too far with the advice. You did get a little upset.'

'No, it was okay.' Charley felt herself blush as she tried to think back to what they had discussed. 'It was good advice.'

'You didn't think I was too harsh?'

'Of course not,' she lied.

'It must have felt good to get it off your chest, though. And I'm always here to listen.' Ella beamed at Charley. 'That's what friends are for.'

'I guess.' Charley smiled back.

'And I'm really looking forward to next Saturday night. I thought maybe we could go into town in the afternoon, if you like? I know you said you had new heels but I wouldn't mind some new shoes too and maybe a pair of jeans – if I can ever find a comfortable pair to buy. It's a nightmare, isn't it, to get a good fit? And I could do with some new lippie and eye –'

'Whoa!' Charley held up a hand for Ella to stop. 'You've lost me completely.'

'Next Saturday, remember? You and I are going out.'

Charley's shoulders dropped. 'Forgive me, Ella. I might have agreed to something while I was worse for wear and I wouldn't want to let you down. What exactly did I say I'd do?'

'You said you'd come out for a drink with me.' Ella's smile faltered. 'Don't worry, I can find someone else.'

Charley was mortified to see the look of rejection on Ella's face. Damn, she couldn't go back on her word now. Besides, even if some of the night was cringe-worthy due to her drunken ramblings, most of it had been fun. She decided to go along with it.

'I don't do clubbing anymore but I'm happy to do a night in a pub, or a couple of pubs?'

Ella brushed aside the remark and turned to leave. 'No, don't worry. It's fine. I can –'

'– find someone else to go out with, I know. But, hey, do you know what? Maybe I can manage a night. It would be fun to let my hair down once in a while. And you're right, I have a great pair of heels that have hardly had any wear.'

'Well, if you're sure …'

'I'm sure.'

Ella smiled. 'It's a date, then!'

Charley smiled too – at Ella's delight. It didn't take much to make her happy, it seemed.

After dozing in the armchair again the night before, Jean too had been woken on Ella's return in the early hours. So she'd been surprised to see her up and about when she looked out of the window the next morning. She had to hand it to her – the girl had stamina.

Jean wished she could have a bit more energy to get her through the perils of old age. Then again, she smiled, she wasn't sure she'd want to live her life as vivaciously as Ella.

She reached for her notepad, noted down that Charley had left, and realised she'd been dozing in the chair for most of the night. Insomnia – not good for the soul but something she'd had for several years now. It had started when her late husband, George, died. She'd been up for a few nights after his death, which had upset her routine, and had struggled to get it back into line again. When she'd visited the doctor in a state of desperation, so tired and bone weary, the doctor had told her it was grief related and given her a course of sleeping tablets to knock her out. They'd worked on and off every time she'd taken a course but, once the course was done, she'd be wide awake again at 3 a.m. It was as if her body didn't know what to do without George to snuggle up to, even after all these years.

Which is why last night she'd been awake again when Ella had arrived home. She recalled hearing a car pull up, the engine die, and car doors slamming before she'd been quick enough to sit forward to look out of the window. He'd been a young thing this time, and his hands had been all over Ella before they'd even got into the house. Ella had run giggling up the steps as he'd cupped her behind, squirmed as he'd tried to get a hand inside her jacket. He'd kissed her neck before turning her round to face him, kissing her again.

As Jean had observed further, she'd had her own private show. A voyeur wasn't something she wanted to call herself but she *had* watched as Ella's stud pushed her up against the wall, his hand up her skirt, the material bunching up her thighs. And then she'd watched in awe as Ella's pants came down, saw her step out of them, quickly picking them up and shoving them into the pocket of her jacket before pulling him near again. She must have undone his belt because the next thing Jean knew he'd pressed her against the wall, pushing himself into her as she wrapped her legs around his waist. Mesmerised, she'd watched them together until they finished. He'd fastened his belt and they'd headed indoors.

As an afterthought, Jean glanced up and down Warwick Avenue. The car he'd arrived in was nowhere to be seen. Ella must have been up to her usual tricks. Bang 'em and chuck 'em out, Jean called it. She sighed – young women these days. They might have more stamina than her but some of them had far less morals and convictions. Jean had only slept with George in her entire life.

She wondered if anyone else in the avenue had seen them coupling outside. It seemed to Jean that Ella wasn't bothered in the slightest if anyone did see her, the way she paraded around naked in her front window. Sometimes, Jean wondered if she wanted to get caught out. Or did Ella think that other neighbours would be watching her, peeping on her like she did? Maybe Ella was turned on by that thought.

Jean moved back to settle in her chair again, hoping to get an hour or so of sleep. Sometimes her life was so mundane, but every now and then, she got a little slice of excitement.

Ella flounced upstairs and closed the door to her flat with an almighty bang. She marched down the hallway and into the living room where she threw herself onto the settee face first. She began to pummel a cushion. Damn that stupid bitch. How dare Charley make promises she didn't intend keeping! Didn't she realise how hurtful it was?

Despite being sore from her encounter with the barman last night, Ella made herself feel better the only way she knew she could. Spent after a couple of minutes of frantic masturbation, she sat up again but Charley was still on her mind. Why would she deny everything? They had a spark – whether friendly or something more meaningful she wasn't sure yet. She'd spoken to her truthfully about her sex life last night. Ella didn't want to come on to her yet but, once she'd been let down by a fella or two, she would be all hers – or rather, all Cassandra's.

A plan began to form in her mind for their night out.

Don't be so ridiculous.

Ella covered her ears.

She won't go out with you. She has far better things to do.

'La la la la la!'

Who in their right mind would want to spend time with you? Look at you; you can't even get a man to call your own, never mind setting anyone else up.

'Go away!' In a desperate attempt to rid herself of the taunts, Ella ran into her bedroom. She went into the walk-in closet, closed the door behind her. In the darkness, she slid to the floor and sat with her head in her hands. Maybe the voice would go soon. If not, she was going to get very, very angry.

Chapter Twelve

Ella had a hard time containing her excitement about the planned night out with Charley that following weekend. So much so that she'd logged onto *One Night Only* and gone out for sex on three consecutive evenings during the week. Continually thinking of the time they would spend together made her horny. She wasn't quite sure what it was about Charley yet – was it purely the need to look after her, as any good friend would? Or was she missing signs that Charley wanted to take things further? Either way, she'd been disappointed when they'd failed to meet up again. Each time she'd caught her coming home in the evening and had asked her to pop up for a drink, Charley had politely refused, saying she had too much work to do.

Lying awake on Thursday morning, Ella turned onto her back, wincing at a sudden pain in her stomach. She groaned. What the hell? Pulling back the duvet revealed a mass of angry bruising below her ribs, easily as big as a tennis ball. She tried to think back to the night before? Who had she met? Damien – that was his name, and, by the look of what they'd got up to, he certainly had been the anti-Christ.

Carefully, she got out of bed and made her way to the bathroom. It was there she saw the full horror of her injuries. There was another bruise on the bottom of her back and a few scratch marks. She touched her stomach gently, grimacing again at the pain. *Think, THINK!* How the hell had she got that bruise? Had Damien given it to her or had she somehow caused it herself? Had they got too rough or had she picked a fight with someone as she was often prone to do? Shit. She wouldn't be able to find out, either – rules were rules on *One Night Only*. Unless individuals passed on details to each other, all contact information on the website was deleted once two people had met. And she hadn't emailed him personally, just through the site. Unless she contacted the administrator to report him for bad behaviour, which she couldn't do because she wasn't sure exactly what had happened, she would have to live with not knowing.

Naked still, she sat down on the side of the bath and switched on the hot water tap. Noticing another bruise on her elbow, she tried to cast her mind back again, but nothing. Ella hated that it was becoming a regular occurrence, getting so drunk she couldn't recall anything.

'Stupid fucking bitch.' She slapped her face as hard as she could. 'You know better than to lose full control.'

It makes you feel better until the next time. You know there'll always be a next time, don't you?

She spotted the red dress she'd gone out in scrunched up on the floor behind the door. She picked it up – there was a tear down its side. She looked again, trying to remember. But everything was blank.

Suddenly, she turned off the tap and stepped into the bath. Then she switched on the overhead shower, turning the dial to cold. Sitting down, she let the water cover her, wash away her fear, take away her anger, cleanse her of evil.

But the water didn't do anything. Not that she expected it to – nothing seemed to calm her down just lately. Maybe she never would be at ease.

She hugged her knees and began to shiver, wondering what would become of her if the blackouts continued.

At the end of a long, but thankfully not too eventful, week at work, Charley logged off her computer at five thirty and rummaged under her desk for her handbag. There were only a few people left in the office but she and Lynne had wanted to finish off some case notes before they left.

'Off so soon, Charley?'

She looked up to see Aaron approaching her desk and smiled. 'Well, it's the weekend and all that.'

'Any plans?'

'As a matter of fact, I'm going out with the new neighbour tomorrow night.'

Aaron clutched his chest and staggered backwards, blue eyes showing mock pain. 'Tell me what he's got that I don't have.'

'It's a she, not a he.'

'Oh, my.' Aaron folded his arms. 'So tell me what does *she* have that I don't have?'

'Nothing!'

'I'm serious. *I've* been trying to get you to come out for months. *You* change addresses, make a new friend and all at once, I'm *forgotten*? Men have hearts too, you know.'

'Yeah, right.' Charley could see where his light-hearted banter was heading. 'And I stole yours – is that what you're going to say next?'

'Well, I –'

'You're such a sweet talker. If you must know, I agreed to go out with her after too many glasses of wine. It's only for a few drinks in Hanley. I doubt I'll be out for –'

'Stop right there!' Aaron held up a hand to silence her. '*You're* going into town?'

Charley nodded.

'For a drink – in a pub?'

Charley knew he was winding her up. 'So will you be there tomorrow night?'

'I was going to give it a miss,' he waved his hand to dismiss her comment, 'but seeing as you might be there ... Any idea where you're going?'

'No, but there's hardly much choice now, is there? Not like when we were younger.'

'Speak for yourself. I'm still young.'

'You're desperate, I'll give you that.'

'Look, do you want me to buy you half a lager and share my kebab with you later?'

'Ha ha, very funny.'

'What on earth are you two wittering on about?' Lynne came bustling into the office, putting a file down onto the desk before sitting in her chair.

'We're going out tomorrow tonight,' Aaron said, pointing first at himself then at Charley.

Lynne looked up in confusion. 'You mean both of you?'

'Hmm-hmm,' said Aaron.

'As in. A. Date?'

'Hmm-hmm.'

'No, we are not!' Charley laughed as he sauntered off backwards, making a heart-shape at her with his fingers.

'The Exchange,' he shouted before he left. 'You'll find me in The Exchange.'

'He's serious about you,' Lynne spoke without taking her eyes from her computer screen.

'It's banter,' Charley told her as she searched in her bag for her keys.

Lynn bobbed her head up and pushed her glasses down her nose.

'It is!' said Charley.

'I'm just saying ... you could do much worse. He's a nice guy and mad about you. Why don't you give him a try?' She laughed. 'Something for the weekend, madam.'

Charley tried to look shocked but laughed too. She thought back to her conversation with Ella last week. 'I must admit,' she said, 'I do miss the closeness of being a couple.'

Lynne shook her head. 'I much prefer a cup of tea. It's far less mess and besides, I'm too old for all that rolling around now.'

Charley smiled. She knew that what Lynne had been through with her ex-husband would scar her for the rest of her life. It was no wonder she'd become somewhat guarded and protected over the years. She'd been through so much; age had nothing to do with it.

'So?' Lynne asked.

'So?'

'I want to hear all about it – every detail – on Monday morning.'

'Give over!' Charley hitched her handbag onto her shoulder. 'Like anything is going to happen that quickly.'

On Saturday afternoon, Ella lay curled up on the settee after taking a nap. Although annoyed that Charley hadn't wanted to go shopping with her – and that she hadn't invited her downstairs to share a bottle of wine while they readied themselves for the night ahead – anticipation fizzed up inside her. She hadn't been out for a girlie night in ages. She cast her mind back ... no, she couldn't remember ever going on one, really. She didn't need any long-term friendships now, though, not since she had found Charley. And besides, she didn't want anyone to find out about Cassandra. The fewer people knew about her and *One Night Only* the better as far as she was concerned.

Lately, it had become harder to keep Cassandra under wraps. Sometimes it didn't do to cross her. Ella ended up in more trouble than if she'd been nice to her and let her out to play. Take last week, when she'd brought home the barman – Matthew, was that his name?

Why do you want to hide me, Ella? I am a big part of who you are.

Ella closed her eyes, trying to rid herself of Cassandra's chides. This was her night out and she wasn't going to let her spoil it. She had a chance to build up a proper friendship, something she hadn't had in a long while. And besides, Charley needed help to get over Dan and move on with her life. *She* was going to see to it that Charley moved on. And she knew exactly how. Her plan wouldn't fail. Afterwards, Charley would be hers and hers alone.

Feeling the urges building up inside her again, she got up quickly and ran to her bedroom. It wasn't time to get ready for at least another hour yet but she stripped, pulled open her underwear drawer and rummaged through it. The first thing to catch her eye was the red number – she'd treated herself to it only last month – a vintage-inspired corset in rich satin, with a lace-up back detail and heavy boning that she hoped would give her some curves. Ella loved its front hook & eye closure, putting her in control of exactly how much she wanted to reveal and when. She found the side-tie thong to go with it. Then she rummaged again. She had a padded plunge bra to match. That would do instead of the corset. It was only for herself anyway. Where was it?

She found it at last, pulling them both on in a hurry. She knew that Charley wouldn't be seeing any of her yet but she wanted to imagine how she'd feel wearing something so sexy, so naughty, sitting next to her. Or maybe she'd be better going commando, sit with her legs open. Thoughts of Alex in Rendezvous came back to her. She groaned in her eagerness, lying back on the bed to relive it all.

Charley had been looking forward to the night out a little more as the week had gone on, but that afternoon, all her doubts suddenly came rushing back. She wasn't sure she was ready to go out as a single woman, facing crowds of people in noisy bars, making a fool of herself again if she drank too much through nerves and ... well, feeling old.

She anguished over what to wear. Not too dressy; not too casual. Killer heels or comfortable wedge shoes. At least she had a natural glow from the weather they'd had recently, although the autumn coolness was in the air now that it was mid-September.

But along with all the panic came a smidgeon of excitement. She *was* looking forward to going out. In the bedroom, she flicked on the closet light, stepped inside, and rummaged through her clothes. For the first time in ages, she felt full of life as she pulled on an outfit of dark skinny jeans and a sleeveless top before slipping into her shoes. She checked herself out in the mirror and grinned back at her reflection – not bad for her age, either. Bunching up her hair and piling it on top of her head, she wondered whether to clip it up or wear it loose. She pulled down a couple of strands for added allure, then let it all drop. She would leave it free.

Glancing at the photo of Dan beside her bed, she reached over for it and ran a finger over the glass. 'I do love you,' she whispered into the quiet of the room, 'but tonight I might have a bit of fun. I hope you don't mind.'

She put the frame back. It was silly, she realised, but knowing he would be pleased for her put her at ease. And Lynne was right – she could do much worse than Aaron. So maybe, if it was okay with Ella, they could head to The Exchange some time during the evening.

Ten minutes later, she was blotting her lipstick when she heard a knock. She checked her watch: it was quarter to eight. Ella was early but she was ready. A final glance in the mirror and she went to answer the door.

Ella stood there in a short black dress, the highest of red heels and a long-sleeved lacy cardigan. Her hair was loose too, shiny, and she looked fresh and younger with a little more make-up, ready for a night out.

'You look amazing!' Charley complimented her. 'I feel so under-dressed now.'

'Of course you're not. You look divine.' Ella held up a bottle of wine. 'One for the road?

'I –'

Ella pressed her thumb and index finger together. 'A teeny weeny one?'

'Oh, go, on then. Why not?'

She stepped through and Charley closed the door behind her.

'I'm so excited about tonight, Charley. I haven't had a good laugh in Hanley for ages. I think it will be brilliant, you and I going together. I thought maybe we could start off in The Exchange and then go further into town. There's not much to choose from but I can show you where I hang around and maybe meet –'

'Slow down!' Charley held up her hand. 'I'm having a job keeping up with you.'

Ella grinned. 'Sorry. It's been a good week and I want to celebrate in style.'

'Oh?' Charley poured drinks while Ella stayed in the kitchen doorway. 'Any particular reason?'

They went through to the living room.

Ella shrugged. 'No, just life in general is going well.'

'That's always great to hear.'

'How about you?'

'Me? Oh, the usual stuff, as in nothing exciting has happened. I'm just deciding whether to do an evening course at Staffs Uni or if it would be too much alongside my work.'

'What would you do?' Ella stood in the window, looking out to the avenue.

'I'm not sure whether to go for something academic that would help me with my job or do something enjoyable.' She laughed nervously. 'You know what I mean.'

'Something that doesn't demand too much attention?'

'I suppose. I'd like to qualify in something but I'm not sure I have the energy to be a student again.'

'I can imagine.' Ella turned back to her. 'All that partying ...'

'I meant all the revising for tests and exams.'

Ella smiled. 'I know. I was winding you up. Besides, I've never been to college or university so I wouldn't have a clue what it's like.'

'Have you never wanted to?'

A taxi pulled up outside, beeping noisily.

'Blimey, an early taxi. Better get a wriggle on.' Ella drained her glass. 'Come on,' she encouraged, pushing Charley's glass up towards her mouth a little. 'Down the hatch in one go.'

'I'll be drunk in no time!'

'That's the general idea. We're going to have an unforgettable night!'

Chapter Thirteen

Twenty minutes later the taxi dropped them off in Hanley. Situated on the corner of Trinity Street and Marsh Street, the Old Victorian Telephone Building stood red and regal, almost out of place as traffic queued up against the lights at the crossroads. The Exchange was spread over two floors. Above the doorway, the words *Telephone Building* were scrolled on top of the brickwork. The plush entrance and stone steps almost made Charley feel like a little girl as she ran into the hallway.

It was a popular venue, with the contemporary feel of a bar similar to one found in London or Manchester – high ceilings, wooden floors, and a laid-back atmosphere. Already it was filling up nicely for a Saturday evening, although it was still pleasant to stand near the bar. People were eating in the dining area, a thirtieth birthday party taking over the bottom of the room; there were pink and white balloons at three tables.

They ordered drinks and moved over to the far end of the room.

'It's great in here,' said Charley. 'I can't believe I haven't been before.'

Ella gave her a look of incredulity. 'You've *never* been to The Exchange?'

Charley shook her head.

'Not even for your lunch? They do great food. The fish finger bloomer is one of my favourites. So when was the last time you came in to Hanley for a night out?'

'I haven't got a clue.'

'When was the last time you went out? Can you remember that?'

'That would definitely be before ... before Dan died.'

Hearing her voice falter, Ella touched her arm gently. 'This is a first for you.' She picked up the drinks menu. 'I think we'd better order cocktails.'

An hour later and they were ensconced in a booth, chatting about everything and anything. Soon more cocktails had been ordered and after another hour, they seemed to have settled for the foreseeable future. Charley's head felt fuzzy as she headed upstairs to the ladies'. Once there, she checked her appearance in the mirror and giggled. Her hair was sticking up where she'd been ploughing her fingers through it; there were flakes of mascara all over her cheeks and not a trace of any lipstick. *Dragged through a hedge backwards* would have been putting it politely. But she was having a great time with Ella. They'd been discussing their first boyfriends and swapping horror stories of crushes and first loves and all that teenage angst.

As she made her way downstairs again, she lost her footing. When she hung onto the banister as well as her dignity, one of a group of men arriving stopped her from falling.

'Whoops,' she grinned. 'Silly heels! Thanks.'

'I don't mind being your knight in shining armour any time,' he smiled, holding the door open for her afterwards.

It was nearing eleven o'clock and the bar was hectic now. As she made her way back to Ella, she sensed someone looking at her and turned to see if it was the guy whose feet she'd practically fallen at. Instead, her eyes fell on Aaron. He was waving to catch her attention. A rush of pleasure ran through her as, in a matter of seconds, he'd negotiated the crowd and was by her side.

'Well, hello,' he smiled. 'Fancy seeing you here.'

'Fancy indeed.' And lucky, thought Charley, that he'd seen her *after* she'd tidied up her appearance rather than before. All of a sudden, she realised how important that was to her. She checked out what he was wearing; she was so used to seeing him in work attire. Jeans and casual shirt, Timberland boots. Hugo Boss again. She took hold of his hand and dragged him over to Ella. After introductions, he slid into the booth with them.

'I have to hand it to you, Ella,' he said. 'I'm surprised that you managed to persuade Charley to come out. I've been trying for some time now.'

Ella beamed at the compliment. 'That's what friends are for – taking care of each other. She just needed a helping hand.'

'I did,' slurred Charley.

'She definitely needs taking in hand,' laughed Aaron. 'She's tipsy.'

'You could take advantage of her, if you like.'

'You mean I need a good seeing too, don't you?' Charley giggled and prodded Aaron in the chest. 'I know what you're after, Mr Campbell.'

'Yes, but I'm not going to overstay my welcome.' Aaron grinned and pointed at their table. 'Can I get you a drink before I head back to the boys?'

'The boys?' Charley snorted. 'You're practically a middle-aged man.'

Smirking, he moved off as Charley and Ella started laughing. Ella leaned forward and whispered in Charley's ears. 'You should take him up on his offer. He's gorgeous.'

Charley looked over at Aaron, who was now with the 'boys.' Ella was right – she might be drunk but he was gorgeous.

Ella nudged her arm. 'Go for it,' she urged.

Charley turned back to her. 'Go for what?'

'Him! You told me you'd never had a one-night stand. Now's your time.'

'Nooooo.' Charley wagged her finger at Ella. 'He's too close for comfort.'

'He's comforting, I'll give you that.' Ella sniggered. 'He's sweet on the eyes.'

Charley glanced through the crowds towards Aaron again. He was looking back at her. She caught his eye and he smiled.

'You see?' Ella was determined to get her point across. 'Look, you need to sleep with someone. It's going to be painful so why not do it with someone who cares about you?'

Charley shook her head fervently. 'I couldn't.'

'You could – and besides, he has some great-looking mates. Maybe one of them might be single, too.'

'I thought you wanted to go somewhere else after this drink!'

'Changed my mind.'

Before Charley could stop her, Ella made a beeline to chat to Aaron and a few minutes later, he and his friends were sharing their booth. Finding that the alcohol had loosened her inhibitions, she heard herself laughing raucously at something funny Aaron whispered to her. It felt good to be a little out of control after so long staying home alone.

The night went on and, at midnight, Charley found herself sitting with Aaron. The crowd in the bar had lightened a little, some people moving downstairs to the basement bar where a local band, Diamonds, was playing. Ella was chatting to someone called Steve whom Charley vaguely recognised from their group, and the rest of them were nowhere to be seen.

Her head was so close to Aaron's that if she turned slightly, he would catch her cheek with his lips. Embarrassed, she moved away slightly. He smiled and she returned it, a woozy feeling overpowering her, something that she definitely knew wasn't entirely down to the alcohol.

'I am so drunk,' she told him, running a finger lightly over his hand as it lay on the table. 'Happy but drunk.'

'I am so drunk too,' Aaron replied. 'But I want to stay here with you forever.'

All at once, a longing to be part of a couple overwhelmed Charley. Rather than upsetting her, though, it excited her. She glanced over to Ella, who was smooching with Steve. His hands were all over her as they kissed.

'Oh-oh.' Aaron had followed her gaze, his eyebrows raised high. 'It looks like those two need a room. Maybe we should be on our way soon?'

Charley nodded, although not wanting to leave him yet.

'Perhaps we could all head back to my place?'

She swallowed. Even unable to focus fully, she could see the desire in his eyes. She knew he'd be able to see it reflected in hers too. She smiled shyly.

'Perhaps we should,' she said.

'Are you sure?'

'I'm sure.'

He leaned forward to kiss her lightly on the tip of her nose and then grabbed her hand.

After they'd hailed a taxi, Charley found herself heading off to Stockton Brook and being dropped off outside a tiny semi-detached cottage. From the outside, it looked like a small two-up, two-down but, once inside, it opened up vastly into a large double room with a staircase down the wall to her left. Laminate floors gave it a vast feel; the walls were cream except for one painted with abstract blacks and violets. The fire and television were sunk into the wall. A cream rug with a glass coffee table atop of it and deep purple curtains pulled it all together.

'Coffee?' asked Steve. 'Or something stronger?' Almost immediately, he and Ella disappeared into a room at the back that Charley assumed would be the kitchen.

'Wow, I'm impressed.' She looked at Aaron. 'This décor is incredible. Did you –'

'I did – and all by myself.' Aaron held his arms up and twirled around. 'This is my creation. Whoops.' He flopped onto the settee in a fit of laughter, pulling Charley down on top of him.

Charley thought the sound of her heart beating erratically might be loud enough to wake the whole street as they stayed that way, neither reluctant to move. They stared at each other, for once no words needed.

'You are so gorgeous,' he told her eventually, touching her cheek lightly.

'I'm drunk,' Charley retorted, not sure if her heart was beating erratically due to the heat of Aaron next to her or their recent twirl. 'It's been a great night. I've enjoyed it so much.'

'Me too.'

He kissed her. Light enough to make her feel that it might not have happened. He gazed into her eyes, almost as if he was asking for permission. Then he kissed her again. Charley wrapped her arms around his neck, entangling her fingers in his hair, drawing him close. Her body responded, making her tingle as she felt his tongue against hers. For some reason, it didn't feel wrong to be kissing him. He ran his hands over her back, pushing her further down onto the settee.

The door opened and Ella appeared with Steve. Her hair was tousled and one flap of Steve's shirt was out.

'Okay if we use the spare room tonight, mate?' Steve grinned at Aaron.

'Sure,' Aaron nodded, not taking his eyes from Charley.

Before they left, Ella gave Charley the thumbs-up. There was a giggle and a thundering of feet up the stairs before a door slammed.

'Peace and quiet at last,' said Aaron. 'Now, where were we?'

Early the next morning, Charley opened heavy eyes, momentarily confused by her surroundings – white walls and a navy blue carpet, her shoes placed together underneath a small window with blue curtains. She moved her head to the right, wincing as a pain shot through it. Then she groaned as she spotted her clothes draped over a chair.

Shit.

She turned over. Even though the curtains were drawn, the room was light. She didn't dare look at the time for fear of waking him. But she did lift the duvet up to see if she was naked.

Shit and bollocks.

'Morning, my sleepy drunkard,' Aaron said, his eyes still closed.

'Morning.' Charley's voice came out as a croak. 'What time is it?'

He lifted his arm. 'Quarter to nine. Did you sleep well?'

'I can't remember.'

'You can't remember.'

'No.'

'You mean, you can't remember *anything* of last night?'

Charley tucked her hands under her chin and curled her knees up a little more.

'Not even a tiny bit of it?' Aaron mirrored her actions.

'Nope.' Charley thought it best to lie until she knew more of what he was referring to. She could remember parts of the evening: having a laugh with Ella in The Exchange, meeting up with Aaron, coming back here and lying on the sofa ... but she wasn't going to let on to him. Then maybe she could deny anything else that might have happened too.

'I am deeply hurt that I'm so unmemorable.' Aaron sighed loudly. 'You've ruined my street cred.'

'Aaron, I ...' Charley cleared her throat. 'Aaron, did we ...'

'We did ... not.'

'We didn't?'

'No, you were a little too worse for wear for my liking.'

'You make me sound like a drunken trollop!'

'You were a drunken trollop! But I've been wanting to get inside your knickers for so long that I didn't want to mess up and take advantage of you and then you'd be mortified this morning and you wouldn't want to see me and think that I was only interested in a one-night stand when I'm not and just the thought of seeing you at work afterwards if you thought that would be agony but I'm scared now that I *did* miss out on the opportunity to sleep with you and –'

Charley put a hand over his mouth. 'Enough,' she cried. Once she knew he'd stay quiet, she removed it.

'What I'm trying to say is that I wouldn't take advantage of you.'

A pause. 'Who undressed me, then?'

'Erm, that would be you.'

'Oh, I –'

He smirked. 'You really don't remember anything, do you?'

'Sorry, no.'

'You paraded around taking all of your clothes off … first came your top.'

'Oh, God.'

'Wait; actually it was the shoes that came off like missiles. I had to duck!'

'Sorry.'

'And *then* came your top.'

'Right.'

'And then your jeans, and your bra and –'

'Enough!'

'There was enough for my liking but –'

'I said enough!'

'I reckon it's a good job we didn't sleep together, then. I'd hate for you not to remember how fantastic I am in bed!'

'So modest.'

'I am! I'm sure you'll find out one day.'

Charley felt her cheeks start to burn. Even so, she was hoping that would be true. She was grateful that he hadn't taken advantage of her. Plus she liked the fact that he was willing to take things slowly.

'Some men would have had their wicked way with me last night,' she told him.

'I was probably too drunk to get it up anyway.'

'You're an idiot, do you know that?' But Charley was smiling when she said it. She'd enjoyed herself so much last night that she would have been mortified if they *had* made love. Not because of the sex but the fact that he'd maybe think all she was after was the one night – to get over Dan and move on – and she wanted it to be more than that. All of a sudden, she was hoping he would ask to see her again.

From across the hallway, loud banging. Then a grunt and a deep groan; at the same time, a moan in a higher pitch. Staring at each other, they listened as the banging became louder and more frantic, the grunts and moans too. A final bang and it was quiet again.

Charley giggled. 'Some people certainly aren't taking their time like us.'

'Maybe we have that to look forward to if we don't rush things?'

'Maybe,' she replied, moving nearer to him a little.

'If you fancy a nice but friendly cuddle, I wouldn't get too close,' he warned.

'I know. I have terrible beer breathe too.' Charley covered her mouth with her hand.

'It's not the beer breath I'm worried about.' He lifted up the duvet. 'Get down, soldier.'

After greeting Ella and Steve coyly in the kitchen an hour later, Charley and Aaron then joined them over coffee and bacon sandwiches as they dissected the night before. Later, Steve had a football match to watch so Aaron offered to drop him off and take Charley and Ella home.

Back in Warwick Avenue, Ella went inside as they said their goodbyes.

Aaron pulled Charley into his arms and kissed her. His mouth caressed her lightly, tantalisingly at first, but she found it wasn't enough. She placed a hand on his back, pulling him as near as she could. She wanted to feel him close to her again, a small part of her unable to believe that the night had happened at all. After all her worries, Charley couldn't have been happier. Well, apart from one thing...

Afterwards, she didn't want to let him go.

'Well,' Aaron spoke finally, 'this *isn't* one of those awkward moments, I'm pleased to say.'

'Really? I wasn't going to remark but I'd rather call it a one-night stand even though we didn't actually have a one-night stand,' she teased. 'One night was enough for me, thanks very much.'

'Like that is it?' He leaned across – she thought to kiss her again – but instead he opened the passenger door. 'Get out, then.'

'Shut up, you idiot,' she grinned.

'Oh, no – the damage is done. Out.'

Charley kissed him instead, shivering as the lust she'd felt earlier returned quickly with one touch of Aaron's hand to her cheek. Her body responded, arching itself towards his. She wanted to invite him in, to continue where they'd left off now that she didn't feel so embarrassed, so out of practice, but, as well, she didn't want to rush things now that they'd started. There would be time, she was sure. Finally, they let go.

As she reached for her handbag, she had a clear view of exactly how much Aaron's excitement had built up. The bulge in his trousers was unmistakable and she stifled a grin.

'I'll call you later,' she told him after getting out of the car.

'You'd better!'

Charley practically bounced up the steps to the house. She opened the entrance door to find Ella sitting on the bottom step waiting for her.

'So?' She stood up quickly. 'How did it go?'

Charley's smile became a goofy grin.

Ella clapped her hands together excitedly. 'I knew it! I knew it,' she cried. 'You've had sex!'

'Actually, we haven't!'

Ella's smile dropped. 'But I thought –'

'Apparently I was so drunk that he didn't want to take advantage of me.'

Ella looked on incredulously.

'I know! I can't believe it.' Charley laughed then covered her mouth with her hand. 'He said once I got upstairs, I took all my clothes off and threw them to the floor. Then I jumped onto the bed and collapsed. I must have been asleep in moments.'

'You mean it was all for nothing?'

'Not exactly.' Charley beamed. 'I'm seeing him on Tuesday evening.'

'But you weren't supposed to see him again.' Ella clenched and unclenched her fists, gnawed on her bottom lip.

'Why not?' Charley felt all the excitement she'd had about hooking up with Aaron slowly evaporate. What they had done wasn't wrong. They'd had fun, shared some intimacy, and she couldn't wait to see him again.

'It should have been a one-night stand,' said Ella. 'A bit of fun to get you in the mood.'

'I don't want to *get in the mood*. I ... I just want to have a good laugh getting to know someone before I –'

'But you do know Aaron! You work with him.'

'Yes, but that's different.'

'I give up! You turned down sex on a plate!'

'It wasn't about the sex. I –'

But Ella was walking away. 'I can't believe you're seeing him again. That's the deal. One night only.'

'What deal?' Charley looked on perplexed. What on earth was Ella talking about? Was she expecting her to sleep with Aaron and then move on to someone else? Put some notches on her headboard? Because if she was, she had the wrong impression of her.

'It doesn't matter.' Ella shook her head. 'I need to catch up on my sleep. See you later.'

Charley watched as she headed upstairs all droopy shoulders and stroppy attitude. She sighed at the sound of Ella's door banging loudly, having a feeling that she'd never be able to understand her strange views on relationships. One minute she was telling her to find a man, make a go of it with Aaron, and now she was accusing her of not taking advantage of him before moving on to the next conquest. Surely she should be able to know her own mind and not rush into things?

She let herself into her flat and closed the door quietly. Then she grinned; she wasn't going to think about Ella. She had someone else to occupy her thoughts right now. Who would have thought she'd wake up in Aaron's bed that morning?

Chapter Fourteen

Ella couldn't believe how wrong it had all gone. She'd been planning on going out with Charley for brunch to chat about the night before, plot their next missions, have a laugh like they did last night, and enhance any good points so that she'd be there for Charley when Aaron didn't want to see her again. That way she could play on the fact that *she* would never let her down; she would always be there for her. But no, all Charley wanted to do was catch up on her sleep because she'd had a really great time with that fucking moron.

It was like before, when she had felt the darkness falling around her; she wasn't good enough. Ella had thought that Aaron would screw Charley and not want to see her again; thought that she'd be the one comforting Charley soon, after giving herself to a man and him not wanting anything long term. Instead, she remembered how she'd looked when she'd left her moments ago. Charley was radiant; she'd obviously enjoyed the night.

That wasn't meant to happen! She was supposed to be your friend. I told you, didn't I?

Ella covered her ears. She *was* supposed to be her friend but maybe Charley and Aaron wouldn't get on as well as they hoped. Charley would need her then and she would be there for her. This was a sideways step, that's all.

Why won't you listen? She doesn't want to know you. You don't deserve her friendship anyway. You're an evil bitch. You need to be alone.

No. Ella slapped at her face. She cried out, knowing she could never hit herself hard enough to take away the hurt. She slapped herself again and again until an angry red patch appeared on her cheek.

She went into the kitchen to pour herself a drink, got out a glass, and slung it at the wall. As it shattered everywhere, falling to the floor like raindrops, she began to cry. Why didn't anyone want to spend time with her? Why?

She reached for the whisky bottle, removed the top, and guzzled down a mouthful. Coughing and spluttering, she took another gulp. She needed to block out the bad feelings that were forming. She'd been screwed last night; she didn't need to be screwed again.

But Steve hadn't wanted to see her a second time. He'd said goodbye, he'd see her around – the usual shit. They hadn't even swapped phone numbers. There was no way they could contact each other, unless indirectly going through Charley to get to Aaron. But she knew Steve hadn't wanted that. If he had wanted to see her again, it was so easy to keep in touch these days. Social media didn't give anyone an excuse anymore, although someone could hide just as easily using an alias. It was a joke, really – Ella had gone online as Cassandra, after all.

In the living room, she fixed her eyes on the avenue but there was nothing going on – a man a few doors down washing his truck, his young son on the pavement pedalling up a storm on a bike with stabilizers. Other than that, the place was dead. Everyone would be tucking into a roast dinner now; people meeting up with family, brothers catching up with sisters, parents seeing their children.

It's Sunday lunch time – what do you expect? Everyone is with someone they love.

Lunch? That was a joke. All she had in was mouldy cheese and out-of-date bread. That would have to do unless she went shopping, which was highly unlikely as she couldn't be bothered to go out. But then again, she might be able to pick up a date at the supermarket. She laughed out loud at the thought. Whoever had come up with the idea of supermarket dating needed their head looked at. If they'd seen the state of some of the single men who roamed the aisles looking for love amongst the ready meals, they'd soon realise why they were loveless.

Like you. No one loves you.

Ella heard the entrance door open and close. She ran to the window just in time to see Charley walking down the steps and heading down Warwick Avenue. She wondered if she should follow her again, see where she was going, but when she didn't get in her car, Ella realised she couldn't be going far. Maybe she was off to the local shop to get a paper, or something to ease the headache she'd been complaining about.

Not wanting to miss the opportunity, Ella grabbed her keys and shot downstairs. Adrenaline rushed through her as she let herself in to Charley's flat.

She'd visited several times since that first morning. In the living room, Ella noticed the colour of the cushion covers had changed, and there was a new glass vase on the fireplace. Running a hand over the side unit as she went past it, she stooped down and opened both doors wide. Was there anything she could play with in here?

She flicked through a stack of paperbacks, mostly women's fiction, and a pile of papers and magazines; she opened envelopes – a few circulars and a leaflet about a college course on counselling. Bits of Blu-Tack attached to the back of a few photos made her look closer at them. Treasured photos had Blu-Tack on the back of them: they'd probably been stuck on mirrors to see every day, or onto the edge of computer terminals or walls in an office. They were all of Charley and Dan: one on a beach, one at a wedding, one with Dan messing around in a garden. Ella speculated if it was their old house, tried to guess what it had been like – their love nest.

Above her on the surface, she saw a glass cube containing more images of Dan. She picked it up and drew it close.

He was a good-looking man, she had to admit. All strong features and a smile that reached his eyes. Ella guessed he'd been fun to be with. She could tell that about a person, the way they held themselves, the way they looked comfortable in their own skin. She'd never looked comfortable in hers. That's why she wanted to cut it off at times. Dig that knife in deeper and deeper to take away the hurt.

Hmm – maybe she could move this. Or hide it somewhere – it might upset Charley enough so that she would turn to her for comfort! And if she was upset about losing it, perhaps it would make her realise that she didn't need anyone like Aaron yet. Ella could then take her time again getting to know Charley more. She wouldn't have to be alone because her plan had backfired.

She looked at the cube again. If she took it, Charley would know that someone had been in her flat. Maybe if she moved it around so that another image was at the top – or even turned it towards the wall. No, Charley wouldn't notice that, would think she'd moved it herself. Maybe …

Very carefully, she slid it as close to the edge of the unit as it would go without falling off. She balanced it, catching it before it dropped on one occasion before pushing it back slightly. When she had placed it right, she stepped away slowly, praying that one false move wouldn't make it fall. She wanted that to happen when Charley was back. She hoped it would unsettle her and maybe, just maybe, get her thinking that it had been moved by another force: by Dan as though he were annoyed with her seeing Aaron. She giggled – that wouldn't work, but she'd have fun thinking about it.

She glanced around again, looking to see if there was anything better that she could do. But all she could see were things that would be too obvious. She went through to the kitchen, opened the fridge – yes, there were two bottles of wine. She pulled one out, read the label, and then did the same with the other bottle. She decided on the second one, a medium-bodied rosé, notes of ripe red fruits, strawberry and watermelon.

Charley would never know. She'd think she'd already drunk it, convince herself that she couldn't remember doing so, because there would be no other rationalization. And Charley would have to have an explanation rather than think that someone had sneaked in while she was out and stolen it.

Served her right, the sneaky cow. She should have just had a one-night stand.

When I was twenty – ah, yes, the Mark episode. By that time, I'd given Mark two years of my life but it seemed I hadn't learned my lesson regarding Brendan. Mark gave me two years of grief, three cracked ribs, and a broken wrist, and left me with a stomach condition that I was stuck with for life, due to the number of times he punched me in it. He was an evil shit, controlling. If he couldn't have me, then no one could have me. Everything I did was wrong. He wanted to be in charge of me and I let him at first because I took his possessiveness for caring. I wanted him to love me and I thought that was his way of showing me.

I can't recall things exactly but I'd been staying at a friend's bed-sit for a couple of weeks when I met him. She was someone I knew from the streets and had been lucky enough to get her own place. It was a doss hole but it was a roof over my head, too. A few nights into my stay, I met Mark. He was one of her friends and he wowed me to begin with. Well, I reckon, back in the day, anyone would have wowed me if they took a bit of notice of me; I was such a mess. I used alcohol to wash away the memories of my shit life, to block everything out. So anyone taking an interest in my skinny figure, my unwashed hair and clothes, got more than a smile from me. They got my body.

I moved in with Mark two weeks after we met. And from that moment on, he owned me. He wouldn't let me go out on my own. If he went out, he wanted me to stay in. In the end, I became his house-maid and bed maid – when he let me sleep in his bed.

By six months, I was so reliant, so brainwashed by him, that I would have done anything he said because he loved me. But he said he could only screw me when he was drunk. I liked it better when I was drunk too; it didn't hurt. When he was drunk and woke me up at three in the morning to force himself into me, that was when it hurt the most. That was when I closed my eyes and went to my special place; pictured myself running through a meadow with my daughter, Amy.

One night, as Mark came at me with his fists, I curled up in a ball in the corner of the room. But after he had done the damage and stood there catching his breath, I grabbed the lamp on the bed-side table and hit him with the base. I think it was a survival mechanism. It knocked him sideways and onto the bed. I wasn't sure if I'd killed him or if he'd passed out but suddenly I didn't want to find out. I grabbed a few things together, dressed quickly, and checked his wallet, stole the money in there – two hundred quid! Where the hell did he get that from?

That two hundred quid got me far away from Mark. Far enough away to give me the opportunity to get cleaned up and clear my head. But I never did. I was too obsessed with why Mark didn't love me. Why wasn't I good enough for him to treat properly? He was just like Brendan – making me beg for love. I did too – when he was drunk and wanted me to screw him, he'd turn the tables around and he'd make me ask him to be screwed. And then he would screw me, good and hard. Brutal and harsh. I hated him but I loved him too. He told me all the time that no one else would want to touch me, that I disgusted him.

He hated me but he would still shag me.

I can't for the life of me think why I stayed with him. I was better than that but he made me feel worthless, like a piece of shit. He used to laugh at me and scream obscenities into my face as he pumped away at me, as he rammed my face into his cock. I was his bitch, his whore, his good-for-nothing girl he could bang and abuse whenever he wanted to. And why did I stay with him? Because I thought he would change. Because I thought he loved me.

Luckily for me, I walked out. Not early enough to come away without any physical damage but early enough for him not to kill me with a punch too many. I heard he got sent down for GBH in the end so who's laughing now, you silly, stupid, little fucker. Who's laughing now?

Why aren't I in control? Do I attract men who will abuse me? Do I look for men to use me? I just want to be loved. Why won't anyone love me? I'm not a horrible person. I would love someone back. I did love someone back once.

I was never safe with Mark but I didn't realise that at the time. I hate him now. He made me doubt myself. He helped me turn into the monster I am today. Him and Billie and Brendan. I hate them. I hate them ALL. Bastards, bastards, BASTARDS!

Jean was coming to the end of a row of knitting when she'd seen Charley leaving the house. Before she started the next one, she noted down the time: 13:23. Her eyes followed her down the pavement towards her car, and on as she walked straight past it. She wondered where she was going; obviously not far by foot. Perhaps she needed some fresh air after her night out.

Jean couldn't believe that Charley had stayed out all night with Ella. Even more so, she'd been flabbergasted when they'd been dropped off by a man whom Charley then went on to kiss passionately. Well, Jean couldn't see that closely, but she could use her imagination. She wondered if he was a new man on the scene or someone she'd been courting for a while. Perhaps he'd been away on holiday, or working abroad since she'd moved and had now come back to rekindle the fire. All the same, she hoped this one would return, unlike the men Ella brought home. It wouldn't do to have two promiscuous women in the same house.

What surprised her most was that Charley had gone out with Ella. She wasn't quite sure why but she didn't look the type to get up to the things that she saw Ella doing. Her mind worked overtime, speculating again about whether they had known each other previously. Perhaps they had been more than friends. For all she knew, Charley might like entertaining men, just like Ella. The place might even become a brothel!

Jean chastised herself. She knew that the woman wouldn't be anywhere near as promiscuous as Ella. After watching Charley's routine for four weeks now, she could tell she wasn't away with the fairies like Ella. Just as well, really.

'Time for a cuppa, I think,' she said to the cat sitting in the window.

Once tea was made, glancing into Ella's window as she settled down again, Jean was pleased to see her upstairs. She didn't like it when she went downstairs to Charley's flat. It wasn't right that Ella stole in when she wasn't there, snooping through her belongings.

She peered closer. What on earth was the stupid girl up to now? She'd slipped off her dressing gown and was naked again – dancing, swaying an arm around and over her body. Her hands touched her breasts and then moved lower over her stomach, down further. Oh, my, it looked like she was going to ... no! Jean wouldn't watch, thank you very much.

'Close your eyes, Tom. You're too innocent for that.'

When Charley arrived back over an hour later, Ella stood by the side of her window. Dressed in her gown, she held high a glass half full of Charley's wine, raising a toast to her as she climbed the steps to the door. Charley had indeed been to the shop – she was carrying a small carrier bag. It didn't look too heavy; probably a few essentials needed to get her through the day. Ella guessed she must have been somewhere else too because it didn't take that long to walk around the aisles.

She smiled widely, already imagining her jumping with fright at the sight of Dan's photo moving all on its own. She sipped the wine – Charley had good taste. It was a lovely blend.

Any second now, Charley would go into the living room and be spooked! She laughed; she couldn't help herself. *Spooked* was such a silly word.

She prayed that Charley would realise the cube had moved. It was only a slight trick, but she would, wouldn't she? And maybe before Ella visited the flat again, she could think of something else to do that would spook her, make Charley come running to her for comfort. It would be easy to wreck her life if she didn't play ball.

Charley let herself into the flat and closed the door quietly behind her. Even a walk in the fresh air hadn't help to ease the throbbing in her head. But she'd just received a text message from Aaron that had her all of a giggle.

She went through to the living room, her heart leaping into her throat when she saw the photo-cube of Dan on the end of the sideboard. She must have caught it on her way out of the room this morning, although she couldn't recall knocking it.

She picked it up, smiling half-heartedly, and wondered if Dan would approve of Aaron. He was ... No, she wouldn't think of the similarities. She didn't need to compare; it wouldn't be fair.

It had been strange to wake up with Aaron that morning but it had certainly broken the ice. She'd felt so warm when they'd kissed and it had been good to be in someone's arms again after so long. To be with a man, feel his need, feel her arousal. Emotions she'd long ago locked away and buried had surfaced in seconds, and it excited her.

It scared her too.

Was she ready to be with someone new? Only time would tell.

Without another thought, she put Dan's photo-cube back in its original place.

Chapter Fifteen

At work the next morning, Charley was at her desk, Lynne at hers, when she spotted Aaron walking through the office. He winked at her as he went past. She grinned like a happy five-year-old, praying he would keep discreet about their rendezvous. She wasn't going to tell anyone yet. But her reddening skin gave her away.

'You okay?' Lynne asked. 'You look a little flushed. Not coming down with anything, are you?

Finding that she couldn't contain her thoughts, she nodded her head in Aaron's direction. 'We had a thing on Saturday evening,' she said.

Lynne gasped. 'You had a *thing!* That's fantastic news. Although about bloody time, if you ask me. He's been laying it on so thick that everyone knows how much he fancies you. He adores you and worships the ground –'

'I wouldn't go that far,' Charley broke in. 'And *fancies*? That's such a teenage word.'

'But it's true! You don't see what I do. I'm so glad you got together. Are you seeing him again? Please tell me you are.'

Charley smiled. 'I am.'

'And what about the whole working together thing?'

'We're only going out for a pizza.'

'I know but a-one-a-pizza-leads-a-to-another.' Lynne's phoney Italian accent had Charley practically spitting out her coffee.

'Very funny.'

'I suppose the only thing I really want to know is,' she leaned forward for more privacy, 'is he good in the sack?'

'I can tell you, but I would have to kill you.' Charley smirked. She knew that Lynne would be after the gossip straightaway so she would enjoy holding back from her. And she'd have to let people think otherwise rather than tell them the truth. Stripping off and then passing out – she was never going to admit to that!

'At least that explains your chin.' Lynne pointed an accusatory finger at her. 'Stubble rash!'

Charley's fingers touched the spot where her skin felt raw. She'd tried her best to conceal the redness with foundation that morning. But she grinned at the memories it brought to mind.

'I haven't had a proper snog like that in a good while,' she admitted.

'Tell me about it,' Lynne piped up. 'I don't miss a man for some things but for others ...'

'So have you never since Derek?'

'No.' Lynne sighed. 'I'm not sure I'd trust a man again after what happened. I feel much safer on my own. Sad, but it's the way it has to be. But, you,' she pointed at Charley again, 'you, my dear, deserve a little happiness. You're far too young to be on your own forever. I have twenty years on you.'

'Oh, no, he's coming over with Gavin,' Charley whispered. She bobbed her head down behind the computer screen, feeling the heat building up on her cheeks again.

Lynne twirled round in her chair with a crafty smile. 'Morning, guys. Did you have a good weekend?'

'Yes, ta, Lynne,' said Aaron.

'Me too – or at least I think I did, from what I can remember.' Gavin screwed up his face. 'I don't think I've slept since Friday.'

'Sounds like someone else not so far from me.' As Charley glared at her, Lynne turned her attention back to Aaron. 'Get up to much, did you? Anything new and exciting?'

'No – pub with the lads on Saturday and football on Sunday.'

'And did you score?'

'Oh, I scored,' Aaron nodded. 'But it was a bit of a home goal. I'm hoping to get a better shot at it next time, though.' He grinned at Charley. 'Did you have a good weekend? Fun in Hanley?'

'I did.' She felt her cheeks burning up again and cursed inwardly.

'Did you score a home goal this weekend too?' Lynne asked with mock innocence.

Gavin turned with a frown. 'Have I missed something?'

'She was definitely playing away.' Aaron threw his head back and laughed. Charley felt her eyes immediately drawn to the neck of his shirt where a few dark hairs curled up sexily on display. She remembered seeing them on his chest yesterday morning, running a hand over them as they had snuggled up together. She wondered when she would see them again, if...

She jumped as he waved a hand in front of her face.

'Dreaming of someone wonderful?'

'I – I...' She picked up her mug, which was still full of the drink she'd made only fifteen minutes ago. 'Coffee, anyone?'

Ella lay alone in her bed, not wanting to get up to face the day. Her fingertips trailed across her chest and up and down her stomach, sending aches through her body. Even though she'd gone out for sex the night before, she couldn't stop thinking about Charley: the way she held her head when she laughed; her bare shoulders as they'd sat close when they were chatting in The Exchange; the way she'd tried to encourage her to look at the positive in everything. She was playing hard to get, Ella was sure.

Last week she'd imagined them going out again this evening or, at least, sharing a bottle of wine and having a giggle. Like friends do – everything together. But that had all stopped because of Aaron. She wondered if Charley had even thought about her the night before, or had all her feelings been about him? Damn the man for getting under her skin. She hoped it would all fizzle out after a couple of dates.

The photograph thing mustn't have worked either. Had the cube stayed balanced on the edge or had it toppled over before she'd got back? Ella had hoped it would upset Charley enough for her to come knocking, distressed by memories and feeling unfaithful towards Dan. But there had been nothing, so at eight thirty she'd gone out. It hadn't been spectacular but at least she'd satisfied the urge – just like old times.

She stretched. What on earth was she going to do with her day? Ah, yes, Google time. With a purpose now, she jumped out of bed. Then she paused – where the hell would the file be? She glanced around the chaos of the room before spotting a yellow cardboard folder on her desk, in the middle of a pile of newspapers. She pushed it all to the floor and flicked through its contents. Then her hand fell on the rent agreement.

She located her laptop and logged onto the internet, clicking first on Google Street Maps. Within moments, she was looking at the house Charley had shared with Dan. It was nothing special in size, one of several detached properties in a line, but it was a home to be proud of. All fresh paint and weed-free block paving on the driveway, with room for two cars. The front door was painted a welcoming pillar-box red, the garden neat and tidy. It had certainly had some love and attention given to it.

But the one thing that stood out to Ella was that it looked homely and inviting. Her eyes brimmed with tears. Why couldn't she have had that? She knew she might have settled if she had.

Like hell you would. You're a waste of space.

'How would *you* know?' Ella wiped at her tears and clicked on print. She'd keep the photo to look at. One day she would have a home like that.

Yeah, IF you can ever act like a normal human being.

'I am normal!'

Not if you stop taking those tablets.

Tuesday evening came round before Charley knew it. Absent-mindedly, she wrung her hands as she glanced up and down the avenue, waiting to spot Aaron's car. Her mind was obsessing over whether it was better to go straight out to greet him or for him to call in for her. If she went out to him, he might think she didn't want him inside her flat. If she invited him in, would he think she was offering more than she was willing to give yet? But then he had been really sincere on Saturday night. And despite the banter with Lynne and Gavin yesterday morning, Aaron hadn't mentioned it to anyone else.

What should she do? It felt as if she hadn't known him for years, as if he was someone she was meeting for the very first time. Should she go out or stay in? The question ate her up inside so much that she felt a little queasy. She rushed to the bathroom, holding onto the sink for support, praying that the nausea would pass.

She grinned at her reflection in the mirror, eyes all bright and shiny despite how she was feeling: better not tell Aaron that she was sick at the thought of seeing him again.

Her mobile phone beeped and she rushed to it, all of a panic again. Don't say he was going to be late – or worse, call the whole thing off. She opened the message: it was from Ella.

'*Do you fancy meeting up tonight? I've made too much pasta this time.*'

Charley sighed. It was the second night in a row she'd had a message like that. Last night, she'd genuinely been tired after the weekend's events caught up with her so she'd had a long bath followed by an early night in bed with Ian Rankin – she'd found it hard to put down his latest book.

At the time, she'd sent a message back to decline but had received no reply. It wasn't that she didn't want to spend time with Ella, just that she didn't want to be with her too much. They were only neighbours – it wouldn't do to be too friendly. She decided not to text her now.

But a few minutes later, there was a knock at her front door. She frowned and went to answer it – had she missed Aaron's arrival?

Ella stood in the hallway smiling at her, barefoot and wearing only a dressing gown. Charley noticed a bruise on her right knee before catching her eye.

'I've ran out of sugar.' Ella held up a cup. 'Do you mind if I pinch a bit from you?'

'Sorry,' said Charley. 'I don't take sugar so I can't help you there.'

'You haven't brought any in for visitors?'

'No, sorry.'

A car horn peeped outside.

'I suppose that's Aaron?' Ella snapped.

Charley frowned. What was with Ella's sharp tone?

'Yes,' she told her, ignoring it for now. 'We're going out this evening. I'm a little bit nervous about it if I'm –'

Ella put up a hand and stopped her in mid sentence. 'Yeah, I know. Off with him again. No time for me.'

Charley couldn't ignore her hostility this time. 'Ella, I think –'

'Have fun.'

Ella was already halfway up the stairs when a knock came at the entrance door. Charley rushed to it.

'Hi.' Aaron smiled, looking as self-conscious as she felt.

'Hi, yourself.' She beamed and then blushed. Shocked by the juvenile feelings taking over her, she beckoned him in. Instantly, she forgot the weird conversation with Ella.

'You look gorgeous.' Aaron drew her into his arms and kissed her lightly on her mouth. 'Mmm, you smell gorgeous too.'

'Thanks.'

Charley cringed inwardly. *Thanks* – is that all she could come up with? She would have been better saying she 'carried a watermelon' like Baby in *Dirty Dancing*. All at once her skin burned up again. If she was blushing now, how was she going to get through the night?

<hr />

From her window, Ella looked down as Aaron opened the car door for Charley; watched her slide into the passenger seat of the car, short skirt, legs on show but covered with opaque black tights, and heels. She scowled – Charley was all smiles and girlish flicks of her hair. A laugh came up through the open window to taunt her. It was just as well they were going out, though, as Michael would be here in forty minutes.

Earlier, she hadn't been thinking of meeting anyone, hoping that Charley would reply to her text message and say she was available to meet this time. But she hadn't, and she'd rudely dismissed her when she'd gone downstairs in search of sugar that she didn't need. In her anger, she'd texted Michael with her address. He was free – although she didn't plan on letting him stay long. Ella intended to spend the rest of the night pleasuring herself. She'd found a new soft porn website that morning. There were lots of interesting pictures and articles that would entertain her for hours.

Suddenly, she spotted a shadow in the window of number thirty-six. Ah, she smiled. Jake was on the prowl again. Ella liked Jake, thought he was cute; wondered if he was a virgin or if he'd popped his cherry yet. Not sure of his age, she recalled seeing him one night in a bar, found him attractive then, too, in an older-woman-shags-boy kind of way. She knew she shouldn't but she really wanted to seduce him. Maybe he'd come up to her flat one day and she would let him screw her in the window, in full view of everyone who wanted to watch. Jean, for one – she was always watching.

Her hand slipped inside her open dressing gown and she began to caress her naked skin above her pubic bone. Across from side to side, gently, never taking her eyes from Jake. Knowing he could see her turned her on even more. She might as well give him something to watch.

While she stroked her skin, her eyes moved across to Jean's window but she couldn't see her. Now, that was a surprise, and a disappointment, she realised. She'd caught her on numerous occasions watching while she masturbated in the window, or once or twice as she'd been screwed by some young stud who wouldn't give up until he'd come three or four times in one session.

The orgasm was quick; she was hot because she knew she was being watched. Ella moved from the window to take a shower. Whilst in there, she masturbated twice more, then again in the bedroom, and had to shower again. At this rate, when her date turned up she would be spent but sometimes the urge took over. She needed release and she needed it now.

She hated being rejected.

This was all Charley's fault.

Chapter Sixteen

Still naked when Michael arrived, Ella pulled her dressing gown on again and went downstairs to let him in. She opened the door, pleasantly surprised. Wearing a charcoal suit, a white shirt open slightly at the neck, and dark hair gelled back enough to look sexy as hell, her date seemed like he was ready to take her out to dinner. Ella liked that – the fact he'd made an effort for her, not knowing what to expect; not knowing whether they would go out or stay in. It was a shame that it would be wasted. All she wanted was to see him naked.

'Cassandra?'

She nodded and he stepped in, greeting her with a kiss on the cheek. He followed her upstairs. Her heartbeat quickened when she realised he'd been checking out her legs, her robe barely covering her bottom for a purpose. When his hand touched her thigh, she stopped. He left it there, inching it up while he drew level with her on the landing.

'You smell nice enough to eat,' he said, as she closed the flat door behind them.

Ella knew he was talking crap. She didn't reply; she didn't need to. That was a big advantage of being a member of *One Night Only* – she paid good money to behave how she wanted.

In the hallway, she grabbed the lapel of his jacket and pulled him close. 'So, where is it to be, Michael?' Her voice was softer than her mood. 'In the bedroom?' She stood up on her toes to kiss his lips gently. 'On the floor in the kitchen?' She kissed him again. 'Bent over the table in the front room?' She ran her tongue across his top lip and bit down on it playfully. 'Or here, good and hard up against the wall?'

'Not much room in here,' he spoke softly back to her, untying her belt and slipping his hand inside her dressing gown.

Ella pressed her body to his as they kissed, wanting to feel skin on skin as quickly as possible, knowing this would do until they were both free of clothes. She stepped back, taking him with her into the living room. Maybe someone else would be in one of the windows. She could give them double for their money this evening, if Michael would oblige. Sometimes her lovers did; sometimes they didn't.

She felt the small of her back hit the top of the settee and she slid off her dressing gown while his hand slipped between her legs. Still kissing, she tugged at his jacket and let it drop to the floor. A moan escaped her lips as his fingers went to work; hers undid buttons on his shirt. Once that was off too, her hands dropped to his belt. He stopped her, turning her round quickly and bending her over. He found her wetness again, and she held onto the settee as the pressure began to build. She was sore from all the earlier fun but she didn't give a stuff. Right now it was all about being taken, being screwed. She needed to be wanted, even if it was only for a few moments.

She needed to feel him inside her.

She reached behind to touch him but he pushed her hand away. Turning slightly, she could see he was pleasuring himself at the same time.

Well, what do you know! He doesn't need you.

Ella tried to face him but he pushed her back. It was always the same, always the fucking same – they would screw her but they would never want to look at her. Was Michael imagining she was someone else? Did the guilt of it all become too much? She laughed out loud. She'd chosen another stupid bastard. What a waste of time.

Still, she let him push her to the limit, climaxing noisily. Then, as he was about to push himself into her, she wriggled out of his way. He huffed, left hanging as she moved to the side of the room.

'Why won't you look at me?'

'What?' Michael looked perplexed.

'You!' She pointed at him. 'You can fuck me but you can't look at me. Why?'

'It's nothing personal. I like it better that way.' He grinned. 'Tighter; firmer; better for me.'

'You can take me now while you look at me or you're not having me at all.'

'Really?' His hand found his cock, moving up and down it as he stared at her. 'Fine, I'll shoot this across your carpet if you don't come and finish me off.'

She watched him for a moment, her eyes never leaving his as he pumped with his hand. She wasn't going to move. He could make as much mess as he liked; she'd make him clean it up before he left.

But a moment later, the urge to join him became too much. *She* needed to give him that pleasure, to be in control of when it happened. She wanted to see his face as she made him come too, know it was because of her. Disgusted with herself, she dropped to her knees to finish him off.

Once it was over, she reached for her dressing gown. She slipped into it quickly and wrapped around the belt.

'Well, that wasn't what I had in mind,' she told him.

'It's what I wanted. You know the rules.'

'Fuck you! I needed more than that.'

'You would have got more if you hadn't thrown a strop in the middle of it. What was all that "I don't want to see your face" shit?'

'It was true!'

'Not, it wasn't. It was the way I like it.'

'Yeah, right.'

'You didn't even have the decency to get dressed for me, make an effort, so it works both ways.'

Ella frowned in confusion.

'You're in your dressing gown, easy access for a quick fuck that tells me; so that's what I gave you. If you wanted more, you would have dressed for me. Not dressing means you don't give a shit who I am or what I do as long as you get your rocks off.'

Understanding now, Ella knew he was right but she would never give him the satisfaction of telling him so.

'You're wrong,' she said instead.

'Am I?' Michael paused, as if weighing up the situation. He shook his head. 'You're weird. So unless there's anything else on offer, I'm leaving.'

'Fuck off, then.' Ella folded her arms.

Michael pulled on his shirt and jacket. She watched his every move.

'That's it, then?' he asked.

Ella nodded. But as he turned to the door, she realised he was actually going to leave. She thought he'd been joking. How dare he! He needed to fight for her. Wasn't she even worthy of that? The selfish fuck-wit! Picking up a book from the coffee table, she struck him on the back of his head.

He cried out in pain. 'What the –'

Seeing him turn towards her, she drew it back to hit him again.

Michael wrestled the book from her hands, threw it to the floor and her onto the settee. He pinned her down with his body as she thrashed about to shift his weight. Then his hands were inside her dressing gown again, fingers searching. She stopped struggling and pulled him close. God, she needed to feel him inside her, no matter how annoyed he was.

She kissed his lips, his cheeks, his lips again. But he didn't respond. Looking into his eyes, she pressed down on his hand, arching her back to greet him.

Then he stopped. 'You'd let me, wouldn't you?'

His breath was shallow but Ella couldn't make out if it was from lust or anger.

'Yes, I'd let you,' she replied. Her eyes never left his. God, she wanted him inside her! 'I need to be fucked.'

He sat up abruptly. 'I'm going to leave.'

'You can't! Not yet.' Desperately, she pulled him back but he knocked away her arm. She followed him down the hallway, levelling with him at the door. As he opened it, she slammed it shut again.

'No.' She pushed him up against the wall and kissed him. Still he resisted, grabbing for her wrists, pushing her away. She tried to remove his jacket again but it was no use; he was too strong. When she knew she was beat, she slapped his face.

'You bastard,' she said, tears now falling. 'You bastard.'

He let her cry for a few seconds and calm down before he pushed her into the opposite wall. He mirrored her actions by pressing his body up against hers, but he didn't try to kiss her. Instead, he looked at her with contempt.

'I know the games we play can be dangerous but you're lucky that I don't hit women,' he seethed. 'Because if I did, I'd have knocked your fucking head off by now.'

Ella didn't dare speak. Her black mood was mounting again, pushing her anger nearer and nearer to the surface. She had to control it; otherwise, she would lash out again.

Eventually, after a few seconds to catch his breath, Michael released his grip and stepped away.

Ella didn't trust herself to move. Her eyes flitted around for something to grab but there was nothing of significance.

Michael opened the door, turning one last time before he left. 'I don't think I'll be rating this visit as five-star-fun on the website. You need to get some help.'

Ella slammed the door behind him and slid to the floor in a heap.

What the hell was happening to her? Michael was right: she did need help. But she couldn't go to see her social worker and be patronised for failing. Every time she went back, it was harder to do it all over again when she went off the rails. It was like someone else's mind took over her body, took control of her thoughts and made her do things.

'All I want is to be loved,' she whispered, tears beginning to build. She pulled herself up and went into the bedroom, stepped into the closet. She closed the door and sat in the dark. Wrapping her arms around her knees, she cried herself to sleep.

I was a shadow back then – a weak individual who let people use and abuse me but then I tried to change. I learned my lesson after that fuck-wit Mark laid into me. The next relationship I had, I was in control.

I was the abuser.

What? You think I should take it all my life but not give it back? I don't think so.

To overpower someone, I chose a woman. Her name was Nina and God, I loved her. I was with her for three years. It was a great time for me. The first two years were good for her, the last one not so much. You see, through all the years of abuse I'd had, I knew where to hit her, where it would hurt but the marks wouldn't be seen.

It started with a harsh push away every now and again when we were bickering. Then it changed to the odd slap when we were arguing. Eventually, I punched her in the face, and bent her arm up behind her back while she begged me to stop. Then a swift kick to the stomach after we'd had sex one night. After that, the violence escalated to a more regular basis, along with verbal use – I was telling her what she could and couldn't do, what to wear, who she couldn't see; taking control of her money. Why did I do that? I don't know.

Yet she never retaliated. She loved me, did Nina. And I turned that love to hate.

I hadn't realised I'd become a monster, that I enjoyed being in control for once in my life. Not that I needed to be. Nina wouldn't have hurt me. She loved ME.

What was wrong with me? Why couldn't I treat someone who loved me with respect? I loved Nina but instead I pushed her away. I wasn't good enough for her.

On the night before she left, high on whatever drug I was on and fuelled by alcohol, I beat Nina bad. I can't remember much about it now. All I can recall is she was in a terrible way and once she'd come out of A&E, she headed off to her mum's. She didn't want to be with me, said she needed space.

We live in the same city yet I haven't seen her since. I called at her mum's but she wouldn't tell me where she was, despite my protests. Maybe she moved away. Maybe she still lives in the Potteries. Or maybe she got a train from Stoke Station and got as far away as she could. She was damaged – by me! I damaged her.

Oh, God, I missed Nina so much. Looking back on this now makes me realise that I was so wrong. I was scared and I hurt her because I was hurting. Was it because she was nice to me? Didn't I feel that I deserved a little happiness?

Why did I hurt her? Because it sure as fuck didn't make me feel any better.

Me – the abuser. ME!

Surely that can't be right?

Jake had been amazed to get two sessions out of Ella that night. Man, the bitch was horny, touching herself to orgasm while staring at him – right at him! It was such a turn-on. He had to have her soon.

And he knew now that she wanted him. She'd started to play with herself more often in the window, wanting him to see what she had on offer. Maybe he could instigate a meeting somehow, bump into her outside when she came out of the house. It would work if she had a set routine, like that other woman, Charley, who was as regular as clockwork now. It was a pity she'd got herself a fella: Jake wouldn't mind a threesome. Even though he doubted Charley would be game, it didn't stop him dreaming of them both.

His phone rang.

'Where are you, mate?' his friend, Will, wanted to know. 'You said you'd be here half an hour ago. I'm standing like a lemon on my own.'

'I'm coming,' said Jake. 'I'll be with you in ten.'

He disconnected the call and sniggered. He was definitely coming. Just one more time and then he'd be gone.

Next door, Jean was certain she wouldn't catch Charley doing what Ella had been doing now. It had been quite a show again; she'd written it down in her notebook.

20:24 Ella had a male visitor.

He'd arrived in a dark grey hatchback, the suit he wore practically the same colour. Jean thought he looked more like he was dressed for work; from what she'd seen of the visitors Ella usually invited, he seemed too smart for a date.

She'd dropped a stitch when she'd next looked, spotting Ella bent over the settee with him standing behind. She'd reached for her binoculars to take a closer look, but by this time they were apart, facing each other like alley cats about to pounce. She'd leant further forward to see what was going on just in time for them to drop onto the settee and she hadn't been able to see any more.

But she'd been surprised to see him leaving some five minutes later. Some date that had been! He must have had his fill and left. Not a very nice man in her eyes.

20:57 Ella's male visitor left.

It was wrong what Ella got up to. Jean didn't disapprove of women having sex, not at all, but she couldn't understand why Ella felt the need to sleep with so many men. She wondered again about her sexual appetite. She obviously used sex as a comfort blanket – Jean had seen it so many times during her working life. Kids and women abused by men whom they should have been able to trust.

Nothing to see at Ella's window now; she looked up and down the avenue and sighed, wondering why she expected anything else. Apart from the odd erotic display from Ella, nothing of interest ever happened in Warwick Avenue. But then again, it was everyday events that triggered off bigger problems, most of the time. She doubted many of the people who committed atrocities got up thinking 'I'm going to kill someone this morning.'

Still, she mused, her knitting needles clickety-clicking away, it wouldn't do for everyone to live the same, day after day. And she should know. The day she lost her job at Ravenside Children's Home had started out like any other but it had ended as anything but.

And she would always keep that hush-hush.

Chapter Seventeen

Ella couldn't believe it when she'd messaged Charley on Saturday afternoon and again she said she was going out with Aaron. She speculated whether she was trying to tell her something in a round-about way but at the same time didn't really want to know. Trying not to dwell on it, she lined up a date for that night with a client from *One Night Only*. Soon she'd be heading to watch a show in the Cultural Quarter of Hanley and then on to a club afterwards. *Dirty Dancing* was showing at the Regent Theatre and if her date was lucky she might get some dirty dancing of her own.

It had been a long time since she'd gone out on a date for anything but sex. Even so, she dressed carefully in anticipation of what was to come later. Her thoughts returned to Charley as she put on a vivid-blue scant bra and brief set, feeling the silkiness against her skin. Ella wondered if Charley and Aaron had fucked yet; had he tasted her, run his tongue all over her, felt every inch of her? She lay back on her bed, seeing them in her mind, almost feeling she could reach out and touch them. It led to a delicious thought which took her to orgasm twice before she'd finished the fantasy. Maybe they would let her watch, she surmised – maybe they would let her join in! It had been a while since she'd had a threesome. Most of the time, her partners found her enough on her own.

She was meeting Sabrina that evening. Her profile picture looked that of a young woman, quite butch in stature but feminine in looks. Her face was fresh – no more than twenty at a push.

She slipped into her heels, knocked back the vodka, and poured another. She wanted to be pissed by the time she got there so she wouldn't be thinking of Charley.

———

Aaron took Charley out for dinner to a restaurant just off Piccadilly. Marlon's had been in Hanley since 1985. Charley had been a few times with Dan before he'd died but not since. It was a small, intimate restaurant, two-thirds full already when they arrived, and would, no doubt, be overflowing come ten o'clock once the show was over. Aaron ordered Quattro Stagioni and Charley chose Pizza della Casa.

Over the past few nights, Charley had enjoyed herself so much with Aaron that her nerves had gone and she felt comfortable with him now. She glanced at him covertly as they sipped coffee afterwards. There was so much she didn't know about him, yet so much she wanted to learn. And she realised, with a childish sense of excitement, there was going to be time to do just that.

The air between them became electric with expectation.

Aaron reached forward and ran the tip of his finger over the top of her hand. 'I've had another great evening,' he said. 'I can't believe you're this much fun!'

Charley snatched her hand away in mock indignation. 'And there was me thinking you were trying to seduce me with that one finger thing.'

Aaron gasped. 'You said the "S" word. You are so naughty.'

'Well...' Charley kept her eyes locked on his, 'it's bound to happen, isn't it?'

'I bloody well hope so!' He grinned. 'But, you take your time. I'll wait another week maybe.'

'You're impossible!'

'Irresistible!' He sighed loudly. 'You should have said I'm irresistible.'

'I wouldn't be telling the truth.'

'I'm deeply hurt by that remark.' Aaron picked up his napkin and dabbed away imaginary tears.

Charley reached for his hand this time. 'I am, however, really glad we got together last weekend. I must admit, I did think you were joking and jesting while we were at work and I'm sure I wouldn't have thought anything more unless we hadn't...'

'Slept together?' He raised his eyebrows.

'Yes, so to speak.'

'We didn't do anything *but* speak,' he teased.

'Like I said, I'm sure we can rectify that later.'

Aaron leaned closer so that the group of women celebrating a birthday at the next table couldn't hear him. 'If you don't stop with the insinuations, I'm going to push everything off this table, bend you over it, and have my wicked way with you right now,' he said quietly.

Charley choked on the wine she was sipping. Aaron certainly drew a thin line between flirting and downright cockiness – he was determined to let her know what his intentions were, even if she hadn't already been sure from the get-go. Still, it was good that she knew he was joking, because she might be ready to be cocky back – well, kind of. She'd really enjoyed spending time with him that week, getting to know him better.

She held up a hand to signal she was okay as a waitress came rushing over. 'You are too funny!' Her voice was laced with sarcasm. 'I might have to persist with the insinuations because of that.'

Aaron paused. 'I think I'd better take you home and we can continue our conversation there.'

'No.'

'No?'

Charley felt a shake in her hand as she put down her wine glass. She wasn't sure if she'd be able to make love with Aaron but if she did make a fool of herself, well, she'd want it to be with him. He would understand; she'd still be able to take things slowly afterwards. He knew what a big moment it would be for her. Her stomach flipped over as she thought about it. But she wasn't going to give up. She spoke out before she changed her mind, her voice sounding more confident than she felt.

'You can take me home but I don't want to talk,' she said softly. 'I think action will speak louder than words on this occasion.'

Another pause. Then Aaron waved frantically to get the waitress's attention.

'Could we have the bill please?'

Ella paced up and down in her living room. She wanted to stop the feeling of betrayal but knew it wouldn't go away – not until Aaron left. He was downstairs with Charley. They were most probably fucking right this minute.

Desperately, she tried to hold in the scream threatening to escape. And she'd had such a great time with Sabrina. For once, the sex had been gentle and kind. She'd been fun to be with – a dream to make love to. They'd enjoyed the theatre and headed for a club, but after a heavy petting session, they'd got a cab back to Warwick Avenue. Ella had been about to take her to bed and, while Sabrina went to freshen up beforehand, she'd been standing in the window when Aaron pulled up outside the building and got out of the car with Charley. The lingering kiss he gave her on the pavement told Ella everything. They couldn't keep their hands off each other either.

Still, it had been okay. Because while Sabrina had skilfully and gently brought her to orgasm, she'd imagined Charley and Aaron lying directly below her in their bed doing the same. But afterwards, she couldn't get the image from her mind, no matter how much fun she'd had with Sabrina. She'd fallen asleep next to her but Ella couldn't rest. Instead, she'd listened for the entrance door, the signal that Aaron had gone home. But there had been nothing. Shortly after three thirty, she'd got up and gone in to the living room. His car was still there when she'd looked out of the window. Damn that fucking man!

She stopped pacing and went to the window again. The car would still be there, she knew. No doubt they would be screwing. And if they weren't screwing, they would be lying together with legs entwined, arms wrapped around each other, or he would be spooned into her back, as new lovers do.

Tears pricked her eyes. It was always the same.

Of course it's always the same. Nobody wants to be with you for more than one night.

She didn't know how long she'd stood in the window but, in the darkness, a hand enveloped her waist. Ella felt a warm body press up to hers, fingers gently caressing her breast and then a nipple, lips spreading tiny tantalising kisses across her shoulder. She pulled back her head and the lips found the side of her neck.

'I wondered where you'd gone,' Sabrina whispered.

'I couldn't sleep.'

'Maybe I could help with that?' From the light of the street lamp, Ella caught the smile on her face as she moved to her side. She smiled back; she might not be good enough for Charley but Sabrina needed her.

Ella kissed her, making it as passionate as the kiss she had seen between Aaron and Charley earlier. Then she took Sabrina's hand and led her out of the room.

When Charley woke up the next morning, she'd been relieved to find that she was in her own bed. The relief continued when she realised that she wasn't drunk, nor had she embarrassingly stripped her clothes off or passed out shortly afterwards like she had last weekend.

Her clothes had been removed, though.

She glanced up at the man whose chest she'd been snuggled up to since and smiled. She had never met anyone who had such a positive outlook. Even in his sleep, Aaron looked happy. She knew she was a moody cow at times but being with him, well, he made her feel content. It was strange to feel that way after just a week. Funny things, hormones, she mused.

Last night it had happened. But even though she'd been tearful thinking about Dan as she and Aaron had made love, it hadn't stopped her from enjoying all those bubbly feelings, still running through her now too. It was so long since she and Dan had gone through their lustful stages – where the touch of a hand would bring a quiver of anticipation, a wink of an eye would have her weak at the knees, where a fingertip with just enough pressure could send her to heaven. But being with Aaron had brought that all back and it felt so good. Charley couldn't – and didn't want to – rid herself of Dan's memory but she sure as hell could make some new ones with Aaron.

She bit her lip. Had she really slept with him after a week? What a tramp! But she was in her thirties, not her teens, and didn't have to justify three dates to move to second base and five dates to move to third. If it felt right, it felt right. Yet, she blinked back tears … What had she to feel guilty about?

'Morning.' Aaron opened his eyes slightly, briefly looking at her before closing them again.

Charley felt a hand touch her thigh lightly.

'I'm awake.' He sighed with relief. 'It did happen, then.'

'What exactly?' Charley teased, knowing full well that this week she could remember everything from the night before. And that she didn't want to blank any of it out.

'You mean it wasn't memorable? You know, the,' Aaron whistled twice and mouthed the word 'sex.'

Charley sniggered.

'So how do you feel about it this morning?'

Last night, Aaron had been gentle with her, pausing when he'd clearly wanted to continue. At first she'd felt shy, resisted her urges, but then she had wanted him and no other man beside her, inside her. As her emotions soared, more tears had followed. Aaron had held her in his arms, no need for words, until she'd fallen asleep. Dan would always be special, but sleeping with Aaron had been the right thing to do.

She smiled now, recalling the second time they'd made love – that had been much better.

'I'm okay,' she told him. 'I'm good with it.'

'Thank God for that. Maybe now I can stop holding my stomach in all the time and relax a little more.' He lifted the covers up. 'And maybe this time when you cuddle into me, you won't mind what brushes against your leg.'

'Cuddle?' She ran a hand over his chest. 'I hope that's not all you want to do.'

———

As soon as Ella awoke the next morning, she headed straight into the living room to check for Aaron's car. Rage shot through her as she found it still there.

He stayed the night. But then, you always knew he would, didn't you?

She slapped at her face. He was going to keep Charley away from her now; he'd want her all to himself. Oh, this was such a bad omen. She slapped her face again.

'What are you doing?' She heard a voice behind her.

'I'm waking myself up.'

'I can find a better way.'

Ella could tell she was smiling without looking at her. Sabrina was sweet, she'd give her that, but she hadn't the patience for her this morning.

Sabrina came to her side and gave her a hug.

Ella didn't return it, taking great pleasure when Sabrina's smile dropped just before her arms did.

'I thought, if you fancied, we could go out for lunch some-where?' Sabrina tried again moments later, when the silence became loaded.

Ella shook her head.

'Look, if it's the *One Night Only* thing you're worried about, it doesn't have to go any further if we meet again. We could –'

'Who says I want to see you again?'

'But I thought ... seeing as you're still naked ... that you might be horny.'

Ella didn't even turn towards her.

'Ok-ay.' A sigh. 'I'll get dressed and go, shall I?'

A moment later, the door closed behind her.

Fuck her. You don't need her.

Ella squeezed her eyes tightly shut.

You only need me. You know that, don't you?

In the quiet of her room, Ella heard a door open downstairs.

Chapter Eighteen

'So, two oatcakes with sausage and cheese?' said Aaron, kissing Charley before taking a step down the hallway. Then he came back and kissed her again. 'Or maybe I'll stay here and we can go out for something to eat?'

'But I'm hungry.' Charley kissed him back, pressing herself into him.

'I've noticed.'

'And I need to keep you eager.'

'But I'm eager now.'

Charley smiled. 'Oatcakes – go! It will only take you half an hour at the most.'

'Half an hour is too long.'

'I have to have them from Foley Oatcakes. They're the best around here.'

Aaron sighed and walked away. By the entrance door, he turned back. 'You're sure I can't tempt you with anything else before I go?'

Charley waved him away.

'I'm going. I know you'll be waiting for …' Aaron looked up the stairs. 'Hi, Ella, how're you doing?'

Through the balustrades, Charley could see the top of Ella's short dressing gown. Brightly painted toenails curled around the step she was stood on, three up from the floor.

'I'm fine,' Ella replied.

'Seen anything of Steve?'

'No. A definite one-night stand he was.'

Charley noted how Ella emphasised the words *one-night stand* but she still decided to greet her politely.

'Morning, Ella,' she said.

'Morning.'

'I'll be off, then,' said Aaron, into the growing silence.

'Yes, push off and give her some peace. You don't have to be so eager.'

'I'm not eager. I –'

'Have you been listening to us?' Charley stepped out into the hallway and across to Aaron. Ella had no right to speak to them in that tone, nor listen to their conversation. Her eyes flicked up to meet Ella's glare and she folded her arms.

It was a moment before Ella backed down and looked away.

'Couldn't help but hear you,' she retorted. 'It was vomit city.'

'I think we have a case of the green-eyed monster,' Aaron whispered to Charley, before pulling her into his arms and purposely kissing her again.

A fresh-faced young woman came down the stairs. 'I'll be off then.'

Spotting her first, Aaron indicated to Charley with raised eyebrows. She turned, smiled when she realised Ella *had* got friends, after all. It was somewhat of a relief to see.

But the woman ignored Ella, almost pushing past her. Ella pulled her back and kissed her passionately, keeping her eyes firmly on Charley.

It was over in a few seconds but enough to embarrass them all. The younger woman stood looking shell-shocked.

'See you soon,' Ella said to her.

Charley saw the woman smile widely. 'Okay, yes, I'd like that. Cool.'

Once she'd gone, Ella stormed back upstairs. Charley stood still for a moment, unsure of exactly what she had been a part of. Oh, God, she hoped somewhere along the line she hadn't given out the wrong impression. Okay, if she'd thought about it more, she might have expected Ella to be bisexual; she had been a bit full on lately. But to do that blatantly, it seemed, to get her attention? She shuddered involuntarily.

'What's got into her?' asked Aaron. 'I thought you two were friends.'

Charley turned back to him. 'I don't want to be that kind of friend.'

'I don't think you could.' He grinned. 'See you in half an hour.'

Closing the door behind him, Charley turned to see Ella standing right behind her.

'Jeez, you startled me,' she cried, hand to her chest.

'That didn't go to plan, did it?' Ella almost growled through gritted teeth.

'I don't follow you.'

'You and him! You've seen him four nights this week.'

'Sorry, I hadn't realised you were keeping a note.'

'You said you wanted a one-night stand.'

Charley shook her head. 'No, I think I recall *you* saying that. That's a little different.'

'Whatever.' Ella glared at her.

Unnerved but feeling the need to fight her corner, Charley continued. 'And really, it's not my style. I couldn't sleep with anyone until I got to know them a bit first.'

'What, like a week?'

'I've known Aaron a lot longer than a week.'

'Not *intimately*.'

Charley felt herself blushing. 'No,' she admitted. 'But I'm so glad that I met up with him last weekend.' She tried a different tack. 'And I have you to thank for that.'

'Oh?'

'I moved here so that I could get over Dan. I hadn't expected to be, I don't know, set free – sounds such a farcical thing to say but that's exactly how I feel. Moving here made me realise that I was hanging on to something that wasn't ever going to come back. It freed me up to other possibilities – something that had been happening right underneath my nose but that I didn't see because I was too scared to be with anyone else, in case they were taken from me.'

Ella gave a bored sigh.

'If I hadn't gone out with you last weekend, I might never have realised that Aaron was serious. I thought he was just doing it to cheer me up after I lost Dan.' Charley grinned. 'I had a great time with him last night.'

'That's amazing!' All of a sudden, Ella smiled.

Charley realised it had been an effort. 'You don't seem happy about it,' she couldn't help but mention.

Ella pulled the belt on her dressing gown tighter. 'I was thinking that we would see more of each other now that you'd moved in here. I didn't think I'd have *male* competition – at least not this quickly.'

'This *isn't* a competition. And you make it sound as if I'm a floozy and have jumped into bed with the first guy who came along.' When Ella didn't respond, Charley gasped. 'Come on now, you don't believe that?'

Ella shrugged.

'You think I'm going to be bringing strange men home every evening to have fun with because I feel I've been set free?' She shook her head.

'There's nothing wrong in that,' Ella almost snarled.

'I'm not suggesting there is. You know how open-minded I am; look at the job I do. I think we should be able to live how we like – if we don't hurt other people, obviously. I'm just saying that it wouldn't suit me. If I give my heart, I only want to be with one man. I'd like a relationship rather than a fling.'

'You don't have to give your heart to be fucked by a man.'

Charley raised her eyebrows. 'I know that too, and I'm not about to give my heart to Aaron but –'

'Oh really? From what I've seen, and so *quickly*, I reckon you're falling for him. Especially if he's in your knickers already, considering not long ago you were crying on my shoulder over your dead husband.'

Charley couldn't have been more shocked if Ella had leaned forward and slapped her across the face. To be angry with her for seeing Aaron was one thing, although she still didn't understand why she should be, but to bring Dan into the conversation like that was out of line. What the hell was wrong with Ella?

Her breathing rapid, she struggled for words. Nothing seemed adequate to show how upset she was.

'I've got to go,' she said, feeling tears well in her eyes. 'I'll see you later, Ella.'

'I suppose that's pretty obvious, seeing as I live about ten feet away from you.'

Ella flounced upstairs, laughing to herself as she recalled the look on Charley's face. *She* had made her feel that way – lost, mixed up, confused after her night of passion. Served her right for spending time with Aaron when she wanted to play instead.

But reality sank in before Ella reached her door. *She* was the one who felt all those things. Damn that woman for getting under her skin. She slammed the door shut.

How dare she think she was better than her – and to judge her too! It couldn't be coincidence that Charley had talked about being a one-man woman, saying that she didn't want to go off with lots of men — like Ella did all the time.

In the living room, she pushed over a pile of books; they scattered like the bricks of a condemned building at a demolition site. Next was the coffee table, up into the air and then over.

Someone must have been blabbing. Who the fuck was talking about her out there? Was it that stupid Jean across the road? If it was, she was going to have words with her — silly bitch. She should be happy enough watching, not interfering.

But worse than that was the knowledge that Charley had someone else to care for her now. Why was it that no one wanted to care for Ella? Why couldn't *she* meet someone like Aaron who would sweep her off her feet? Not Sabrina, though — she didn't want to live with another woman again after Nina.

It's happening all over again. Someone's stealing your thunder.

Ella pressed her hands to her ears and screamed.

You know what to do.

So many people interfered with my life, you know. Social workers, case workers, therapists, police, counsellors. Doctors, nursing staff, psychiatrists — you name them, I had one or another at any given time in my life. Often I had more than one. Sometimes I wished I had none. Because none of them helped me in the long run, did they? Oh no. I was a drunk — an alcoholic.

And as money was always tight, I'd go out to make a few quid on the streets. Sex had become a means to an end by then so why not make use of my body? When I was arrested and charged with soliciting, I started doing it with Brendan's mates then, or any of the neighbours, for whatever they would give me in return.

I'd been caught shoplifting three times too, when I was too drunk to react quickly enough. Three fines for thieving from Morrisons supermarket. I don't know why I continued to do it. Maybe it was the

buzz it gave me, taking something from someone else. Right under-
neath their noses.

So I was an alcoholic, a thief, and a prostitute!

I was told I was schizophrenic, too, by the people in the know,
but I didn't believe them. They would often gang up on me to make
me feel bad. But no one wanted to know why I was so drunk all the
time, what I was trying to block out – the fact that I'd had no child-
hood and had been dragged up through the system. No, it was all
about how out of control I was – addicted. I wasn't addicted! I just
needed someone to love me. Was that too much to ask, after all I'd
been through?

I remember one social worker named Tanya Smith. She was nice
but she couldn't help me. She tried her best to get through to me,
going out of her way to visit me, see how I was doing or encouraging
me to come along to the next meeting. After one of the group sessions
we'd had – Alcoholics Anonymous type of thing but we all knew
each other – Tanya took me to one side, asked how I was coping. I'd
had a little outburst, you see, in the meeting, in front of everyone,
and she was worried.

I wasn't worried. I just needed more booze. After each session,
I would go and get blotto, ha ha ha!

Tanya wondered if it would help if I wrote my thoughts down in
a diary or a notebook. So any time I felt angry or sad, I could write
about it. Like I'm doing now.

Really, what was the use in that?

We'd discuss these notes at our one-to-one meetings, when I
turned up for them. Sometimes I'd write things just because I knew
she was going to read it and it would piss her off. Like I'd go into
detail about fucking someone. Or write down how many drinks I'd
had – just to see if I could annoy her. But she never retaliated.

Am I am angry now? Am I sad? Who the fuck knows? What
I do know is that this writing lark? It doesn't work. You think you
can write down your thoughts and get them out of your mind? They

won't leave you – not even if you screw up the papers and set fire to them. They're stuck inside your head. Forever.

I wrote in another notebook too for a while. This one was just for me. I wasn't going to share that with anyone. ANYONE.

Like they gave a shit about me anyway.

Silly fuckers, the lot of them.

Ella cried uncontrollably, comparing herself to Charley. Everything had started to go wrong from the minute she'd turned up. And if she hadn't rejected her friendship, had wanted to spend more time with her, there would have been no bad days. She wouldn't be slip-sliding off the rails with no one to catch her on the way down, circling the drain into the depths of despair.

You know what you should do, don't you?

This was all Charley's fault. Why had she rejected her?

Don't you!

Ella nodded then. 'Yes, I do,' she said into the empty room.

She went through to the kitchen, opened a drawer, and pulled out a box of tablets. Inside were two full strips and one half-empty one. Grabbing a mug from the draining board, she hammered the bottom of it onto the tablets over and over. Then she put the remains in the bin, wiping her hands in satisfaction.

Way to go, girl. I knew you'd get there again.

———

As soon as Aaron returned, Charley rushed outside to greet him.

'What's up, gorgeous?' he piped. 'Missed me already? Or are you after my oatcakes?'

Charley sighed with relief, her shoulders dropping in dramatic style. 'Who cares about oatcakes?'

Aaron's eyes widened. 'How can you say that?' Then, 'Are you okay?'

Charley nodded. 'Yes, but that whole thing with Ella and the girl she insisted on kissing in front of us has really unnerved me. Did she have to be so obvious?'

'Did you realise she liked a bit of both before today?' Aaron closed the front door behind him.

'Not really. But it was strange, don't you think? The way she wanted us to see. And she was with your friend Steve last weekend!'

'She has a bloody active sex life, then!' Aaron kissed her lightly on the nose before heading down the hallway.

Charley slapped his bottom playfully.

'She's jealous, my love,' he added.

Charley dismissed the thought. Ella couldn't be envious of her and Aaron already. Could she? Determined not to let the incident ruin her mood, she smiled up at him.

'Why don't we have a nosy around Trentham Estate after we've eaten breakfast? It's only twenty minutes walk from here.'

An hour later as they set off along Warwick Avenue, Charley still couldn't get Ella's outburst from her mind. As she walked away, her hand tucked inside Aaron's, her eyes were drawn up towards the top floor.

Ella was standing in the window.

Chapter Nineteen

Ella watched Charley and Aaron until they were out of sight, wondering where they were off to now. She thought about following them but couldn't be bothered. It would only remind her of what a failure she was.

She turned back to face the room, feeling its emptiness and chaos seeping into her bones. Maybe they'd be back soon and she could imagine they were having sex downstairs. Or maybe they were going out to buy a picnic, finger food to eat in bed as they cuddled together before screwing. That's what couples did of a Sunday afternoon, didn't they?

How would you know what other couples do? No one wants you.

'Shut up!'

You're a freak – a pitiful example of a woman on the edge. Charley will see through you now – you've messed up by having a go at her, you stupid bitch.

'No!' Ella removed her dressing gown, shoved on a tracksuit and trainers, and ran out of the house. She wasn't going to stay there to be insulted.

And if she was quick, she might be able to catch up with Charley and Aaron.

The Trentham Estate was a place that Charley had visited umpteen times since she'd been a small child, although it had been mainly gardens then. During that time, its seven hundred plus acres had developed into so much more, attracting over three million visitors per year. But it was the Shopping Village that was Charley's favourite place to stroll around. Once she and Aaron had wandered around the garden centre, they made their way across the car park towards it.

In between the timber lodges selling local pottery, woollen attire, and all sorts of accessories to delight any home, Charley couldn't help wondering if everyone would see how happy she and Aaron were just by looking at them. It was often obvious to her when she'd seen other couples; surreptitious kisses, holding hands, wrapping arms around each other, feeling the need to be close again, in constant contact. A ludicrously warm feeling flowed through her.

'Wow, there's such a great choice of food in here,' Aaron said, after they'd been inside Brown and Green's for a few minutes. He picked up a pot of Beetroot and Cracked Black Pepper Chutney. 'We should take some of this for later, perhaps? Be nice to have it with some of those breads catching my eye over there.'

'Assuming I let you stay around later. I might have things to do on my own,' Charley teased.

'I doubt that.' She felt his arm slip around her waist. 'You can't get enough of me.'

'You're so smug.'

'*Attractive*! I'm so *attractive*. You need to learn that word!'

Charley giggled, almost high with lust. God love those happy pheromones. She picked up a basket and placed the chutney inside it. A picnic in bed – now, there was a thought for later.

A few feet away, in the throng of Sunday shoppers, Ella cursed when she saw them head into David's Brasserie. How the hell was she supposed to keep an eye on them now?

Out of sight, she sat on a bench in the middle of a large paved area while people walked past her, oblivious to her angst. Hidden behind a white flowering hydrangea bursting out of a wooden planter, she waited for them to reappear. She'd sit there for an hour if she had to until they came out again.

But a minute later, she saw a young waiter showing them to a table outside. He handed them both menus before moving to the next table to take down an order for another couple. Ella locked her eyes onto them, seeing Charley move her head forward, laughing at something Aaron had said, leaning across the table to touch his hand.

'It's so obvious they've been screwing,' she muttered. 'They can't keep their hands off each other.'

As if to prove her point, Aaron wiped a strand of Charley's hair away from her face, cupped her chin in his hands. Envy rushed through Ella as he kissed Charley gently. For fuck's sake, they weren't even sitting opposite each other at the table; they were next to each other, as close as close could be.

She doesn't need you. I told you so.

Seeing the waiter return with coffee and two slices of cake was more than she could bear. Ella stormed off back towards the garden centre.

'Move!' She pushed rudely past a young couple out with a newborn baby in a pram.

Oblivious to their protests, Ella strode away, unable to look at them. She couldn't stand to see any more – couldn't stand to see *anyone*. It was all so lovey-dovey. It made her sick!

Once back at the house, Ella tore up the stairs and into the flat. She marched through her bedroom and into the closet where she sat on the floor, hoping to calm down. But the darkness overwhelmed her, giving her a sense of foreboding, and minutes later, she was out again, pacing the hallway.

It was all her fault, Miss new lodger. Ella needed sex now, would have to go out on a mission later.

No, it had to be now.

She raced through to the bedroom where she stripped, leaving her clothes in a heap on the floor. Talking dirty, she masturbated harshly while in the shower, crying out loudly as she came. Still, it wasn't enough. Thinking of them together angered her. If she went out, she could pick up a fuck – someone had to give her what she needed.

Someone had to want her eventually.

You're feeling sorry for yourself now. You don't need anyone else but me.

But once out of the shower, Ella lost interest in her plan and opened a bottle of vodka instead. She stood in the window, looking out onto the avenue. Across the road, she could see a figure in the window of number thirty-six. She squinted. Was it him? She staggered to the right slightly, holding onto the window frame for support. Yes, it was Jake.

Ella undid her dressing gown. Then slowly, she slipped it from her shoulders and let it drop. Might as well give him something to look at, she mused.

⌣

'Fucking hell!'

'See, I fucking told you,' Jake said, hardly able to keep the excitement from his voice. 'I said I wasn't making it up.'

'Fuck, yeah, I see her.' Will peered through the binoculars again. 'She's got her hands on her tits.'

'Let me look!'

Jake tried to grab the binoculars but Will dodged him.

'No, this I have to see.'

After a few seconds, Jake was beside himself. 'For Christ's sake, let me look!' he said again.

'In a minute!'

'What's she doing now?'

'Ohmigod, she's – she's playing with her pussy. Fuck, I'm so horny watching this. Don't your olds ever see her?'

'If they do, they don't say anything. Mum and Dad sleep in the back room. Mum would go mental if she saw her anyway, so no telling anyone.'

'I won't. Don't want to spoil the fun. What's her name – do you know?'

'Ella.'

'Well, hello, Ella.' Will turned briefly towards Jake. 'You should film her – so you can watch it when she isn't there. It's awesome.'

'I have.'

'What – doing that?'

'Yeah. I've got her screwing some lucky bastard against the wall outside her door, too.'

'Fuck. Off!'

Jake nodded. 'I've been watching her for about a month now. It beats bashing the bishop over a magazine.'

Will paused, licking his bottom lip. 'You filmed her doing that?'

'Oh, yeah.'

'Let me see.'

'No way.' Jake shook his head fervently. 'You can watch the real thing and that's it.'

'You're such a lucky bastard.' Will looked through the binoculars again.

'Two more minutes and I want them back.'

'Jake!' a voice shouted up the stairs. 'Can you give me a hand for a moment?'

Both boys moved from the window quickly. Jake threw himself on top of the bed and Will crashed down into the chair at his desk, the castors rolling him across the laminated flooring. A moment later, they burst into laughter.

'Jake!'

'I'm coming!'

Will sniggered. 'Ella seems to be.'

'I'll be back in a minute.'

As soon as he was gone, Will grabbed Jake's phone from the desk and rushed to the door. Keeping it ajar so he could see when his friend was coming back, he searched through the files until he located the ones he was after. Bingo! Not knowing which one he needed, he synched his own phone with Jake's and began to copy one.

It took less than a minute but it felt like forever. 'Come, on, come on,' he whispered. When he'd done that one, he wondered if he'd have time to do the other. He started, but aborted it when he heard Jake thundering up the stairs towards him.

He put the phone down and raced back to the window. Annoyingly, Ella was nowhere to be seen now.

'She's gone,' he told Jake.

'What?' Jake snatched back the binoculars and looked for himself. His shoulders dropped. 'Did you see her finish off?'

'Oh, yes.'

'Shit.'

Behind him, Will sat on Jake's bed and grinned, his hand on the phone in his pocket. Yes, Ella might have gone, but he'd be able to watch and enjoy her later on his own. Then maybe Callum would like to see it, and Phil, and Mitch. Fuck, he reckoned most of his mates would burst while viewing the clip if it was anything like what he'd seen her doing in the window just then.

Over the next week, Charley and Aaron saw each other most evenings. Ella kept her distance and Charley didn't see Sabrina visiting again. The following weekend was spent mostly at Aaron's house so on Sunday evening, Charley cooked him a meal at her flat. Afterwards, they sat together on the settee.

'Want a cuppa?' she asked after a while.

'Hmm?' Aaron didn't take his eyes from the football match he was watching on the television.

Charley stood up. Still he watched the screen. She laughed.

He looked at her then. 'What?' he said eventually.

'We've only been dating for a fortnight and already we're like an old married couple.'

'We'll be visiting IKEA soon, then.' Aaron grabbed her hand and pulled her onto his lap. 'It's called contentment.'

'It's called football fanatic.' She pushed him away playfully. 'Tea or coffee?'

'Coffee, please.' Aaron sat forward and raised his hand in the air. 'Aw, come on! Did you see that? The ref must be blind – he was definitely offside.'

Charley smirked and went through to the kitchen. Despite the football match taking his attention, she did feel content. She reckoned it was a good sign that they felt so comfortable together already.

As she filled the kettle with water, she noticed the outside light glaring across Ella's garden. It was still on once she'd made the drinks so she stepped outside to investigate. In the quiet of the evening, she could hear crying from Ella's garden. She waited for a moment, unsure whether to let her know she was there or not. But as she heard another sob, she couldn't help but open the side gate.

'Ella?'

She was sitting on the doorstep, arms wrapped tightly around her knees. She looked like she was trying to make herself seem smaller.

'Yes, s-me.'

'Are you okay?'

Ella shook her head.

'Would you rather I left you alone?'

'No.'

Charley sat down next to her on the step. Ella's cheeks were wet with tears. From the smell of her breath, it was clear she'd been drinking.

'What am I going to do, Charley?' she said. 'My life – it's so fucked up.'

'I bet it isn't,' Charley spoke softly to her. 'We all mess up but it's how we choose to handle things afterwards that builds character.'

'Then I have no character because I've messed up all my life.'

'I bet you haven't,' she soothed, although inwardly she'd begun to wonder.

Ella snorted. 'You don't know the half of it. I don't know why I care about it, really – no one cares about me.

'Of course they do!'

'They don't.' Ella shook her head vehemently. 'I wish I could get so drunk that I'd pass out and forget everything. And I don't want to keep going out to ...' She paused.

There was silence for a moment.

Charley couldn't help but pity her. Here she was spending an evening laughing and joking with Aaron and here was Ella, lonely and turning to drink for a companion.

'I don't mean to pry,' she said, 'but haven't you any friends that you can visit, or maybe family? I bet if they knew you were so unhappy, they'd want to help.'

'I haven't got any family, or friends. No one can help me anyway. I'm beyond help, apparently.'

'Who told you that?'

'Lots of people.' Ella pointed to her temple. 'I have mental scars that will never heal. No matter what I do to myself, or what other people do to me, I'm fucked up anyway.'

'Maybe there's someone I can get to –'

'She's coming back to get me.' Ella began to cry. 'And there's nothing I can do to stop her.'

'Who's coming back?'

'She is – she takes over my life, my head! I have to do what she says and I don't like it. She scares me, Charley. I don't even like her.'

'Who scares you?' Charley leaned closer. 'Ella, has someone hurt you?'

'No.'

'Then what?'

'It's her! I just told you! She messes with my head and makes me do things. I don't want to do what she says. I want to be normal and have friends and a boyfriend like you have Aaron and I want a house like you used to have and I want another baby and I want to be in love and –'

'Everything all right out here?' Aaron appeared in the gateway.

'What the fuck does he want?' Ella muttered.

'Ella!' Charley admonished.

'Well, everything was good until he showed up.'

'That's not a nice –'

'Leave me alone!' Ella stood up and went inside. 'Mind your own business, both of you.'

Charley shouted after her but Ella shut the door. With a shrug, she turned to Aaron.

'What was all that about?' he asked as she drew level with him.

'I'm not sure.' Once back in her own garden area, Charley closed the gate behind them. 'She's so manic,' she went on. 'One minute she's smiling and laughing; the next she's having a go with the sharpest of tongues. I don't think I'll ever understand her. I'm sure she's just said something about a baby too.'

'A baby?' Aaron looked perplexed. 'Are you sure?'

'Well, yes, I'm sure, but she's never mentioned anything before.'

'Perhaps she doesn't want you to know about it. Or perhaps it isn't true?'

'Perhaps.' But Charley wasn't convinced. Wasn't she already questioning Ella's constant attention seeking? Maybe it was another cry for help, letting her know a little more of her background.

'She'll be fine,' Aaron said soothingly. 'I doubt she'll remember any of it in the morning.'

'I know, but –'

Aaron took hold of her hand. 'If you're that worried about her, talk to her when she's sober and see if you can help.' He pulled her towards the door. 'Come back inside.'

'So you don't miss any of the match, you mean?'

'Don't be daft,' Aaron grinned. 'It's half time.'

Charley looked up as a light went on in Ella's kitchen, heard water gushing from a tap. She hoped she was making black coffee to clear her head. Charley knew the drinking was a coping mechanism; she'd seen it so many times in her job. And if she was going to figure out if Ella needed help, she had to know some of what she was dealing with first. Even if she couldn't do anything for her, maybe she could signpost Ella towards someone or some agency that could. She was a sweet person when she was happy. It was a shame that she couldn't be like that more of the time.

She wondered what had happened to make her drink so much again, and why she had to be so rude to Aaron all the time. For some reason, she seemed threatened by his maleness.

What was her background? Was she one of the lonely souls who lived forgotten after a traumatic childhood, trying to get through their lives, pushing the right people away, clinging on to the wrong people for affection? Or maybe Ella was a manic depressive, her mood swings a constant. It didn't all stack up yet. Charley hated it when she didn't have answers to all her questions.

Aaron's hand slipped inside her top and she tingled at his touch on her skin. He drew her into his arms and kissed her passionately, leaving her breathless. She pressed herself into him, not wanting to end the embrace. God, she couldn't get enough of him – his scent, his taste, his touch.

Yet, as they went back inside afterwards, her thoughts quickly returned to Ella. It wasn't pleasant to see her so unhappy, especially because she knew exactly how lonely she'd be.

Charley had only recently got rid of that feeling herself.

Chapter Twenty

Charley grinned when she heard her phone beep the next morning. Aaron hadn't left until two a.m. She hadn't wanted him to go last night, nor did she suspect that he'd been too eager to leave, but it didn't seem right yet to spend every night together. Taking it slowly was good for her, even though her heart wanted to rule her head. Or was that still lust ... She knew the dizzy feelings wouldn't last forever.

But the message wasn't from Aaron: it was from Ella.

'You were with him again last night. You should have been there for me. I needed someone to talk to.'

Charley sighed. She wasn't going to reply to that; Ella was most probably still drunk from the night before. If she ignored it, maybe Ella wouldn't even recall sending it.

She got up, went about getting ready for work, and the phone beeped again, then again a few seconds later. Then as she buttered her toast, another message came through, and another. In exasperation, she picked up her phone.

Ella: *'Can I see you tonight?'*

Ella: *'You'll probably be going out with him, won't you?'*

Ella: *'Come out with me instead.'*

Ella: *'You needed me until he came along.'*

Charley read them one by one and then scrolled through them all again. She sighed. Ella must be feeling really low to send such messages. But, drunk or sober, there was hardly any need for the accusatory tone. Charley decided she might ask her about them when she next saw her, see if she couldn't get to the bottom of things.

When another message came through as she was leaving, she thought for a moment about ignoring it. But luckily when she looked, this time it was from Aaron. She smiled as she read it, feeling herself blush at its bluntness. God, that man really had changed her life for the better already!

Upstairs, Ella was pacing the living room.

'Answer me, you bitch. Answer me!' She checked her mobile phone for the umpteenth time but no messages had been received. She threw it down onto the settee. Then she walked the room again, picked up the phone, and repeated the procedure.

Damn that woman – why wasn't she good enough to be her friend? She should want to spend time with her too, surely? It wasn't right that she would ignore her; she wouldn't let her either.

She was about to check her phone again when she heard the entrance door open downstairs, close again moments afterwards. Racing to the window, she was in time to see Charley walk towards her car and sling her bag onto the back seat before getting in. She waited until the car was out of sight. Then she picked up her phone again and sent another text message.

'*Why won't you reply?*'

And then another. '*What's wrong?*'

The final one: '*Why are you ignoring me?*'

It was two thirty on Tuesday afternoon. Drunk, Ella sat sobbing, knocking back more alcohol as she tried to blot out her non-existent life. She was losing control again, she could tell; knew this obsession with sex was tearing her apart. But wanting to kick the habit of sleeping around and doing it was another thing entirely. All she longed for every day was the release it brought. It was as if with every orgasm, every coupling, a piece of the bad inside her was released too, but it didn't last long. Soon, she'd be feeling like shit again and the circle continued.

She wondered whether to seek help from her social worker, maybe go back to the group counselling sessions. She hadn't seen Tanya Smith for a few months now, not since she'd shown her the notebook she'd written in. She'd been scared to go back in case Tanya was tempted to lock her up. Section her and put her into a mental institution; say she was losing her mind. Ella was certain that she wouldn't find her anyway. She didn't know she was living in Warwick Avenue. She'd go to the wrong address, if she was still after her.

She knocked back another mouthful of vodka straight from the bottle, wishing there was someone she could trust enough to tell her secret. Someone who would encourage her to get help and then guide her so she could get better – not the likes of Tanya or that stupid sex therapist she'd seen in the past. Someone who would be there for her all the time and not just when she had an appointment.

Someone close to her that she could call on to chat to when the urge to get used struck her.

Someone as close to her as Charley.

Yeah, as if that's going to happen.

'I KNOW!' Ella screamed.

Charley had kept her distance since she'd caught her crying in the garden on Sunday evening. Since then, Ella had gone further and further into a spiral of chaos. All of the text messages she'd sent had gone unanswered and that riled her – along with Aaron invading the space that should have been hers.

There had been a bit of light entertainment between her periods of drunkenness. Ella had seen Sabrina again last night. It had been fun – she'd made her laugh as much as she'd made her come – but that was all it would ever be. The young woman seemed a little smitten with her. Sweet Sabrina would be good for her. But Ella didn't want good: she wanted bad and nasty.

October was upon them, the nights creeping in, the recent Indian summer forgotten. The week was turning out to be a wash-out so far but although the sky was grey and rain splashed at the window, it was still warm enough for her to lie naked and uncovered on the settee, fingers idly stroking her skin as she fantasised about Charley. It would have been fun if she could have orchestrated it for real. But it wouldn't happen now that she was keeping her distance.

Charley was pulling away – and all because of that bastard, Aaron. If he hadn't come along when he did, she and Charley would be great friends by now. It was more his fault than hers. If Ella ever had the chance to harm him, she would hurt him as much as he had wounded her by taking Charley away.

Frenzied by alcohol and bad thoughts, she slipped downstairs. It took a few times before she could see clearly enough to put the key in the lock but finally she managed to get inside Charley's flat. She headed for the living room, noticing different things along with familiar objects. There was a pile of paperwork on the desk this time, with several manila folders. She flicked one open, saw notes about someone called Margaret Owen who'd been sexually assaulted by her partner. Ella wished she hadn't drunk so much now or she would have read them all.

Trying to read, she brought the paper nearer to her face. The address looked familiar – Uttoxeter Road, Meir. Of course, she realised. It was where she had followed Charley to when she was out visiting, where Charley had touched the woman's arm to comfort her.

Feeling drowsy, she dropped onto a settee and thought about what Charley and Aaron must have got up to in this room. Had he fucked her at the desk, or shagged her on the carpet in front of the fire? Had they screwed on this very sofa? It made her feel aroused again. She dropped the empty bottle to the floor, touching herself to orgasm, imagining them both with her.

Satisfied afterwards, she congratulated herself. This was fantastic – why hadn't she thought of it before? She could come down here, see them in her mind everywhere in this flat, touch herself standing in the exact same spot and come over and over again. Not even have to leave the house. It was perfect and so fucking rude.

Her eyelids fluttered closed as she slipped back into her fantasy. Moments later she was asleep.

Jean couldn't believe Ella was in Charley's flat again. What was wrong with that woman? She had hoped it would be a phase of Ella's, that once she'd got to know Charley she wouldn't feel the need to snoop around. She knew there was nothing she could do about it but it made her sad. It was one thing to do as Jean did, stare out of the window all day every day, but it was another thing entirely to be in someone's home when they didn't know about it. She didn't invade anyone's privacy, go through their belongings, and search through personal possessions. Jean couldn't imagine that Charley would be too excited about it if she did find out any time soon. It was deceitful.

She heard the door go downstairs.

'It's only me, Jean!' Ruby shouted up to her. 'Wait a couple of minutes and you'll smell something nice that I've bought you.'

Jean smiled. On her last visit, Ruby had said she'd call in at the chip shop the next time she was due. Knowing she would keep her word, Jean had been looking forward to it all day. So too, she imagined, would Tom if he knew what leftovers he could expect. He was curled up on her lap; she stroked the top of his head.

'Fish for tea, Tom,' she told him. 'Far more important than looking out of the window.'

She noted down Ruby's arrival time and closed the notebook. That one completed, she took out another from the cabinet by her side, excited about starting a new first page all over again. With all Ella's comings and goings lately, she'd used up the last notebook much quicker than usual.

Ruby placed the tray on her lap, her eyes scanning the room. 'Where is it?'

'I haven't the faintest idea.' Jean looked on in amusement.

Ruby pushed her hair behind her ear and pouted. 'It's called a Lifeline system for a reason.' She spotted what she was looking for and went to retrieve it. Jean had a cordless telephone and a pendant which were attached to a twenty-four-hour call-out system, so if anything happened to her, help would be at hand. It allowed Jean to be independent. The emergency pendant hung by a cord over the corner of the headboard. But the phone was nowhere to be seen.

'What's the point of having this if you don't wear it – or at least keep your phone nearby in case you fall?'

'Consider me told off,' Jean said, as she placed the pendant around her neck. She knew she'd remove it as soon as Ruby had gone; she didn't want to be a burden to anyone.

'Right, then,' Ruby reached over and pinched a chip. 'I'll find your phone and whether you like it or not, at least I'll feel better knowing that someone is looking out for you!'

By Wednesday lunchtime, her messages still unanswered, Ella drove into Hanley and hung around Stafford Street window shopping. Just after twelve thirty, she saw Charley come out of her offices and head into the centre of town. Ella stayed well hidden until she saw her go past and then set off, keeping a little way behind.

Two minutes later, Charley crossed over the road and headed into TK Maxx. Ella followed, walking briskly up the next aisle and then down to her as if she'd been in there all the time.

'Hi, Charley,' she beamed. 'I'm on my lunch break. Fancy seeing you in here.'

'Hi, Ella.' Charley smiled. 'I'm just after a couple of pictures to put up in the hallway. How are you?'

'Fine, fine.' Ella tried to keep her voice from squeaking excitedly. 'So what've you been up to? Still getting on with the lovely Aaron?'

Charley nodded. 'Yes, so far so good.' She picked up a framed image and began to study it.

An awkward silence fell between them.

'Do you fancy grabbing a coffee? We could head over to –'

'Sorry.' Charley stopped her. 'I've been on my lunch break far too long now; I'm due back at the office in a couple of minutes. Another time, maybe?'

'Sure.' Ella stopped herself too, from slapping Charley across her face for lying. As she turned to look at the picture again, it took her a while to realise she was being dismissed.

'Right, then. I'll see you again soon, yeah?'

Charley nodded. 'Sure, Ella. See you.'

'When will you see me?'

'Sorry?'

'I could call for coffee later this evening? It's been ages since we had a good chat. I know you're seeing Aaron but it would do you good not to live in each other's pockets. I mean, you've only been seeing him for nineteen days. It's not like you're marrying him or anything, is it?'

She paused for breath, long enough to acknowledge the astonishment on Charley's face. She grinned. 'Sorry, I'm being too forward again, aren't I? It's such a bad habit.'

Charley put down the picture and made a big gesture of checking her watch. 'Blimey, I really have to go. Bye, Ella.'

'Bye, Charley. See you soon.'

Ella watched Charley scurry off before heading into the city centre to get a drink. She needed a shot of something to calm herself, to erase the memory of Charley's rejection. But inside The Reginald Mitchell pub, she found that she couldn't walk towards the bar. Tears welled in her eyes as she ran into the toilets. Finding them empty, she locked herself in a cubicle and let her grief out.

Why didn't Charley want to make time for her anymore? All Ella had done was be friendly and that friendship had been rejected since Aaron had come on to the scene. Nineteen days she'd had to suffer, watching them together. And she had a feeling it was going to get much worse.

Why couldn't Charley see that she didn't need Aaron? She sobbed, wiping her eyes with the back of her sleeve. She just needed Ella. Ella would be enough for her, good for her.

Why couldn't she see that?

'If you're worried about Ella, you need to notify someone,' Aaron said when Charley went over the incident with him later that evening. She was at his house, having followed him home in her car after work.

Charley sighed. 'I'm not sure it's my place to get involved. Maybe she's lonely and latching on to me. I feel like I want to keep my distance but I don't like being unfriendly. You know how I like to help people.'

'Yes, but she's clearly not acting rationally. It wouldn't do any harm to check if she's known to social services, either.'

Charley had already had that thought but misgivings had crept in. 'She isn't my client.'

'I wouldn't *want* her as one of my clients.'

Charley turned to him sharply but realised he was winding her up when she saw him grinning. Their jobs ensured they were both open-minded, non-judgemental; helping people was what they did.

Charley hadn't told anyone about Ella's erratic behaviour with the text messages on Monday morning, mainly hoping that they would stop. And they had. But, ever since Ella had caught up with her, the messages had started again. Her phone had beeped constantly every ten minutes or so, to the point that Lynne had asked her to put it on silent as it was making her lose concentration.

'Why don't you fancy a coffee this evening?'

'We could do another night instead?'

'How about tomorrow?'

'She knew exactly how long we'd been seeing each other,' Charley decided to tell him. 'Nineteen days – even I wouldn't be that specific. I'd say nearly three weeks if anyone asked, not an exact number. Why is she keeping track of us?'

'Bloody hell, Charl, that's eerie,' Aaron remarked.

'I know.' Charley sighed. 'She's obviously lonely. I'm going to look into what I can do for her.'

'Well at least you don't have to worry about it this evening.' He pointed to her overnight bag. 'I hope you remembered to bring your toothbrush, too?'

'I sure did.' Charley grinned cheekily, thankful that she was staying over with him. 'There is one thing you won't find in there, though.'

'What's that?'

'My pyjamas.'

Ella woke up with a start when she heard a car door slam outside the window. She stretched and opened her eyes. She got up quickly, falling to the side and rolling onto the floor in her haste. Shit, she was in Charley's flat! After retrieving the bottle, she let herself out quickly.

Back upstairs in her living room, she checked the time. It was quarter past seven. She looked out into the dark. Where was Charley? She had never stayed out during the week before. She'd always come home first if she was going out later, either changing from her work wear into more casual clothes or emerging ready for a workout at the gym. This was unlike her.

Ella's mind went into overdrive. Had Charley been involved in an accident? Shit, she could be lying dead in a morgue for all she knew.

Or had she gone to see Aaron instead of coming home? If she had, things might be more serious than she'd imagined.

She's screwing him. She doesn't need you.

Why hadn't she rung to tell her where she was, damn her!

Why should she? She's not your friend, really.

Five hours later, Ella was still standing in the window. Charley wasn't home; nor had she seen Aaron or his car.

She'd come to the conclusion that it could only mean one thing: Charley must be staying over at Aaron's house, without telling her. How dare she!

How fucking dare she!

Chapter Twenty-One

All day Wednesday, Ella paced up and down in her flat, continuing to drink whatever she had in. She'd been awake for most of the night thinking of Charley and why she hadn't come home. One minute, she'd imagine her hooked up to a breathing machine and lying in intensive care; the next she had her sleeping curled up with Aaron or them having sex without her.

What angered her most was that Charley hadn't thought to contact her. A simple text message, that's all it would have taken. Thirty seconds, tops, and she would have been fine, not have to worry. But no, she'd been too busy fucking Aaron.

Why hadn't she come home?

By the time Ella saw her parking up outside that evening, she had to fight the urge not to run outside and punch her full in the face. While Charley reached for her belongings from the back seat of the car, she took a few deep breaths to calm herself down. But when she saw her coming up the steps outside, she thundered down the stairs and waited for her to open the door.

———

Charley jumped when she saw Ella standing behind the door as she pulled out her key.

'Where the fuck have you been?' Ella cried. 'I've been worried sick.'

'Why, what's wrong? Has something happened? Are you okay?' she asked all at once.

'How would I know? You didn't come home!'

Charley frowned. 'Sorry, I'm not sure I –'

Ella pointed at her. 'You stayed out all night! How was I to know if you were alive or dead? I mean, anything could have happened. You could have had an accident, be lying in a ditch. You could have been kidnapped and raped – worse, you could have been murdered! Why didn't you tell me where you were going? I shouldn't have to spend the night not being able to sleep because I don't know –'

'Ella! Stop!' Charley raised her voice. 'I'm fine! I stayed over at Aaron's.'

'But I wasn't supposed to know that!'

'No, actually you weren't.' Shocked at her manner, Charley decided she needed to set some boundaries. 'I don't have to tell you where I'm going and when I'll be back. I don't answer to anyone, especially not my landlady.'

'I thought I was more than a landlady to you,' Ella pouted. 'I thought I was your friend.'

'Friends don't come tearing down the stairs and start swearing at –'

'I was worried!'

'You shouldn't be. I'm a big girl. I can manage, thanks.'

'So it was okay for you to cry on my shoulder when you needed it, and go out with me until you found Aaron, but it's not okay for me to worry about you? It's the first night you've stayed out since you moved in.'

'I know, but ...' Charley paused. 'How do you know that? Are you keeping tabs on me?'

'No, I –'

'Well, how else would you know that this is the first night I've stayed out?'

'Because I hear the entrance door!'

Charley wasn't convinced but she didn't feel like arguing with a woman who was saying that she didn't have the right to do anything unless she cleared it with her first. It was absurd – and a little bit odd. She moved past Ella towards the door to her flat.

But Ella blocked her way. 'Where are you going?' she asked.

'Into my flat – let me pass.'

'But I thought you'd come upstairs to have a chat with me. We can open a bottle of wine, have a laugh.' Ella's eyes widened with excitement. 'Hey, we can dissect your dates with Aaron – I'd love to know how you're getting on.'

Charley frowned. Which Ella was she talking to now – happy-go-lucky or paranoid manic? It was ridiculous trying to keep track of her moods.

She didn't like it. And right now, she wanted to get away.

'Ella, I'm tired.' She smiled, hoping to show friendliness rather than hostility. 'Thanks, but if you don't mind I'm heading for a bath and an early night.'

Ella moved to one side. Charley was at the door when she spoke again.

'That's because you were fucking him all night, I suppose.'

Charley recoiled. 'I beg your pardon?'

'Tired because you were fucking him –'

'Yes, yes, I heard you the first time. I just couldn't believe you'd say such a thing.'

'It's true, though, isn't it?'

Before she could reply, Ella pushed her up against the wall. Her hand went inside her jacket, found her breast and squeezed it hard. Then she brought her mouth close to hers.

Charley turned her head to one side, screwing up her face, repulsed as Ella's lips missed their target and touched her cheek.

Bile rose in her throat as she pushed her body as far into the wall as it would go. She pulled away Ella's hand quickly, still feeling the imprint of where it had been placed on her clothes.

'What the fuck are you doing?' she cried. 'Get off me!'

Ella stopped and glared at her. 'I thought you might want to get intimate.'

'No!'

'But what does Aaron have that I haven't? I was watching over you until he came along!'

'I don't need anyone to watch over me!'

'Yes, you do. You're lonely and that means you're vulnerable. I could have cared for you. You didn't need to go out with him.'

'I … I …'

'Oh.' Ella dropped her arms and took a step away. 'I must have read the signs wrong.'

Charley couldn't speak. She was sure she hadn't given out any signals at all.

'I thought you'd gone with Aaron to make me jealous,' Ella added, 'like you were playing hard to get.'

'Of course I wasn't! I don't –'

'I've always liked a bit of both, I must admit.' Ella paused. 'You should try it sometime. You don't know what you're missing.'

Charley didn't know what to say to that, either.

'I'm really sorry.' Ella grinned, looking embarrassed. 'I'll leave before I make more of a fool of myself.' She paused again. 'Friends still?'

Charley nodded. She let herself into the flat quickly, drew the lock across the door, and leaned on the back of it for a moment.

Afterwards, she walked around as if in a daze. The place felt strange; for the first time since she'd moved in, she didn't feel safe there. It had suddenly turned into something sour, somewhere she didn't want to come home to.

And what had all that been about? After making a pass at her, Ella was trying to brush the incident off as if it hadn't happened. Charley thought back to the times when she'd been alone with her. Had she given her any unintentional ideas? She could only remember them hugging when she'd been upset about Dan. Had she got the wrong end of the stick from then? Oh, God.

She went through into the living room. Knowing Ella was upstairs above her was freaking her out. Of course Ella couldn't see her, but she couldn't shake the feeling that she could. Christ, she'd seen a lot of things in her line of work, but nothing had alarmed her like that. She definitely felt the need to talk to someone about Ella's behaviour now.

Yet again, Ella had spoiled Charley's return after a good time with Aaron. It had taken her a long time to pluck up the courage to move out of her home and into Warwick Avenue but, if anything else happened, she would have to find somewhere else to go. It wouldn't be easy to find another place so quickly, and she would lose her deposit here, but if she didn't feel safe, no money in the world would make her stay.

———

Ella wallowed in self-pity all evening after Charley's rejection. Memories of Susan Reilly came back to her mind. She'd seen the same look on her previous tenant's face when she'd made a pass at her, too. She'd thought Susan was game. The signs were there. She was single, and she was always friendly. But Ella had acted too quickly, frightened her off, especially when she'd been waiting downstairs in the flat for her to return that evening. Ella couldn't help but giggle as she recalled the fearful look on Susan's face when she'd found her sitting on her settee drinking her wine. She hadn't thought she would move out so quickly afterwards, though.

Finally succumbing to her needs, Ella logged on to *One Night Only* and arranged another meet. Arriving home shortly before two a.m. she made as much noise as she could to let Charley know that she'd been out having fun. She didn't need her; she didn't need anyone as long as she could go out and get screwed. Tonight, she'd found a man who'd been willing but it had been too gentle and too quick for her liking. And he'd been too old – which is why she'd come up with her plan to get someone younger next time, someone closer to home. Someone across the road from her.

She had to wait all the next day but the thought of what she was about to do kept her on edge. Finally, she spotted Jake walking up the avenue towards his home. Even though it was half past three, Ella was still in her dressing gown. Some days there seemed no point in getting dressed. Barefoot, she ran down the stairs quickly and out the entrance door.

'Jake, have you got a minute?' She waved to catch his attention, hoping she wouldn't seem too drunk when he came over to her. She'd had a delivery from Tesco that morning, with far more alcohol than food, but at least it meant she didn't have to go out and fetch anything. She really couldn't be bothered.

She watched as he came across to her, her heart quickening as he drew near. From his smart yet casual attire, Ella assumed he'd most probably been to college or maybe Staffordshire University. Towering over her, at least six feet in height, he was neither lanky and lean nor too bulky. Olive-skinned with short dark hair, he had the odd blemish that gave away his youthfulness, yet he showed signs of a five o'clock shadow. Two lines had been shaven into one eyebrow and there was a hole where she assumed he'd taken out a stud or a ring. Ella licked her lip, praying he had a pierced tongue – there was nothing better than feeling something alien when it flicked over her most delicate of places.

He stopped on the bottom step as she stood at the top.

She spoke first. 'You couldn't help me out with something, please? I need to change a bulb and I can't reach it.'

'Sure.' He smiled shyly.

'Great. I'm on the first floor, but you already know that, don't you?' Not giving him time to answer, she beckoned him in.

They went into the house and up the stairs. She knew he'd be checking out her legs so she walked a little more slowly than usual, waggling her hips that little bit more. In her flat, she closed the door and led him through to the living room.

'Would you like a drink?' she asked.

'I – yeah, go on, then.'

'Whisky?'

'Sure.'

She poured two drinks, handed one to him.

'Where you've been all day. College?'

'Yeah, at the new Sixth Form in Stoke.'

'You seem more of a man than that, if you catch my drift.' Ella put the glass to her lips, staring intently at him. 'How old are you?'

'Seventeen.'

'Seventeen.' She knocked back the whisky, poured some more, and drank that too, while Jake sipped at his.

'And are you a virgin, Jake?'

He shook his head.

'So, you *are* all man, then?'

'I suppose.'

'You suppose.' Ella nodded slowly. 'Jake?'

'Yeah?'

'You realise I don't really need a bulb changing, don't you?' She stepped closer to him.

When he nodded, Ella saw his Adam's apple move as he gulped. Laughing inwardly, she took the glass from him.

'You like watching me, don't you?'

'I – I might do.'

She wagged a finger at him. 'I can see you. But you know that too.' She lifted up his jumper and T-shirt, ran her fingers across his stomach, feeling him pull it in at her touch. 'I really like you. Do you like *me*?'

'I guess so.'

She moved a little closer and giggled. 'I can see how much by that shape in your trousers.' Pressing on his erection caused him to jump back a little. She laughed. 'Don't worry, I won't bite. Well, not too hard.'

She reached for his hands, placed them both on the ties to her dressing gown, urging him to pull them apart. When he'd done that, she slipped it from her shoulders, revealing her nakedness. Hearing him gasp, she placed his hand on her breast, almost shivering at his touch.

'I bet you've dreamt of doing this, haven't you?' she purred.

Jake could only nod again.

'Kiss me.' She drew him near.

He didn't need any further encouragement. Ella tasted him, sweet on her lips. He faltered at first, unsure whether to continue, but as instinct took over, he came into his own. She pulled his upper garments above his arms and over, needing to feel his bare skin against hers. Then she pushed his head down until his mouth found her nipple. Ella groaned as he sank his teeth into it, stood on her tiptoes so he could take in more. He moved to the other one.

'That's so good.' She gave a moan. 'Now, do something with your hands at the same time.'

Jake's hands dived between her legs, his fingers slipping into her. At first, he moved too fast and she slowed him down with a hand over his. Then when he had a rhythm she was happy with, they kissed while she let the passion build. Suddenly, she arched away from him.

'Now you can move your hand faster,' she moaned. 'Make me come, Jake. Make me come over and over again. And then we can fuck. I want you inside me. I have to have you inside me. And then...' Words failed her as her body quivered. She threw back her head, trying to keep her balance as she reached orgasm noisily. Satisfied with her last quiver, her head came forward again and she smiled at him. He was good.

'Well, that was much better than anticipated,' she said, watching his chest puff out with pride. She rested a hand on his zip, then pulled it down slowly. 'Every bit a man, I feel.' She went down on him, holding onto the back of his legs to steady herself as she took him to her mouth.

It was a matter of seconds before he came. Ella stood back up again, wiping her mouth with the back of her hand.

'Eager little fucker, aren't you?' She pointed at him in an accusing manner. 'Don't move. I need another drink.'

Naked, she padded through to the kitchen, congratulating herself on such a good idea. Being young, Jake would be able to go over and over. Maybe she could teach him a few tricks to make him last longer, too.

Far more unsteady now, she grabbed a half-empty bottle of wine from the fridge and closed the door with the bump of a hip. As she wrestled to untwist the top, she heard the front door close. She tore into the living room to find it empty. Where the fuck was he?

She raced to the front door, opened it in time to see the entrance door closing again. No, no, no – he couldn't have gone! She clenched her hands into fists and screamed as her body went rigid.

'You sneaky little shit!' She tore down the stairs after him. Losing her footing at the bottom, she fell onto the floor, bashing her knee as she came down hard on the tiles. Crying out in pain, she burst into tears. 'Wait 'til I get you,' she sobbed. 'Wait until I fucking get you. Nobody leaves me!'

They all leave you eventually.

'Nobody leaves ME!'

Jake legged it across to his house, took the stairs three at a time, and bolted into his room. Over by the window, he paced the floor before peeking around the edge of the curtains to see if Ella had followed him out. When he couldn't see her after a few seconds, he flung himself down onto his bed.

Fuck, that had been one scary experience. He couldn't quite believe his luck, couldn't believe it had happened – or that Ella had come on to him first. He knew there'd be no bulb to change: she'd come downstairs in her dressing gown, for fuck's sake. She knew he'd seen her drop it to the floor in the window while she touched herself.

She'd wanted him.

He grinned. He'd felt her tits; he'd *sucked* on her tits. His fingers had been inside her pussy! And she was willing to let him screw her. Wait until Will heard about this!

But he'd never expected it to happen that quickly.

Christ, why the fuck had he lost his nerve? Okay, he'd only had sex with a couple of girls so he could hardly call himself experienced. But Ella could have shown him what to do. He could have learned from her.

It was the way that she'd come on to him so quickly that had scared him away. Knowing what he'd seen of her too, he'd watched her disappear out of the room so self-assured that he'd panicked, thinking he wouldn't be good enough for her. He could have had her, he was sure. He could have had so much more.

Then he grinned again. Fuck, she'd given him a blow job! Maybe next time, she'd forgive him for his nerves and let him fuck her. Yeah, next time, there'd be no stopping him. Next time, he wouldn't bottle it. He would be all man.

Jean sat forward when she saw young Jake running out of Ella's house. He was tucking his T-shirt into his trousers, his hair a tousled mess, cheeks flushed. She roared with laughter – that would teach him to mess with the likes of Ella. Jean had guessed what Ella was up to as soon as she'd seen Jake going over, and the look on his face confirmed that she'd either got what she wanted or he'd bottled out. She wished she knew which one, even though she expected that Ella had been too much for him, probably frightening him away with her forwardness.

All the same, Jean did think it a little odd that she had shouted him over, too close to home even for Ella. She wondered if they'd met before, or if Ella had just seized the opportunity. It had been obvious from her stance that she was under the influence. Maybe she'd seen Jake walking up the avenue and fancied her chances. Strike while the iron is hot, so to speak.

Jean picked up her new notebook, giving Tom a quick tickle on his head as he slept on her lap.

'He was terrified, Tom, poor thing.' She laughed again, remembering the look on Jake's face. 'I really wish I knew what had gone on.'

Ella sat down on the settee and hugged herself, preparing for the onslaught. It started almost immediately.

He didn't want to screw you.

She covered her ears.

Are you listening? He didn't want to screw you.

As the voice inside her head grew louder, she took the rest of the whisky and went to hide in the closet. Afraid to turn on the light, she sat in the dark. But the voice became more insistent as she lost all sense of sight; her hearing heightened.

You're breaking down again, aren't you? You're a stupid cow!

'Enough,' she cried. 'Leave me alone!'

I will never leave you alone. Not until you do as you're told.

'No!'

But you know what you have to do, don't you?

'I can't,' she sobbed.

'*You have to end this farce, once and for all.*'

Chapter Twenty-Two

Ella drank well into the evening as she fought to block out the voice taking over her mind. Clenching and unclenching her hands, she sat down on the settee, and then she stood up, went to the window. Then she sat back down again. But the more she stared at the wall in front of her, the more she was convinced it was moving towards her, blocking her in, like a caged animal. She stood up again and paced the room.

Jake had rejected her now – Jake, a young slip of a boy! He'd used her to have his fun and then fucked off and left her all alone. And after all the effort she'd put into letting him see her in the window – fucking pervert. She would get him for that. But first she needed to get out, rid herself of the resentment building up.

Heading out on foot this time, she walked along Trentham Road. Even though it was dark, the night air felt pleasant, the sharp wind taking her breath away but failing to remove her drunkenness too. She wished it could blow away her building anger but she knew she was stuck with it.

She continued until she came to the Hem Heath pub that marked the site of the former colliery of the same name. Here she turned off and walked on to Stanley Matthews Way. There was a pub down there, behind the Britannia Stadium, Neck End. Ella didn't go there often as it was a dive, but it would be good enough for tonight.

Normally she didn't go out close to home. Picking up locally had its disadvantages in that most men weren't out for sex – Jake being a perfect example of that this afternoon. Not that it usually stopped her from finding someone. You only had to ask the nosy cow across the road about that.

She walked into the pub, luckily unable to focus on the stained wallpaper that had been there since the smoking ban came into force. Neck End was an old man's pub, or at least it seemed that way with its seventies flock wallpaper, swirly Axminster carpeting, and dado rails around the middle of the room that had all seen better days.

At the far end of the bar, Ella managed to hitch herself up onto a stool, ordered a double vodka. Glancing round the room, she began to look for a suitable target. Even at eight thirty, the place was two-thirds full, mostly groups of men without any dress sense. She noted a woman on her own at the other end of the bar and wondered whether to change her plans. But minutes later, disappointment made her shoulders sag as the blonde was greeted by a man, and they made a quick exit.

She sat for what seemed like an age, topping up her glass with vodka, to the point that she wouldn't be able to see if anyone was suitable for her, even if someone came and prodded her in the chest.

Annoyed by the lack of prospects, she turned when she heard laughter. Straining her eyes, she noticed a group of young men huddled near the fruit machine. Then she saw them look in her direction before laughing again. What the hell was wrong with them?

She needed to use the toilet and dropped from the stool as elegantly as she could muster, knowing she'd have to walk past them.

One of them nudged another as she did so. 'It is her!'

Ella turned to them slowly, trying to focus on them now that she was closer. But no, she didn't recognise any of their faces. Still, maybe one of them would be game.

'Hello, boys,' she slurred, giving her sexiest smile. 'Whatcha up to?'

'Thinking about you,' one of them said. Another snorted; another hid a smirk behind his pint glass.

She spoke to the nearest one. 'What's your name?'

'Will.'

'And what exactly are you thinking about doing to me?' She stepped closer and, before he could react, pressed a hand to his crotch. 'My, that is some bulge you have there, young one.'

Intimidated by her openness, he pushed her hand away, causing her to lose her balance. She stepped back, knocking into someone behind her.

'Watch out!' the man said. 'You nearly soaked me, you stupid cow.'

Ella turned to him with a frown. 'I'm not a stupid cow.' She prodded a finger into his chest. 'I stumbled.'

The man flicked the spilt drink from his hands.

'Don't waste his beer, love,' a man with trendy-styled greying hair said. 'He'll turn into a bear, if you're not careful.'

'With a sore head if he calls me stupid again,' Ella replied, swaying slightly. They all laughed and she joined in, unsure if they were laughing at her or with her but not caring either way. She checked the group out. Six; all middle-aged. Maybe one of them would screw her. She turned back to the giggling teens, who weren't giggling anymore.

'Sorry, boys,' Ella pouted. 'I guess I'm going to stick with the men now. So, what's your name?' she asked the one she'd nearly drowned.

But it was a bad idea. After a few minutes, they grew tired of her and moved away pointedly. She looked over at the fruit machine. The boys had gone too. In the middle of the room, she sighed loudly and pulled her watch up nearer to her face. Half past ten: she could take a chance and mingle some more or call it a night. Wiping her hair from her face, she headed for the exit. Fuck it, she was too drunk to care now.

She walked a minute along the road, staggering slightly and taking moments to catch her breath while she moaned to herself along the way.

'Waste of fucking space, the lot of them,' she said. 'Each as bad as the other.'

'Cassie!'

Ella stopped as she heard a name she'd buried a long time ago.

'Cassie!'

It had a sobering effect in an instant. More footsteps behind her, getting closer. Her heart began to palpitate, hurting her chest as it beat out a loud rhythm. Oh, please God, don't let it be him.

She turned slowly.

'Hello, Cassie,' he said, drawing level with her.

Even after all this time, she'd recognise his face anywhere. Gaunt, beady eyes set too close together. Strong nose, stubble on his square chin. He had a tooth missing to the side of his mouth; Ella hoped someone had punched it out of him and it had hurt like hell. She recalled the stench of his breath as he'd pushed into her at such a tender age, bullied her into marrying him when she was seventeen and out of her brain on one drug or another, then chucked her out with little thought to her well-being.

Even now, older and wiser, the anger she'd been holding back began to bubble at the surface again.

'Hello, Brendan,' Ella spoke eventually.

'It is you!' Brendan Furnival shook his head in disbelief. 'I can't believe it. I saw you in the pub!'

'I've never seen you in there before.'

'I don't come up this way often but it's my mate's birthday; he lives round the corner in Magdalen Road. You looked familiar as soon as I saw you but I couldn't place you at first.'

Ella glared at him. 'I was your wife. Remember?'

He sniggered. 'It's been a while, though.'

'Not long enough.'

He laughed now. 'See you haven't lost your sense of humour.'

'That's because I'm not joking. It wasn't my face you were used to seeing, though, was it?'

'No, I don't suppose it was. And when I saw you with those lads back there, and then hitting on those men, I realised that you don't seem to have changed.' He looked at her pointedly.

Ah. Ella understood now, the sneaky bastard.

He wants to screw you! Fucking lowlife!

Ella shook her head, as if she had a twitch. 'So you thought you'd follow me when I left?' she said.

'Yeah.' Brendan glanced up and down the road at the passing traffic. 'I thought you might have headed home in a car but –'

Loser.

'In this state? I can't see my feet, never mind a steering wheel.'

Another smirk. 'Then I saw you were walking, figured I could catch you up. Live around here now, do you?'

'Yeah, over in Warwick Avenue – in a huge big house that I own.'

'Really?'

Ella could hear the doubt in his voice.

He thinks you belong on the streets!

She tried not to slap him. How dare he think she had no right to live anywhere respectable! Just because she'd been dragged up through the system didn't mean she couldn't make a better life for herself.

She wasn't going to tell him anyway. 'Well, where've you been hiding then?' she asked, hoping to steer him away from prying further.

'Around.'

'Around …'

Brendan shrugged. 'I'm settled now. Live over in Longton.'

'Settled?' Ella felt sick to the pit of her stomach. 'As in another wife?'

'Yeah.' He puffed his chest out like a peacock. 'And two boys – six and eight. Cool kids.'

He's remarried and had children while you have nothing?

Ella drew in breath. She closed her eyes momentarily to stop herself from crying, trying not to think of their beautiful daughter, Amy. He hadn't wanted her either! The fight they'd had, resulting in Brendan trying to kick her enough to miscarry, came flooding back. He hadn't been successful, not that it had mattered much in the long run.

But then again, Brendan had always been a selfish bastard, so why should this surprise her? And if he was so happily married, why had he come after her?

He's after something.

Ella took a step towards him, stumbled. Brendan caught hold of her arm.

'So why did you follow me?' she asked, once upright again, trying not to react to his touch.

He showed a row of nicotine-stained teeth. 'After all this time, I couldn't just let you walk away.'

Give it to him.

Although she knew what he was getting at, she still posed the question. 'What do you mean?'

'You know.'

Give it to him!

'Tell me. I want to hear you say it.' Ella stepped closer, her mouth inches from his now.

'You really need me to beg?'

'I want to hear you talk dirty again. Tell me what you want.'

No hesitation this time. 'How about a fuck for old times' sake?'

Ella nodded her head.

Bingo.

As they walked back towards the pub, with every step Ella began to remember more. Memories flashed before her eyes – punches flying at her, black eyes, split lips, and bruised stomachs. Brendan had taken what was left of her sanity and trodden it into the ground. It made her want to lash out at him. She was stronger now.

Everything is his fault.

'I know.'

'What?' Brendan looked down at her.

Ella realised she must have spoken aloud. 'So how come I've never seen you around since you kicked me out and divorced me?' she asked, hoping to keep her anger at bay.

'I've been away for a while.' Brendan's tone was light, as if they were indeed old friends catching up. 'Her Majesty's pleasure at first – but then I had kids and, well ..,'

All his fault. You do know that, don't you?

Ella tried to keep her cool.

Just before they arrived back at the pub, they turned off down a muddy track. Ella knew it led onto an overnight car parking area for articulated lorries and would be perfect for what she was about to instigate. In the dim lighting she could see seven cabs, five with trailers, parked up for the evening. The curtains were drawn across the windows; Ella wondered if there was anyone sleeping inside or if the drivers would be having a late night tipple at Neck End or at the Hem Heath pub back there at the traffic lights. She hoped for the latter – the fewer people who saw her with Brendan, the better. Ella was going to enjoy herself tonight – for old times' sake.

She stopped for a moment.

'What's up?' he asked.

'I'm listening. I'm hoping no one will be in these cabs; no one to tell us to move on.'

'More likely they'd want to join in.' Brendan smiled lasciviously. 'You remember that, Cassie? You used to join in lots of dirty things we'd get up to.'

'I remember, all right,' she muttered.

They inched their way down between the sides of two trucks. Once at the back and out of view, Ella turned to face him.

Brendan shook his head in disbelief. 'Never thought I'd ever see you again, never mind screw you,' he said.

Before the rage shrouded her completely, Ella moved forward and kissed him. His rank breath mingled with the smell of stale ale; his tongue ran a line from her mouth to her neck and to her chest, his hands rough as they found their way into her blouse and underneath her bra. He pressed his mouth to her breast before thrusting his hand up her skirt. God, he was another eager bastard.

Do it.

She kissed him again, trying not to gag at that sour taste she remembered so well, all the time wondering about his wife waiting for him at home; his boys, tucked up in bed, oblivious to how their lives would change by morning after she'd finished with their father. In one move, she yanked down both sleeves of his jacket, leaving his hands inside at the cuffs to limit their use. She heard him moan but it didn't heighten her passion. Nothing felt familiar to her, despite having spent four years at his mercy.

Do it.

Sober now from the reality of what she was about to do, she let him think she was game. Unbuckling the belt to her jeans, she slid down his zip and slipped her hand inside. She took him out, caressing him for a while before stooping down to take him in her mouth. Moments later, her breathing quickened, veins pumping ready to explode as she fought to control the urge.

Do it!

Finally, when she knew he couldn't hold back much longer, Ella sank her teeth into him, biting down as hard as she could.

His cry of distress encouraged her to bite down further.

Brendan pawed at her face, urging her to release him. When she did, he grabbed his cock and dropped to his knees, rolling over onto his side.

'You mad … fucking …' he coughed, 'bitch!'

Ella stooped down beside him and punched him in the face, and again, and again, and again, relishing the sound her fist made when it connected each time.

Brendan curled up into a ball. One hand covering his genitals, his trousers hanging loose hindering his moves, he held up the other hand to protect himself. But it was no use.

Feels good to get your own back?

A fury in Ella burst forth, something she had held in for too long. For every man who had used her over the years, she kicked him. For every person who had badly treated her, she punched him. The anger and hurt of over twenty years came out in those few moments. She couldn't – wouldn't – hold it back. She wanted revenge.

Afterwards, she sat beside him. The night was quiet – it seemed no one had heard a thing. No one had interrupted them, therefore no one was able to save Brendan from further humiliation and pain. She wondered if he was dead or alive – found she didn't care.

A minute passed before she pushed herself to her feet. Brendan wasn't making a sound. She nudged him with the tip of her shoe but he didn't stir. She kicked him swiftly in his back. Still he didn't rouse.

Her breath coming easier now, she stood over him for a while, wiping her mouth with the back of her hand. It came away with specks of his blood, mingled with hers. It made her retch.

Leave him. He got what he deserved.

She drew back her foot as far as it would go and gave him one final kick.

'For old times' sake, Brendan.'

Chapter Twenty-Three

It was nearing midnight when Jean noticed Ella running up the avenue. She was about to turn in, having spent a couple of hours dozing in the chair. Her knitting had fallen down by her side. She pulled it up quickly, hoping she hadn't lost any stitches.

As Ella drew closer and into the light of the lamp, Jean sat forward. What were those marks all over her dress? Had she fallen over – or worse, been in a fight? She shook her head. Why on earth would a woman of her age pick a fight? Ella should be in bed now, settled down with a husband by her side and one or two children asleep in the next room.

Jean pushed her glasses up her nose, no point in trying with the binoculars; they didn't have sophisticated night vision. Ella was at her house now, running up the steps, in a panic trying to find her keys. She could see clearly that she was crying, wiping at her cheeks before opening the door and going into the house.

She waited for a light to go on upstairs before she pushed her aching legs, willing them to work so that she could stand. Ella really had looked like she'd been dragged through a hedge backwards. What had she been up to now?

Ella ran into the house with the slam of a door and took the stairs two at a time. Sobbing uncontrollably, in her haste to get inside she struggled again to fit the key in the lock, kicking out in temper. But at last she managed it.

Inside, she removed her clothes quickly. She pushed them all into a plastic bag, along with her shoes, and shoved them underneath her bed. It was too late to do anything with them now; ideally, she should burn them but Charley was downstairs and might hear her in the garden and come out to see what she was doing. Charley could alert the police and then Ella wouldn't be able to keep it a secret any longer. No, she'd have to get rid of them in the morning; she couldn't risk them being found here.

Then she sat on the bed with a thump. 'Please don't let me lose control again,' she whispered.

Ella knew that if she hadn't seen Brendan, she wouldn't have been reminded of her past. The sex addiction she could just about cope with – it was a means to an end. But Brendan had been such an evil bastard to her. Attacking him had only been what he deserved.

You stupid bitch. What have you done now?

Ella covered her ears.

Everyone will know it was you.

'Shut up!'

They'll come after you and they'll lock you up and who will protect you from me then?

Ella ran to the closet. Pulling the door shut behind her, she pushed herself as far into the corner as she could go and slid to the floor. Then she put her head in her hands and sobbed.

Why had she chosen to stay local? If she had gone into Hanley, none of this would have happened. She gagged. She could still taste Brendan on her lips, still smell his breath. Still remember what he'd said to her when she was younger, hear him talking to her, coaxing her at first to do the things he wanted. Then when she had, he'd forced her to do much more. She'd been young, vulnerable. He should have known better.

He should have been there to protect her. Instead, all he did was expose her vulnerability. And he made her think of Amy. She'd shut her away in a box a long time ago too, never to be let out. But seeing him, seeing the father of her daughter again, it had all come hurtling back. The hurt, the humiliation, the fear.

Ella recalled being the happiest she'd ever been when she found out she was pregnant. She pressed her hand to her stomach, remembering the feel of the tiny human being growing inside; ran a finger over the silvery stretch marks that showed where her skin had expanded.

At first she'd kept it a secret. It was her baby, someone who would love only her, cherish her. But eventually, when she could hide it no more, she told him. Nothing could have prepared her for his hostility. She shuddered at the thought of how he'd dragged her onto the floor by her hair, screaming in her face to get rid of it. She told him she would, to get him to stop. But she knew she was lying.

Instead she'd gone to see a nurse at the local health centre, who explained how the baby wouldn't grow if she didn't look after herself. From that moment on, she'd tried to stay away from the drugs and alcohol. But Brendan would often coax her into it, though; she couldn't help it. She tried! God, she tried.

She would have made the perfect mother.

Ella pulled at her hair, all the time talking aloud, trying to drown out the words going round inside her head, putting the blame on to her. It wasn't her fault. It was people like those social workers – people like that bitch Charley downstairs – who poked their nose in where it wasn't wanted, interfering and making things worse. All Ella had ever wanted was to be loved. Why wasn't she good enough for that?

But she knew why: it was because she pushed people away. She made people dislike her so that they wouldn't get close to her, so they couldn't hurt her. She made women despise her by the way she looked at their men. She made the men feel wary of her – unless they screwed her. If they screwed her, they were hers for that moment in time but gone soon after. No one wanted to see Ella again afterwards. She wasn't good enough for more than that.

It was a while later when she took a shower. The water cascaded over her, taking with it splashes of blood she'd returned with, bits of Brendan that she didn't want. The side of her face stung where he'd scratched at her, trying to get her off him as she'd bitten down harder on his cock. Her head hurt, too, where he had pulled her hair. But she'd been too strong for him tonight.

At one time she would have let him do anything to her – she'd thought it proved how much he cared for her. Every cut, every bruise, every bite. Saliva built up inside her mouth as panic coursed through her. Suddenly, she was out of the shower and throwing up into the toilet.

Fuck, what had she done? If anyone found out it was her, they'd find out she had a criminal record and lock her up again. They'd make her take drugs, do tests, tick boxes, and conform to how they thought she should act. She could never go back to that regime.

You're in so much trouble.

After working late into the previous evening on a report for a meeting, Charley left home early the next morning to continue with it at her desk. It was just after half past seven as she locked her front door and headed along the hallway, stopping as she noticed a smear on the banister. Peering closer, she put out her hand before snatching it back. She shouldn't touch it. It could very well be ... She moved a little closer.

It was blood. Oh, God, what had happened to Ella now?

Thankfully, there didn't seem to be a lot of it – from a cut hand, maybe, as she'd leaned on the rail to go upstairs. She'd heard her banging around as she'd come home last night, and she had been quiet after that.

Charley paused at the bottom of the stairs. She sighed. Ella was a weird one but she couldn't go to work without seeing if she was all right.

At the top of the stairs, she hesitated, a hand in the air. But then she brought it down onto the door.

'Ella?' She knocked loudly.

There was no answer.

She knocked again. 'Ella, are you okay? Did you fall over last night?'

'Go away.' She heard a faint voice from behind the door.

'But there's blood out here, on the banister rail. Are you sure you're all right? Do you need help?'

'No, I can manage.'

It was a whisper but Charley would have to be satisfied. She stood for a few moments, seeing if Ella would come out. But there was no movement from inside the flat.

Ella had been dozing on the settee when Charley had knocked on the door. She'd been there all night since she'd had a shower, curled up with another bottle of vodka, trying desperately to keep Cassandra out. She couldn't let her back into her life. But as the voice became louder and louder, Ella knew she wouldn't be able to continue batting it away for much longer.

Surprised by Charley's concern, she wondered what she'd meant by asking if she was okay. It wasn't anything she would do of a morning normally. She dragged herself into the bathroom, her head fuzzy again.

Rinsing her face, she winced. Going to the mirror, she pulled away her hair to reveal a deep scratch down the side of her face. How the hell had that happened, now? She touched it, winced again, trying to remember what she'd done the night before. Then she paled. She'd blacked out again, hadn't she?

She sat on the settee, hoping to remember eventually.

A few minutes later, it all came back. Shit: Brendan Furnival. Fear coursing through her, she ran through to her bedroom and looked under the bed. She pulled out the bag and burst into tears when she saw the blood all over her clothes.

'No, no, no, no, no!' she cried.

Worse than that, she remembered why Charley had checked on her.

In the kitchen, she ran a bowl of hot water and added detergent. Then she took it out onto the stairs. She could see it – more blood, all down the handrail. It could be hers or it could be Brendan's. How would she know?

She had to get rid of it. It could be evidence. Manically, she scrubbed at the wood until there were no remains of Brendan, trying not to think about what she had done. He wasn't moving when she'd left him. Had she killed him? If she had, she'd be in so much trouble.

No, she shook her head to rid it of its confusion. It wasn't her; it couldn't be! She'd have to blame Cassandra. Yes, Cassandra had attacked Brendan, not her.

It was you, you evil bitch. Don't try and put the blame on me!

She ignored the voice. This *was* all Cassandra's fault.

No! I won't have you saying that. Do you hear?

'Look at what you've made me do now!' Ella screamed. 'Look at what you've made me do!'

Chapter Twenty-Four

'Did you hear what happened to Brendan Furnival?' Lynne asked Charley, arriving at her desk at nine in a flurry of wet coat and dripping umbrella.

Before Charley had a chance to speak, she continued. 'He was beaten up last night – left for dead, apparently. Someone found him on the spare ground behind Neck End pub.' She laughed. '*Your* neck of the woods, isn't it, by the Britannia Stadium?'

Charley looked up from her work in confusion. Lynne was right; it was about half a mile from Warwick Avenue.

'Police say he was getting dirty with a fella – can you imagine that? I hadn't clocked that he was into men – just thought he was a mean bastard with the ladies. Mind, he did spend a bit of time inside. I suppose it could have turned him.'

'Slow down!' said Charley. 'I can't take it all in.'

Lynne glanced around before whispering to her. 'Someone tried to bite the end of his knob off.'

Charley gasped.

Lynne smiled widely. 'Great, isn't it?'

'And they're sure it was a man he was with?'

'Police aren't ruling anything out yet.' Lynne switched on her computer. 'Although I reckon the attack was too vicious to be a woman.'

'I don't know so much.' Charley shook her head. 'There's nothing like a woman scorned, or so they say. Having said that, Furnival is a rough nut. I wouldn't fancy a woman's chances with him.'

'Not if she was going down on him – I've often wondered what it'd be like to sink my teeth into one. I would have done so on quite a few occasions if I was brave enough for the repercussions. I –'

'Ladies, please!' Aaron had come over to them. He grimaced.

'Serves you right for sneaking up on us,' Lynne retorted.

'Back to the subject of knob biting.' Charley sniggered, enjoying the look of anguish on his face. 'It couldn't have happened to a better bloke, if you ask me.'

'Sometimes there is justice in this world.' Lynne took off her jacket and put it over the back of her chair. 'I don't dislike many people but he's an evil bastard. I still can't believe he did what he did and got away with it.'

Furnival was known in their circles as 'the cruel bastard that got lucky.' During her time at Striking Back plus her previous years in social work, Charley had come across him on several occasions. The time that stuck in her mind was when Social Services had received complaints from a teenage girl who was staying at the home where Furnival was working at the time. With the help of the police, he'd been charged with indecent assault on a female under sixteen. Everyone was convinced Furnival was abusing her, but there had been no proof and the child hadn't been able to stand up to the interrogation in court. To everyone's dismay and anger, the case had been dropped. Since then, there had been several incidents reported around him. One day, Charley knew he would have his come-uppance. She hoped every part of him was hurting today.

'Have the police anything on CCTV?' asked Aaron.

'I'm not sure if it will be covered back there. And if it is, it'll be too early yet,' said Lynne. 'I only know so much because there was a Police Community Support Officer in reception and he told me about it. But apparently Furnival's wallet was still there, money still in it.'

'So with his pants being around his knees, they've ruled out robbery as the likely motive?'

'Hey, a recent survey said that men in Stoke-on-Trent have the biggest willies in the UK,' said Lynne.

'Get real!' Charley laughed.

'It's true! Everything in the newspapers is gospel, isn't it?' she added with raised eyebrows. 'I'd be shocked if it wasn't.'

'No, I'd bet my life on him not being gay,' said Aaron. 'Maybe he was just in the wrong place at the wrong time.'

'Maybe,' said Lynne.

'Pity, that.'

'Hmm, yes, pity.'

They all grinned at each other.

After the meeting in the conference room upstairs, Charley was stopped by one of the social workers. Tanya Smith was in her early thirties and they had worked for the local authority at the same time. They'd always got on well, sharing information or helping with each other's cases whenever it had been necessary.

'I wanted to know if you'd made any progress with Cassandra Thorpe,' Tanya questioned just before they got to the doorway. 'She was a client of mine but she disappeared from her address, about six months ago.'

Charley paused. 'I don't know anyone of that name.'

'But I saw you walking down Stafford Street with her the other day. I meant to ring and ask you about her but you know how it is. I got caught up with something else and I knew I'd be seeing you today anyway.'

Charley shook her head. 'I don't know anyone called Cassandra.'

'When would it be?' Tanya frowned. 'It was earlier in the week, Tuesday – no, wait a minute, it might have been Wednesday. You were coming out of TK Maxx. I'm sure it was near lunch time.'

Charley thought back, then she realised. 'Oh, yes, I saw my neighbour – she's my landlady really. I'd bumped into her. Actually, I wanted to –'

'Your landlady is Cassandra Thorpe?' Tanya's mouth dropped open. 'I thought she was one of your clients.'

'Of course she isn't my client. You've obviously got her mixed up with someone else. Her name is Ella – Ella Patrick.'

'Are you sure?'

'Yes, unless she's using a different name now – hardly likely, though. Who's Cassandra Thorpe?'

'She's someone I was working with. She has a background of abuse and addiction,' Tanya explained. 'Both her parents and her sister were killed in a car accident when she was young and she was taken into care etcetera, etcetera. Had a couple of breakdowns. I'd been working with her for about two years. The last time I saw her, she worried me, if I'm honest. I asked her to keep a diary of what happened to her during the course of the week in between that and our next appointment. You know, not what she got up to but how she felt.'

Charley nodded in recognition. 'A mood diary, you mean?'

'Yes. I thought I'd get a page or two if I was lucky but what I got was quite unnerving. She came back with a notepad, every page filled with rambling thoughts – it was a diary of her whole adult life! Not just her moods but what had happened to her, where she'd been. It mentioned she was married. She even talked about having a baby but, like I said, I wasn't sure if it was true or random thoughts.'

Charley went cold. Since Ella's recent outbursts, she'd started to question the truth in anything she had told her. But there had been mention of a baby.

Charley pointed to the table. They pulled out chairs and sat down again.

'What did she say when you asked her about it?' she asked Tanya.

'I haven't seen her since.' Tanya sighed. 'She didn't turn up for the next appointment or for any after that. I wrote to her and visited her address a couple of times –'

'I live in Warwick Avenue.'

'Ah. Cassandra lived in Penkhull.'

'And she didn't register for benefits anywhere at a new address?'

One of the ways their organisations kept up with people who went missing was to check with housing benefits to see if there was a new address on file. A lot of their clients were on income support so had to claim from somewhere. It was a tactic often used when a tenant had left quickly without informing anyone, or the property had been in a state of disrepair. As soon as they registered some-where else for benefits, a re-charge bill for any damage or missed rent would be issued.

Tanya shook her head. 'As far as I was aware she wasn't entitled to them. She had money from her parents' firm when she sold it.'

'Which is why when you saw her with me, you thought she was my client and that I'd found out where she was living now.'

'Yes.'

Charley paused. Some of this was ringing true about Ella. But she shook her head in disbelief. 'Oh, wait a minute.' She reached for her mobile phone. 'I have a few photos here, from a night out.'

'From a night out, hmm? So how is the lovely Aaron?'

Charley smiled. It seemed news travelled fast.

'Seriously, I'm delighted,' said Tanya. 'He's such a great guy and he's had a crush on you since time began.' She took the phone from Charley and looked at the screen. She drew it closer. 'That's Cassandra Thorpe!' she exclaimed.

'But it can't be!' The smile dropped from Charley's face in an instant. Could it really be Ella that Tanya was referring to? It would certainly explain things, but ..., she didn't want to think about it.

'I'm telling you, that is Cassandra Thorpe,' said Tanya. 'Have you ever seen the burn on her arm? You wouldn't mistake her then. It's quite a nasty scar.'

'I *have* seen it – shit!' Her stomach flipped over as she shook her head. 'It can't be her! Her name is Ella!'

'Cassandra's sister was called Eleanor – that can't be a coincidence?'

Charley shuddered, thinking of Ella's recent erratic behaviour. 'She isn't dangerous, is she?'

Tanya shook her head. 'From what I saw of her, she was okay. But she did have her angry moments – which is why the diary freaked me out a little. Here, I brought it with me. I'll leave it with you for a few days.' Tanya reached into her bag and handed her a thick booklet. 'Just make sure you get it back to me.'

'That's some notepad,' said Charley as she took it from her, recalling piles of similar ones in Ella's flat. 'I thought you meant a tiny thing – maybe an A6 or something. This is huge!'

'Wait until you see what's inside.' Tanya screwed up her face. 'Honest to God, it's like a stream-of-consciousness. I didn't think it was too bad until I read it back. I felt sorry for her all over again after I'd seen it. I mean, I knew about some of the things that had happened to her when she was younger, like the accident, but even now I still can't make out what is real and what isn't.'

Charley flicked through the pages. Sometimes the writing was neat and tidy; others it was large, and some paragraphs were illegible altogether. 'So it all stems from the accident and being taken into care and ... Was she abused, did you say?'

'It seems that way, although some of the things in this diary can't possibly be real.'

'Why not?'

'It seems so dark. Like something from a novel more than actual life.'

'Tanya, nothing surprises me anymore. We've seen most of it before.'

'I know – which makes it hard to distinguish between the two.'

'But why would she do that?' Charley puzzled. 'There's no point in her lying to herself.'

'I don't know. It seems to be written in a kind of frenzy, though. I think I'll go and see her on Monday. If I go on spec, she might open up a little to me. She certainly seems as though she still needs support.'

'She does.' Charley told Tanya about Ella's recent behaviour. 'It would be great to know I'm not living near to a psychopath, if you can get to see her,' she said afterwards, with a half-hearted grin.

'She is schizophrenic, although she'll deny it if you ask her. She's prescribed medication. It works, but often she wouldn't take it. I had to try and cajole her. That, and she's a sex addict, as well as drugs and alcohol.'

Charley's eyes widened. She didn't want to tell Tanya about the episode with Ella but it certainly explained it. 'I can see how it would affect her, losing her family so quickly at such a young age. How old was she, did you say?'

'Nine when the accident happened. Her sister was four. Cassandra – Ella to you – was in hospital for two weeks with head injuries and then went into care at Ravenside.'

Charley grimaced. Ravenside Children's Home had a reputation of its own. It had been closed down in 2000 due to numerous complaints. Ella wasn't the only person who had been a victim of its regime.

Tanya stood up. 'I'll give you a ring on Tuesday; see if I gained access or if I was to go away to do one.'

Charley went back to her desk and checked for the name Cassandra Thorpe in their database. There was no mention of it, so she wasn't known to the organisation. Sometimes clients were referred by the local housing office or one of the charities in the city but there was no mention in their shared files either. Out of curiosity, she checked for Ella's name too. But there was nothing. If Ella was Cassandra Thorpe, then neither of them was in their system.

Charley made a note in her diary to visit the local housing office next week to check their records. She wondered if Ella might have a police record too. Maybe someone at the police station could shed some light on things. And it would certainly explain some of her recent behaviour if Tanya hadn't seen her for six months.

If she was Cassandra and had been rejected year after year, then perhaps Ella *would* feel inclined to cling to her. With a diagnosis of schizophrenia, Charley could understand that. And looking back now, there were classic symptoms that she'd missed. Had Ella really been married at seventeen and divorced a year later? Had she got a job? Was that even true? And all those people she mentioned she'd slept with? Were they figments of her imagination, to get the attention that she craved?

But the one thing that stuck in her mind was the car crash. Ella had said that her parents had died but not that many years ago, and certainly not when she was a child. And she'd never mentioned having a sister.

Chapter Twenty-Five

It was nearly four o'clock when Ella felt able to leave the flat that afternoon. She needed to get more alcohol. She would start with vodka and then move on to whisky. Maybe she could pass out by six p.m. and sleep for a while – get rid of the images her mind kept throwing up: being locked in a cupboard and banging on the door to be let out; being held down by strong hands while someone pushed themselves into her; being beaten for daring to talk back in her defence. Everything was coming back.

As she walked along Warwick Avenue, she saw someone coming towards her. He looked familiar; she couldn't place him straightaway but as he drew closer, she realised it was Jake.

'Hi, Ella,' he smiled, giving her a cheeky wink.

Ella stared at him for a moment before smiling slyly. 'It's *you*. My peeping Tom.'

'Keep your voice down!' Jake ran a hand through his hair.

Ella laughed loudly as he glanced up and down the street to see who was around. Luckily for him, there was no one in hearing range. An elderly man with a pushchair and a child ambling alongside. A group of teens dressed in school uniform. The woman who looked after Jean next door.

'So why did you run?' she wanted to know.

'I – I got nervous,' he replied.

'Nervous?' Frowning, Ella tried to focus on him, wishing he would stay in one place and not keep moving around.

Jake nodded, bouncing the toe of his trainers on the wall beside them. 'I wanted to, but, well – you're older than me and I've not been with as many ...' He stopped.

'...partners as I have,' Ella finished off for him, annoyed by his accusation. How dare he think she was a sleep-around. He didn't know her! She was after love – that was it. Love was what she craved. But he would never understand that. And he'd just ruined his chances of the repeat performance she'd been planning on treating him to.

He thinks you're a slag.

'You think I'm a slag,' she seethed, her right hand clenching into a fist.

'No, I didn't mean that! I meant –'

'You meant that I'm not good enough for you, is that it?'

'No, the opposite, actually.'

But Ella didn't hear him. Feelings of rejection pulsed through her. How dare he run away, leave her to her own devices? She was going to get him for that.

'Don't worry. I won't tell anyone.' She leaned forward, touching his arm before whispering in his ear. 'It will be our little secret.' She waited a moment, gently blowing on his ear. 'Maybe you and some of your friends might come and visit me one evening? I could turn their fantasies into reality too. What do you reckon? Or will they run out on me as well?' Ella popped a finger into her mouth. She locked her lips around it and pulled it out suggestively.

'I reckon I could handle you this time.' Jake nodded. 'I won't run out on you again.'

Like hell he won't. Get him for that, the silly little shit.

Ella smiled. 'You're an ambitious fucker, I'll give you that. Come closer.'

With a nervous expression, Jake stepped forward.

'Closer.'

Another step.

Hit him! Make him bleed.

'Now, come down to my level. You're a little tall for me.' Ella giggled coyly.

Jake hesitated for a moment but then he did as she said.

Ella brought her head back and butted him in the face.

Good aim! That'll teach him.

Jake dropped to his knees, clutching his nose. Blood began to trickle from a nostril, a small cut at the bridge pouring too. 'You mad bitch.' He wiped at it. 'What the fuck was that for?'

Ella grabbed a handful of his hair and dropped her face to his level. 'You think you can get me to suck you off and then leave me to my own devices, you selfish little shit?'

'Get off me!'

'I'm warning you, you stay away from me or I'll tell everyone that you pushed me into the hallway of my house and sexually assaulted me.'

'I never touched you! You wouldn't –'

'I'll have the police on you in minutes. A police record for sexual assault – that won't be a nice thing to start your working life with when you leave Sixth Form.'

'Let go!' Jake punched at the side of her leg. Ella cried out in pain. Seeing a car approaching, she loosened her grip and pushed him away. As he fell backwards, she ran down the avenue.

Jean had been curious as soon as she'd noticed Ella doubling back to talk to Jake. Through her open window, she could hear them chatting but, even though she strained to hear more, they were too far away for her to make out their conversation.

But when she saw him fall, she put down her knitting and leaned forward. It had happened so fast that she'd missed it. Had he stepped backwards and tripped over the edge of the kerb? And then she saw that his nose was bleeding when he pulled his hand away. And when Ella grabbed his hair, Jean didn't know what to think. Was this his punishment for running out on her the other day? Oh, dear. Ella was always in a rage about something.

She watched her run off, almost knocking her home help out of the way; heard Ruby cry out in annoyance before turning back to Jake. She offered him a hand to help him to his feet but he refused and stormed off and into the house.

'Not sure what that was all about,' Ruby shouted up to her after she'd opened the front door. 'Would you like a cuppa bringing up before I start?'

'You are a darling,' Jean shouted back. She looked down onto the avenue again. There was nothing going on now so she completed the entry in her notepad while she waited.

Jean wondered what the poor lad had done. Ella's face had been really close to his and she'd been almost snarling. She seemed to be telling Jake off, by the look of her body language. He'd definitely annoyed her about something. That wasn't a wise move. He'd found out the hard way.

16:15 – Ella and Jake had words. Not sure what happened; it looked like Jake had fallen over. But Ella was mad about something. Couldn't hear what was being said, though.

'Hell hath no fury like a woman scorned,' she said to Tom, who was snoozing on the bed as if he didn't care either way.

A few minutes later, Ruby appeared with a tray: a mug of tea, a small plate of digestives, and that evening's newspaper.

'Thanks, duck,' Jean smiled gratefully.

'Really bad headlines, Jean,' Ruby said. 'Some bloke came a cropper last night just around the corner.'

'Let me see.' Jean unfolded the paper so that she could read the story in full.

'Says he was left for dead.' Ruby sorted through Jean's washing basket to see if there was enough for a load. 'Beat up beyond recognition, apparently.'

'Oh, dear, Ruby. I do wonder what the world is coming to, so many decent folk getting hurt. I can't believe anyone –' Jean stopped as she read the victim's name. 'Well, I never.'

Jean hadn't heard the name Brendan Furnival in a long time; never really wanted to hear about him again, either. When he was working at Ravenside Children's Home at the same time she was there, he'd threatened to cut off her fucking tongue and shove it where the sun don't fucking shine if she breathed a word about what she'd seen to anyone. Never intimidated by the actions of a horrible young man, Jean had told the home manager and the rest was painful history, swept under the carpet so that no one got to hear about it. A month later she'd been let go.

What she'd seen was Furnival in bed with one of the young girls – Cassie, she was called. A troubled soul who became worse the longer she'd stayed at the home. Furnival was sacked soon after, once Jean had made a formal complaint but before anything was done about it.

In a way, Jean had been glad to leave Ravenside and all it stood for well behind her after that. But she'd never forgotten that, until the home closed, she'd left children in the hands of animals. That would haunt her until the day she died.

'Well, I never what?' Ruby stood waiting for the rest of the sentence.

Jean smiled at her before picking up a biscuit. 'Just a case of what goes around comes around.'

Once she'd turned onto the main road, Ella slowed her pace, laughing to herself as she recalled the look on Jake's face. It was classic: he really did believe she'd make stuff up about him. Silly boy – maybe that would teach him not to take advantage. One thing she knew for certain was that she had the upper hand. He'd keep his mouth shut about their little episode.

Still giggling when she arrived at the shop a few minutes later, she sidled down the aisles, adding junk food to her basket as well as the bottles of alcohol. It was when she went to pay for them that she stopped dead in her tracks. The headlines in that evening's *Sentinel* came at her as if they were written in three feet tall letters.

'*Man left for dead in Trentham.*'

She paled when she saw it, a layer of sweat erupting all over her body.

'Are you okay?' the woman behind the till asked. 'Would you like a glass of water? You've gone a really funny colour.'

Ella did her best to seem normal and thought of something quickly to put her off the scent. 'No, I'm fine, thanks,' she smiled. 'A bit of morning sickness in the afternoon. A delight – not.'

The woman smiled back sympathetically. 'Tell me about it. I had an awful time with my first.'

As the cashier scanned her items through the till, telling more tales of woe about her second and third child, Ella prayed that the sudden rush of nausea would pass. All she could see in her mind's eye were the smears of blood on the banister. If Brendan did tell the police it was her, they'd be at her door soon. She'd seen those gadgets on television programs, used to detect blood that had been washed away. They would know it was her and lock her up for good! She'd go mad for certain, then.

But you're already mad. You do realise that, don't you?

She avoided looking at the headline again until she was going out the door. It made her sob. Not wanting to cause a commotion, she quickened her pace with every step until she was in danger of tripping over her feet.

Shit, they were on to her already. Ella had to get away before they caught her, locked her away in a mental institution. They would. She knew they would. They wouldn't have a choice after what she'd done, wouldn't be interested in why she'd attacked him so viciously.

Once off the main road, she ran, not stopping until she was back in Warwick Avenue.

I had to stay with Brendan until I had my baby. I didn't have any choice, really. I mean, where would I have gone? Even I, a master of hiding and coping with pain, was scared shitless to give birth on my own. But she died anyway.

She fucking died! She was stillborn, something to do with all the abuse I'd put my body through; I can't really remember now. When they said she was too tiny to survive, I remember I cried and cried. Social Services had been worried about the effects my alcohol intake would have on the baby before it was born. They should have stopped me abusing my body.

I named her Amy. And yes, you all know by now what a selfish bitch I am but even I knew she'd be better off dying than living with me.

For a long time, I remember thinking that they would hate me for what I had done. I don't even know who 'they' were. I only ever saw Brendan and a few of his mates if they called round to see him, or to shag me.

And no one warned me about the grief. I felt like a part of me had been ripped away, taking my heart with it. She was my baby, my daughter! A tiny piece of me that I had created, that I had made, that was something good in my life.

I wanted to love her. I needed someone to look after, care for: someone who would give me unconditional love; someone who would need me. I would have protected her with my life. I would have, if I'd had the opportunity.

I never got the chance to have another baby. I got pregnant again three times but I miscarried them all. Even my babies rejected me!

I reckon losing Amy was the start of the downward spiral for me. I tried to block out the grief with drink. Anything I could get my hands on. I stole whatever I wanted, whenever I wanted. I shagged men for money to buy alcohol. That's when Brendan attacked me and left me for dead one night.

When I came out of hospital, I started to protect myself. I went inside myself, away from what was really happening, took my sister's name and became Ella. I didn't want to be Cassie anymore. As far as I was concerned, Cassie didn't exist; she was gone. I'd left her far behind. I wanted to be Ella.

And none of this would have happened if my family hadn't been wiped out. Even they all died and left me all alone. Why would they do that? It was the cruellest thing ever! Couldn't they see what it would do to me? Abandoned – that's what I was.

Why hadn't I died in the accident too? If I had, I would never have met that fucking bitch. Billie started all of this; she didn't want me in the way. She is the evil bitch not me. I hate her. I HATE HER! If she hadn't come along, I would have been fine. I would have had a different life. I wouldn't have had Amy but I would have had other children and a husband and a dog and a big house and I'd have had the dream. Everything would have been perfect. But Billie changed all that. I fucking hate her and all she stands for.

And now, I live in fear of Cassie. Cassie tries to take over Ella all the time. She frightens me. She makes me do things that I don't want to do. She puts words into my mouth. She makes me screw men I don't want to. She makes Ella cower in the corner. She is evil. NOT ME.

I am not evil.

Chapter Twenty-Six

Later that evening, Charley tried to relax on the settee, watching trashy television. Casually flicking through a magazine, she wondered whether Aaron would stop by later. He was out on a stag night; it had been planned for months, but he'd told her that he wasn't looking forward to it.

Shock, horror – she was missing him! She couldn't help but grin. It was strange to think how much he was in her life now, as if he'd never *not* been a part of it. Every now and then, she still got pangs of missing Dan when she was with him but somehow over the past few weeks, her life had become complete with Aaron. It was as if she was meant to find him. Life was perfect again. She doubted anything could make it better at the moment. Although their relationship was so new, she realised that Aaron could be a keeper. Maybe that was why she'd been so reluctant to get involved with him earlier, on the rebound from Dan: she'd realised how good they would be together so she had kept him at arm's length until she was ready to move to the next stage. He'd certainly made her life a lot more exciting. And she had Ella to thank for that, despite her going on about the power of a one-night stand.

She thought back to her conversation earlier that morning with Tanya, wondered how much she should be worried about it. Ella seemed to be far more vulnerable than she'd originally thought.

Charley had taken her time reading through all the entries in Ella's notebook. It had felt like a car crash waiting to happen – she'd wanted to read it, knowing that she shouldn't but knowing that she would.

The first pages spoke of a relationship when Ella was eighteen. A man called Brendan who had abused her – Charley wondered at hearing the name whether it had anything to do with the attack on Brendan Furnival last night, although Lynne had said the police were looking for a man. Ella wrote of Mark and Nina, names familiar to Charley if she thought of their earlier conversations.

In every entry, Ella wrote about people letting her down, rejecting her, abandoning her. Some of the pages had been so hard to decipher that Charley couldn't make out what she'd been trying to say. It was as if Ella had been writing so fast that she couldn't get her words down quickly enough. And there was reference to someone called Amy all the way through it. Perhaps that was the baby Tanya had mentioned.

Curiosity overwhelming her, she went over to her laptop, deciding to search out what she could find out about the family. She Googled the name Cassandra Thorpe and made a guess at the year of the accident. Finally after a few attempts, she found what she was after.

The article explained what had happened on that fateful day in 1987. Annoyingly, it seemed that Tanya had indeed told her most of it. There had been a head-on crash on the M6, and Cassandra had been the only survivor from a family of four – a little girl without anyone to look after her.

Charley thought back over her time in Warwick Avenue. During the eight weeks she'd been there, she had never seen Ella with a friend, a boyfriend, or a girlfriend – apart from the girl she had kissed on the stairs – and she hadn't seen her since. She hadn't seen any family members, either.

She thought about the diary pages again – maybe they had been written in one desperate melancholy sitting. Could Ella have penned it when she'd had a drink, perhaps, when she was feeling low? Charley knew from listening to some of her clients what they had gone through in their painful lives, so she had no doubt that some of it – even all of it – could be true. But the fact that Ella could be nice one minute, a bit full-on the next, and angry the next, she wondered if she had been having a psychotic episode while she'd written it, feeling upset with the world.

Or maybe she *had* made it all up.

Or was it all true?

If it was, no wonder Ella felt like everyone had abandoned her. Charley thought back to the time when she'd come tearing down the stairs at her when she had stayed over at Aaron's. It all made sense now. It was impossible not to feel pity for her. Maybe, once Tanya had called to assess Ella, Charley could make more of an effort to get to know her – encourage her to get help. With Tanya on board once more, Ella could stabilise again.

Her phone rang, and a warm feeling came over her when she saw the name flash up on caller display.

'Hello, you,' she said.

'Can I come over yet?'

She grinned. 'Okay, fella. You have a deal.'

'Good, because I'm already outside.'

Charley opened the entrance door and Aaron greeted her with a kiss. 'I've missed you.'

'You only saw me this afternoon.'

'Your point being?'

She heard a noise behind her, turned to see Ella walking down the stairs towards them. 'Hi, Ella,' she smiled. 'You off out on the town?'

'You sound like my mother,' Ella retorted. 'What's it got to do with you?'

'Ella, I was only trying to –'

'Considering you haven't been bothering with me lately, I suggest you mind your own business.'

'Oh … right. Well –' The door slammed as Ella left the house. 'Yeah, thanks. I'll have a good night too,' Charley muttered.

'Yes, you will.' Aaron pushed her gently towards the door of her flat.

———⌣———

Ella spent a troublesome Saturday alone. She'd returned last night to find Aaron's car parked outside and then watched as they'd left together this morning. Realising she only had vodka to keep her company, she drank all day as she waited for Charley to return home. She wanted to talk to her. She needed to tell someone what had happened with Brendan.

Images of the attack kept flashing back; her knuckles were still sore from mashing up his face. She struggled to control her anger as she remembered kicking out at him, how good it had felt to pull back her foot and bring it forward with as much force as she could muster. She could see the blood coming from his mouth where she had split his lip more than once. Her eye began to twitch. No, she didn't want to see it.

In the window now, she looked down onto the avenue, over towards Jake's house, but he wasn't there. Ella smirked; served him right for abandoning her, the cheeky bastard.

Next door, she could see Jean. She'd seen so much of her lately: should she show her some more?

She slapped at her face. Of course she shouldn't.

She undid her dressing gown.

Of course you should.

But then she spotted Aaron's car coming along the avenue. She peered at her watch, tried to make out the time. Was it late, was it early? Was it Friday still? Was Charley coming in from work? No, it was Saturday – had she lost a whole day again?

Spying her chance as Aaron drove off, leaving Charley alone, she decided to go out to say hello. Maybe she could strike up a conversation long enough to invite her upstairs to her flat. Then she could talk to her. Charley would listen, she was sure.

But after staggering down the hallway, by the time she got to her front door, she lost her nerve. She couldn't hang around on the landing as if she'd just come out. Charley would see right through that. Instead, she dropped to the floor and listened for her to come in.

The entrance door opened and closed. Ella held her breath, listening intently, hoping she'd come up to see how she was.

She won't bother with you!

'She will, she will, she will,' Ella mouthed silently. But then she gasped as she heard Charley letting herself into her flat. She scrambled to her feet, opened the door this time, and ran down the stairs, almost tripping in her haste.

There was no one there.

Charley *had* completely ignored her.

See, what did I tell you? You're not worth the bother.

Ella ran back into the flat and slammed the door. Clenching her fists tightly, she dug her nails into the palms of her hands. How dare Charley take no notice of her! She wouldn't be ignored, damn it. Who the fuck did she think she was?

She caught her reflection in the tiny hall mirror: skittish, ugly, angry. In one swift move, she drew a hand across the shelf below it and scattered the miniature bottle collection, sending them crashing to the floor. Some smashed; some bumped and bounced down and into the boxes and containers piled up.

She pulled at her hair and let out a roar.

Charley was putting away food in the fridge when she heard a loud crash. She paused, listening attentively. But there was nothing else. She padded through into the living room and looked outside. It sounded as if someone had bumped into a car or something. But the avenue looked as quiet as usual.

Pausing, she glanced up to the ceiling. Could it have been Ella? Should she go and see if she was okay?

She wasn't sure what to do. It could be something or nothing. She wasn't even certain the noise had come from upstairs.

Back in the kitchen, she flicked on the kettle, deciding to make a cup of coffee. If she heard anything else, she would go up.

Paying no attention to the mess in the hall, Ella went through to the closet, closed the door, and sat down. Maybe if she stayed in there, Cassandra would leave her alone. She needed time to get her head straight, too. It wasn't right being too agitated about Charley.

Who the fuck does she think she is, ignoring you?

'La la la la la la.' She covered her ears with her hands. Despite trying not to, she was losing control; knew it could only get worse. Bad things always happened when she was out of control.

You need to teach that bitch a lesson.

'La la la la la LA!' Ella banged the back of her head on the wall behind her, again and again.

You know what you must do, don't you?

'I can't.'

Let me in.

'I can't!'

Yes, you can.

Chapter Twenty-Seven

Ella spent all Saturday night curled up on the floor in the closet, fighting the voice inside her head. Resisting the urge to go out, she finally fell asleep around dawn.

When she next woke up, she knew.

Cassandra was back, and she was here to stay.

Chapter Twenty-Eight

Charley rolled over on to her back and took time for a luxurious stretch. From the kitchen, she could hear Aaron singing to a tune on the radio; the smell of toast still lingered in the air. They'd already had breakfast in bed and he'd gone to make more tea.

With a satisfied sigh, she snuggled back down underneath the duvet, missing the warmth of his body next to hers already. This is what Sundays were meant for, she mused. Funnily enough, she couldn't recall the last time she and Dan had made the effort to lie in bed of a morning. Dan had been an 'early to bed, early to rise' person, so was usually up at the first signs of light. She'd long ago forgotten what it was like to curl up and go back to sleep, having always felt guilty while he was doing stuff. Even since his death, she'd still done it out of habit.

Now she was having fun doing it again. This was all new and deserved to be enjoyed. Content – that's how she felt. For a long time, she'd seen Aaron as a friend, but she had been drawn to him recently for no other reason than he was a nice guy who wanted to spend time with her. Already, she couldn't wait to see him again when he wasn't there, hear his voice, feel his skin next to hers; that kiss on a bare shoulder, that touch of a fingertip. All of it something she thought she'd never have after Dan.

She smiled to herself. Who would have thought that Aaron would rock her world and she would love every minute of it?

'More tea, m'lady?' Aaron smiled as he came into the room.

He'd slipped on his T-shirt, but other than that he was naked. As he drew level with her, Charley ran her fingers over the side of his thigh, feeling his coarse black hair standing on end from her touch. She felt a familiar pulse of lust between her legs.

He placed the tray down on top of the bedside cabinet and slid into bed beside her. She lifted his arm and placed it around her shoulders, returning to lie next to his chest as they shared a comfortable silence.

'So what shall we do today?' she asked eventually.

'I'm taking you to the place that does the best roast dinners ever.'

'Sounds like a great plan. Anywhere I know?'

'Yes, but I don't want to spoil the surprise.'

'You're always spoiling me! Not that I'm complaining.'

'That's because ... oh ... I think ... Well, I know ... Charley Belington ... I'm falling in love with you.'

'Oh!' Charley stared up at him, unsure of her feelings as a million thoughts flashed through her mind.

'Yes, and I'm a little embarrassed that I blurted it out now!' Aaron pressed a finger to her lips as she went to speak. 'I can't help the way I feel, but I don't want you to burst my bubble and say this is all too quick for you. As long as you're enjoying my company, that's good enough for me. So, while my cheeks and that tea cool down ...' He lifted up the duvet and disappeared underneath it.

As she felt his lips travelling from her neck down her chest and cleavage, ever so slowly, Charley's eyes filled with tears.

Of happiness.

―――⌒―――

Watching through the window as Charley left with Aaron later that morning, Ella began to rant.

'Look at them,' she said. 'I bet they're off out for lunch again, somewhere romantic and lovey-dovey. It's enough to make you puke. They've been together all weekend! It's always the fucking same, though, isn't it? Always me seeing someone else fall in love from the sidelines.'

All you're good enough for is a quick screw and away they go.

Ella waved a hand around, clutching a fresh bottle of vodka. 'I can't even get that lately. Home a-fucking-lone again.'

You're such a loser.

In a rush, she felt sick to her stomach thinking of the last time she'd gone out, meeting that bastard again, after all this time. But she'd soon sorted him out.

Revenge was sweet – she smiled then.

She saw an unfamiliar car draw up outside and came away from the window quickly.

Someone's after you – it has to be!

Fear coursed through her as she held her breath, hearing car doors slamming and expecting a knock on the entrance door. Seconds later, when it hadn't materialised, she sneaked a look around the frame. But the occupants of the car were nowhere to be seen. She looked downstairs to the steps in front of her property, but there was no one there either.

No one knows what you've done – no one! So you're okay for now.

She stared across into Jean's window. Jean would be watching; she always was. Ella scowled. Did she see her come in the other night, after she'd laid into Brendan? If she did, she'd be able to tell the police about her. They'd find out she already had a criminal record and lock her away again.

Or then again, maybe Brendan wouldn't want the world to know it was her. After the viciousness of her attack, he might be scared that she'd spill the beans on what really happened at Ravenside. He'd be sent back to prison. And even if he was stupid enough to say anything, the police wouldn't know her as Ella Patrick so they couldn't trace her that easily.

Could the police get dental records for teeth marks, she wondered? There must be plenty of them around Brendan's knob. She laughed again before her mood changed.

It's all her fault. That Charley. All she wants to do now is screw him.

'They think I don't see them but I do. I see them all the time, screwing in the bedroom.'

While you have to go out to get laid.

'And look at ME! I even get rejected by the ugliest-looking freaks I've ever set eyes on. No one wanted *me* when I needed to be screwed.'

Ella paced the room again, clenching and unclenching her fists. 'And now I have to go out or I'll spend all day and all night thinking of them. Screwing, that's all they do. I know.' She pointed to her eyes. 'I can see them. Screwing all the time.'

Yes, you are so sneaky.

It was my fault that Andy left me. I pushed him: I knew it, he knew it. You see, when I met him, I was clean. I was off the drugs and the drink, had been for six months. So I looked good, I felt fantastic, I was beginning to enjoy life. Meeting Andy topped it all.

I hadn't felt so happy in a long while. It was one of the only times in my life that I felt sort-of normal. I trusted Andy with all my being. We did things that couples do: went out for dinner, to the cinema. Even basic stuff like cuddling up on the settee to watch a film was great with Andy. I suppose it was the closest I've ever come to ordinary domestic bliss. I always dreamt that I would have a relationship like my parents' one day. Love and marriage and happy ever after, that's what I wanted. Looking back on how they were together, I see how much they loved each other. Fate is such a cruel bastard at times!

I was with Andy for ten months until I fell off the wagon and changed back into the monster I thought I'd left behind. When the lustful stage of wanting sex every time we met wore off, I still craved the closeness. Andy was content with a few times a week but I wanted it a few times a night. There is nothing like the buzz of sex for me, the rush of an orgasm, the look on his face when he was at the height of pleasure I had given to him.

I began to drink heavily again.

Andy loved me unconditionally. He knew about my past and wasn't repelled by it. He just wanted to make it better, show me that life could be good. That being part of a loving couple, just like my mum and dad, was what I deserved. But I messed up. And screwing his mate had been the last straw.

Why couldn't I have controlled my urges?

It was pretty obvious that he wouldn't put up with my behaviour, and he left when he found out. You see, I told him that too, about fucking his mate – one night when I was pissed out of my brains, picking a fight because I wanted to hurt him. Stupid bitch, me.

Why did I always turn people against me? I didn't want anyone to leave me yet I pushed people away because I didn't want to get hurt. But it hurt a lot more this way, believe me! Stupid, stupid!

When Andy left, not only did he take my heart but he took my sanity. I dipped drastically after that. And that's when my addiction to sex became much worse.

'You could always move in with me,' said Aaron.

Charley glanced over the top of her coffee cup into sincere eyes, honest eyes – eyes full of concern for her.

'Or spend a few nights with me,' he added, 'if you don't feel safe there.'

'We haven't been seeing each other long.'

'I know that – and it doesn't have to be anything permanent. But we've known each other for years, haven't we?'

She nodded.

'So we know we can trust each other. Only time will tell if we'll get past the lust stage,' Aaron smiled, 'but why not run with it for now? Enjoy what we have. You, for one, know how short life can be.'

Charley felt tears well in her eyes – not at the mention of Dan, but because of Aaron. It was silly, really, and scary too, how another person could invade your world, become a part of it so easily, and bring out such happy feelings. And she was still glowing from his earlier confession.

Was all this happening too quickly or, because both of them were older and more experienced in relationships, were they destined to be together because they knew what needed to be worked at?

Charley had been at Aaron's for a few hours now. As promised, he'd taken her somewhere special for lunch. She'd thought he'd forgotten something when he'd pulled up outside his house, but he'd led her into the kitchen, where she found a table set for two and everything he needed ready to cook. He'd sat her down at the breakfast bar and insisted she couldn't help at all. The dinner had been delicious – lamb chops, mint sauce, roast potatoes, the works, and followed by apple crumble and custard. She was fit to burst with food.

The gravy had been lumpy; no one was that perfect.

'I'm just saying that if you're uncertain of Ella and you need a place, the offer is there.'

Charley finished her drink in silence.

'Stay over tonight while you think about it?' Aaron leaned across the table, kissing her tenderly on the forehead.

She nodded. She wasn't sure she trusted herself to put into words what she was thinking anyway, without making a fool of herself.

Because she'd realised something fabulous.

She was falling in love again too.

On Monday morning, Ella woke up, rubbing at her eyes before opening them slowly. She glanced around. Where the hell was she now? She sniffed, nearly gagging as the stench of the room caught her nose. Jeez, it smelt rank – not just of stale sex. Who the hell had she slept with this time?

She pulled back the covers but there were no bruises on her, no blood anywhere. There were no patches on the bottom sheet either; maybe they hadn't had sex in here – whoever *they* might be. She hadn't got a clue.

She lay on the bed. The place was quiet. She checked her watch: ten past nine. Had the someone gone to work and left her there? She tried to recall the night before. She knew she'd headed for Newcastle this time. Somewhere she could disappear into a crowd where no one knew of her existence. But it had turned out that no one could actually see her – well, that's what it had felt like to her. She'd hit on several guys but not a one had shown an interest in taking things further. It was ridiculous, really – how more obvious could she have been than when she told one of them she wanted to be screwed, right now, real hard? No strings attached.

In the end, she'd resorted to walking into the men's toilets to see if she could find anyone willing in there. But all she got was a nose full of the stink of piss, as disgusting as the stench of the room she was in now.

Even then, no one had been interested. So instead, she'd drunk herself into oblivion and wandered off to get a taxi. And…Shit, she remembered. She'd started chatting to a man in the queue, a scrawny-looking git, and headed home with him. Well, at least now she knew it was a man.

She dragged herself out of bed twenty minutes later. God, her head felt rough; her throat was sore too. Was she coming down with something?

Unable to find her clothes, she wandered into the next room in search of a bathroom but there wasn't one. She looked out of the window into a street jammed with parked cars on either side; she was in a row of terraced houses. It seemed clean and tidy out there, a respectable street. But she couldn't place it from such a small view. She'd have to wait until she went outside to read the street sign, figure out which area of the city she had crawled into this time.

Downstairs amongst the chaos of dirty crockery, takeaway cartons, and stale bottles of milk on a cheap wooden side unit, a couple of photos showing an elderly couple were the only personal items she could see. A lumpy settee, a coffee table littered with more rubbish, and a huge plasma television on a stand. Obviously, whoever he was had got his priorities right, she mused ironically.

Next to a pile of his clothes thrown to the side of the settee, and alongside a screwed-up used condom, she finally found her own things. Pulling them on quickly, she went through to the kitchen. Formica units with bottle-green doors that had seen far better days, hanging forlornly, drawers not shutting properly. The soles of her shoes stuck to the dirty cord carpeting under them. She dared a peek into the washing-up bowl, crammed with dirty dishes and a frying pan with the remains of a meal. It added to the stench of stale grease hanging in the air. She gagged again. Time to go. There was no way she'd have a drink or anything to eat here: she'd wait until she got home. She wasn't even going to risk taking a pee; the dirty scrote mustn't have cleaned up in months.

Before she left, she walked to the television and pulled it over, enjoying the splintering sounds as it caught the edge of the coffee table before crashing to the floor.

'You should be more careful who you bring home with you,' she sniggered before letting herself out.

At the back of the house, the naked body of a man lay folded up in the bath. One foot hung over the side, eyes wide open in an expression of shock. An attempt had been made to mop up the blood from the floor, clean the walls up afterwards; cloths left to soak in the tiny, cracked sink, a faint tinge of red in the water now. His killer had taken a shower to swill his blood away; scarlet droplets of water were all that was left in the bottom of the tray.

The knife used to kill and mutilate him had been washed, too, and put back in the kitchen drawer. It was the only thing to have seen detergent there in weeks.

Chapter Twenty-Nine

Just before midday, Ella walked down Warwick Avenue towards her home. After realising she was in the north of the city, in Goldenhill, she'd headed for the main road and into McDonald's for breakfast and to use their bathroom. Knowing it would cost a fortune to get home from one end of the city to the other by taxi, she'd then taken a bus to Hanley and another back home to Trentham.

But as she approached the house, she spotted a woman on the top step, a familiar face she'd hoped not to see again.

Not that interfering bitch.

Putting her head down quickly, Ella turned back in the direction she had come from.

But the woman had seen her.

'Cassie!' she shouted after her. 'Wait!'

Ella stopped, turned again and continued up to the house, all the while fuming inwardly. How the fuck had *she* found out where she lived?

You don't tell her anything, do you hear me?

She looked across to Jake's house: had that imbecile grassed on her after she'd head-butted him?

She glanced up at Jean's house. She was in the window. Was it her? If so, the nosy bag would wish she hadn't said anything by the time she'd finished with her.

Or maybe it was Charley. She'd said there was help out there for her. Perhaps she had stuck her nose in where it wasn't wanted and come across Tanya. Well, she would deal with her later, too.

They're all turning against you now.

Then her blood ran cold as the fear and dread swept through her. She shook uncontrollably for a moment. Were the police here? Were they hiding behind the cars parked near the pavement? Maybe this was a trap! Ella looked around but she couldn't see anyone. It seemed like a normal, quiet day.

She was level with the woman now.

'Hello, Tanya,' she smiled brightly.

'Hi, Cassie.' Tanya dropped down a step. 'Oh dear, what happened to your face? Are you okay?'

Ella had forgotten about the scratch. She touched it absent-mindedly, hoping there were no clues to how she'd got it yet. She stared at Tanya, not trusting her even though she was showing concern. Ella would have to bluff her way out of this. She needed to be indoors, somewhere safe where she could barricade herself away from everyone.

'Can I come in and talk to you?' Tanya added. 'I'd like to catch up with things and see what's been going on.'

Ella nodded. 'Sure you can.'

***

Jean could almost feel every goose-bump rising individually over her body, up her legs, then her arms, and finally all across her chest. It set off a shiver and, for a moment, she froze. Oh, my – had she heard right?

She shooed Tom from her knee and stood up, hoping for a better view as Ella went into the house with the woman. Her visitor was small and plump, dark hair fastened away from her face with a clip, and glasses. She carried a large black bag and a leather file.

Jean wondered who she was; to her eye, she looked fairly official, wearing smart trousers and a jacket.

She picked up her notebook, her hands shaking so much she wondered if she'd be able to write anything legible.

11:55: October 15. Woman in red car RB 59 DUC arrived and went into the house with Ella. But I'm sure I heard the woman refer to Ella as Cassie.

She let out a sob, thinking back to the last time she had seen a child called Cassie. The child whom Jean remembered had been a blonde. The woman who lived across the avenue had auburn hair. But that could easily be a dye, couldn't it?

Upset by the memories the name evoked, and recalling the recent attack on Brendan Furnival, she wondered if the two were connected in any way. It had happened not a mile from Warwick Avenue. She struggled across the room as fast as her legs would carry her. She looked through the newspapers in her green refuse box until she came to the issue of *The Sentinel* reporting the attack on the front page. It was dated last Friday – was it Thursday that she had seen Ella running back, looking as if she'd been in a fight? She reached for her latest notebook – there! It *was* the same night that he was attacked.

No, it couldn't be her, could it? But Jean realised only too well that if it was the Cassie she knew, she would fight back hard if she was cornered.

There was a sure way she could find out if it was Ella. But she wouldn't be able to instigate that from here.

She shook her head. It was too much of a coincidence.

Surely it couldn't be Cassandra Thorpe?

⌣

Ella made coffee, her brain ticking over all the while. Tanya Smith was here to check up on her. Tanya Smith was here to trick her into confessing that she had attacked Brendan Furnival. Tanya Smith was here because Charley had sent her.

What did she want? Why was she here? It wouldn't be to help *her* in any way. She knew the score. Tanya Smith had been sent to fetch her, lock her up.

Get rid of her!

Ella slapped at her head a few times.

Quickly!

'I don't want to hurt her,' she whispered.

You don't have to. Think about it – use your head to get her out of the house.

Ella paused for a moment. Then, smiling, she picked up the two mugs and took them through to the living room.

'It's such a beautiful property, Cassie,' Tanya said as they both sat down. 'I love how it has a lot of its original features.'

'Well, I was outgrowing the house in Penkhull.' Ella pointed at the paraphernalia around the living room, the books still all over the floor from one of her recent tantrums. Luckily, she'd had the sense to tidy up a bit, sweep away the broken glass for fear of cutting herself when she was next drunk. 'I was lost for somewhere to put everything. I've still not settled in yet, hence the mess, but yes, it's all mine.'

'But I can't see that you're registered for housing benefit anywhere on the system? Are you still working to pay the rent?'

'No, the house is mine.'

She thinks you shouldn't have it.

'Pardon?' With a confused look, Tanya opened her case and took out Ella's file.

'The house is mine,' Ella repeated.

'You *bought* it?'

Ella ignored her scepticism. 'Yes, don't look so surprised. You know my parents had money.' Then realisation dawned. 'Ah, you don't know how much they left me, though, do you? Well, I'm not going to tell you but let's just say that I fibbed about having to work.

I have far more than I'll ever need – but I'm always embarrassed to tell anyone. Plus it took me years before I would even accept that it was mine. I didn't feel worthy of it, you know?'

Tanya gave a faint smile of confusion.

'I was going to use the flat downstairs to store my things but when I moved in, I figured it would make more sense to rent it out. I know I don't need the extra income but this house is so big. Good idea, yes? So what did you want to see me about?' Ella tried to keep Tanya on her toes.

'I wanted to see how you're feeling.'

'I'm fine, thanks.'

'Have you been keeping up with your medication?'

Nosy bitch.

'Of course,' Ella lied. 'And feeling much better for it.'

'That's good to hear.' Tanya paused. 'I also came to see if there was anything else that you need. I've been worried that I hadn't heard from you in a while.'

Ella pouted, trying to keep her emotions in check. 'You could have fooled me. You didn't do a very good job of that the last time I saw you. You asked me to write down how I felt. I gave you my notebook and I never saw you again.'

Tanya shook her head fervently. 'I visited your address on several occasions but you weren't at the property in Penkhull. Each time I called, I left a card asking you to get in touch. I've been trying to contact you for ages.'

Always poking her nose in where it's not wanted.

'But I left my new address for you!'

'Did you?' Tanya looked down to the file again.

'Yes, I brought it into your office. Did no one pass it on to you?'

'No, I didn't get it.' Tanya sighed loudly. 'I'm sorry.'

Ella wondered if her bluff had worked as Tanya began to leaf through her notes. She certainly looked bemused as she tried to figure things out.

'I actually thought we were getting on quite well before we lost touch,' Tanya added, still looking through the papers. 'You seemed to be opening up to me, and I was hoping that you'd like to start up our meetings again.'

Ella didn't flinch.

Play the game. The sooner you get rid of her, the better.

'Yes, maybe we could,' she nodded.

'And perhaps we can talk through that diary?'

Ella smiled. 'When would you like to see me?'

Perfect.

Jean rummaged through a pile of boxes in the back bedroom until she found what she was looking for. She took the old black box file through to the front and sat back in her chair. Opening it up meant letting out secrets and memories she'd kept hidden away for years, but she had to look inside.

Anxious of the pain it would conjure up, she pulled out a sheath of papers and flicked through them. Solicitor's letters, tribunal letters, appeal letters. After losing her job at Ravenside Children's Home, she'd taken the authority to court for unfair dismissal. They couldn't just finish her like that, without any reason, no proof that she had done anything wrong. Because she hadn't – all she'd been interested in was the welfare of the children.

But her manager, Malcolm Forrester, had been too clever. Just as he had had no proof, she'd had no evidence to back up her claims of cruelty and neglect, either. There was hardly any staff left at Ravenside to serve as witnesses; others were afraid to speak out for fear of suffering the same fate. Not that she imagined for one minute that anyone would ever look out for her. They were all as bad as each other.

Jean hadn't been able to fight them, and it had haunted her for months afterwards. How she had left children there to suffer at the hands of those...those monsters. How she couldn't help Cassie Thorpe because no one would believe her. How she had left her to the Billies and the Malcolms and the Brendans of this world.

That poor child had suffered since the day she'd arrived at Ravenside Home. Jean had often wondered how Cassie's time there would affect her in later life. It seemed that now she was about to find out exactly how much.

Jean put the box to one side, letting the tears welling in her eyes roll down her face. If that was Cassie living across the road, the system had created a monster.

———

With the social worker shown out, Ella ran upstairs and slammed the door, dragging the lock across before flouncing down the hallway. Tanya had fixed up a time for her to go in to the offices next week. Ella had played the happy-to-oblige client she knew Tanya had wanted to see perfectly, but, as she watched her drive away, she took the piece of paper that she'd written her appointment details on and ripped it into tiny pieces, letting them scatter to the carpet.

That bitch, Ella fumed, slapping at her face. That fucking bitch! Tanya Smith calling after all this time was no coincidence.

It must be her.

Had Charley seen Tanya at work somehow and told Tanya where she was? She must have done – or else how would she know where Ella was living now? She'd hoped that by keeping the property in Penkhull too that Tanya would have given up looking for her. It was still furnished. For all intents and purposes, it looked as though she was still there. But now that Tanya knew she was in Warwick Avenue, she couldn't even hide there. She'd want to poke her nose into Ella's business again.

That Charley is heading for trouble.

Ella covered her ears as the voice droned on.

You're heading for trouble too, because of Charley.

She started to yell: it turned into a scream

She shouldn't have interfered. You know that, don't you?

Of course Ella knew that – that was the problem! Charley should never have stuck her nose into her business. Now she would have to start visiting offices again, have people prying into her life, because if anyone suspected anything, she'd be in big trouble.

Ella had to stop Charley from talking. If she could do that, everything would be fine.

Congratulations! Finally, she gets it!

She nodded. Yes, it was about time she sorted things out.

You know how to do that, don't you?

'Yes, I fucking do,' said Ella.

⌣

After spending Sunday night at Aaron's, Charley had gone straight to work. She'd been in the office only half an hour when she'd found out another weekend had gone wrong for one of her clients and she'd ended up visiting North Staffs University Hospital. After staying there for most of the day while she dealt with the police and then tried to fix up temporary housing, she'd rung Aaron as soon as she was out of the main building. Knowing she was stressed by what she had seen and had to listen to, he offered to come round later with a takeaway.

She thought back to his proposal the day before. It had been wonderful when he'd asked her to stay over for a while but Charley wasn't sure she wanted to give up her independence yet, not even for a few days at a time. Just hearing Aaron suggesting it had been heart-warming, but she needed a little space, time to think it over. Plus, she'd felt better after Tanya had called to let her know that she had spoken to Ella as planned. Ella had also agreed to come and see Tanya again. Tanya sounded hopeful that she would keep to her promise.

Back home by six, Charley was putting her key into the front door when she heard her name. She looked up the stairs to see Ella standing there. Her skin was pale, hair unkempt, and the grey jumper she was wearing had a stain all down its front.

'You couldn't help me for a moment, please?' Ella gave a strained smile. 'I have a problem with my washer and I don't know what to do with it.'

Charley paused. 'I'm not sure I'm the right person to ask. Have you rung for a plumber?'

'Yes. He's calling in the morning but I'm wondering if I can't sort it myself. If I could get the clothes out of the drum, I think I'd be better getting a new machine anyway. Mine's years old and I bet I could get one fitted for the price of a man coming out to replace any parts on this. What do you reckon? Do you think I should force it or wait?'

'I'm not sure,' Charley said truthfully.

Ella was already heading back upstairs.

Charley paused for a moment and then followed her. 'I can take a look, I suppose, but I doubt I'll be of any use.'

'Great!'

Ella closed the door behind them and Charley followed her into the kitchen.

'There it is,' Ella pointed. 'The bloody thing is jammed stuck.'

Charley stooped down to look inside the washing machine, but all she could see was an empty drum. Wondering what Ella was playing at, she turned back with a frown. 'I thought you said –'

Ella curled her hand up into a fist and brought it up hard underneath Charley's chin. A punch to her face followed it.

Searing pain engulfed Charley and she fell back onto the floor, landing heavily. Eyes blurred from the force of the attack, she tried to focus. Christ, why hadn't she seen that coming? And what the hell was it for? She thought back to the last time they'd spoken, wondering if Ella thought she had betrayed her somehow. Confusion set in as she couldn't remember.

'It's all your fault!' screamed Ella.

'Oh – I...' Charley stuttered, unable to form her words into a coherent sentence. Lights flashed before her eyes and she cried out. Seeing Ella take a step towards her, she put her hands to the floor and tried to push herself up. But they wouldn't work to support her weight.

Eyes still barely focusing, Charley felt panic rip through her as she watched Ella come nearer, saw her arm go up in the air. In disbelief, she realised she was going to hit her again. She put up her hands in a desperate attempt to block her.

Another two punches to her head rendered Charley unconscious.

Ella pulled Charley up to sitting, placed a hand underneath each arm and dragged her out of the room. The sound of teeth smashing on teeth had thrilled her, sending a rush of euphoria through her body. But Charley's top lip was split; she didn't want any blood on the kitchen floor, She couldn't afford any tell tale signs or giveaways until she'd put the other part of her plan into action first.

She wasn't going to slip up this time.

Glad to hear it.

Chapter Thirty

Charley woke up in darkness, rough carpeting against her cheek. She lifted her head but the pain shooting through it stopped her momentarily and she laid it back down. The dark invaded her senses. She wanted to scream but it was too quiet; she didn't dare. Where the hell was she? She listened but couldn't hear anything.

Her feet were bare although she couldn't remember removing her shoes. Using her hands to push up from the floor, she tried to sit. When she eventually managed, she took a moment while her head became less fuzzy, still trying not to scream as the dark shrouded her. She could feel her lips and nose beginning to bulge, her right eye struggling to open fully. Gingerly, she laid her fingers on its source, rubbed away what she thought must be dried blood. She sniffed: the metallic smell made her retch.

Biting down the panic, she held a hand out in front but could feel nothing. Her ears began to buzz as she concentrated. To her right, she felt a wall; she splayed her fingers out over the plastered surface and felt her way along. She was about a foot away from a corner.

Moaning in fear, she scrambled over and pressed her back into it as far as it would go. Her eyes filled with tears as the noise of her heart beating madly filled her ears. She held a hand to her nose this time – God, it hurt. What the fuck had happened?

And then all of a sudden she remembered.

Ella tricking her, getting her upstairs to her kitchen, attacking her, hitting her in the face, another fist pummelling her head. Blacking out.

Why had she lashed out at her like that? There had been no explanation, no build-up to it. One minute she'd been fine; the next, Ella had punched her.

She recalled dropping to the floor and then...nothing. Ella must have dragged her into here...Where the hell was here?

It hurt to squint in the dark but, even though Charley's eyes had now adjusted to the gloom, she still couldn't see where she was. She felt the wall again, as far as she could to the left this time: there was nothing on it. Her hand went up and she flinched when she touched something, moving it away quickly. She touched it again: it was thick material. She could feel a wide hem at the bottom. Was it a coat?

Images ran through her mind. If it was a coat, there could be someone wearing it! For the next few seconds, she froze in the quiet, not daring to breathe. Then she sighed into the darkness as she came back down to earth. The coat must be hanging on a wall. If someone was wearing it, they'd hardly be leg-less, now, would they?

Carefully, she turned her body and, using the coat, wrenched herself up to standing. Searching around again, her hands felt over that one, next to it another. Next to that a scarf.

Laughing to herself seconds before bursting into tears of relief, Charley realised where she might be. She put a hand out to the right and yes, there was a door.

She was in Ella's walk-in closet.

Locating the handle, she pushed it down. It was locked. She pushed it down again and again but nothing.

Why would it be locked? Why would Ella put her in there?

Her hand went out to the right again. The layout of this flat was identical to hers downstairs, so the light switch should be in the same place. Her fingers searched it out, found it. She switched it on, praying there would be a working light bulb.

When the light came on, Charley squinted at first. The bulb was naked and shone bright in her eyes. She blinked, looking down for a moment until she could see better through the pain. Now she had her sight back a little, she could see clearly from one eye; the other still swelling by the second.

Slowly, she moved her head to the right: two coats and a scarf hanging on a coat rail. Above them, a shelf with a few shoe boxes. She looked around for her bag but there was nothing. She had no phone, no way of letting anyone know what had happened.

Crying now as claustrophobia built to a crescendo, she banged on the door.

'Ella! Ella, are you there? Let me out!' She pummelled with her fists. 'Oh, God, Ella, please let me out! Ella!

In the bedroom, Ella sat with her back to the closet door, her hands covering her ears, her shoulders bouncing every time Charley's fist hit the wood.

'No,' she whispered. 'No, no, no, no, no.'

She could hear Charley's fear rising at the same time as her voice, experienced her terror as she realised she was powerless. It brought back memories but she pushed them away. *She* wasn't locked in the closet. *She* would never be locked in anywhere again. It had been a horrible experience and Charley needed to relive it, see what Ella had gone through as a child.

You mustn't let her out.

Ella wouldn't let her out until she had learned her lesson. Not until she'd been a good girl and promised not to be sneaky anymore and tell everyone her secrets. No one came out of the closet until she said so – and that was if they were lucky.

She looked at her watch; it was nearly six thirty. She poured the last of her wine while she thought about what to do when Aaron arrived. It wouldn't be long now. Usually when he called, she'd see him park up outside between seven and eight, so she knew she had a bit of time yet. Then the real fun and games could begin.

She was going to get her revenge on him for taking Charley away, for coming along and spoiling everything. He knew what he was doing and Charley, being so weak and vulnerable, had fallen for his tricks hook, line, and sinker. She should have been stronger than that, not let him in so easily.

Yes, it's all his fault.

Charley needed protecting from Aaron.

And Ella knew just how to do that.

Charley knew she wouldn't be able to kick her way out without wearing shoes but still she had to try. She lashed out at the bottom panel of the door over and over until she burst into tears again. Why couldn't it have been one of those cheap ones, all frame and a bit of plywood? She might have had a chance with that if she used her heel.

'Let me, out, Ella,' she sobbed, knocking loudly again. 'Please, I have to get out.'

After a minute or so, spent and waiting for her breathing to return to whatever normality it could, given the situation, Charley evaluated her position. Having her shoes removed and being left with no phone, no way of contacting anyone, and locked in the closet made her realise that Ella was more calculating than she'd originally thought. She had purposely isolated her. Any way she had of alerting people to the danger she was in had gone. If Ella knew to do that, then she wasn't so innocent after all. She was more likely psychotic.

She guessed at the time. Had half an hour passed yet? An hour maybe? Would Aaron have arrived? Normally he would ring or send a text message when he was leaving but she wouldn't hear it from here.

Would he turn up as usual, and then start to worry? Maybe try upstairs first, considering their conversation yesterday about Ella. She could only hope that he would.

What the hell was she going to do in the meantime – could she use negotiation tactics? With all her expertise, she was great at persuading clients to talk; equally, she was a good listener. Maybe if she could get Ella to let her out of the closet, she could talk to her, calm her down enough to get out of the flat and into safety. It seemed like her best shot.

She knocked on the door again.

'Ella?' she said. 'Ella, are you there?'

Silence.

'Ella, we can talk about this – see why you're so upset with me. I'm not sure what I've done, why you would want to hurt me like this.' She knocked again. Then she banged on the door with the palm of her hand. 'Ella! Where the fuck are you? Let me out of here!' She began to sob. Oh, God, so much for keeping calm. She was stuck at Ella's whim.

'There's no point in making a noise, you silly girl. No one can hear you.'

Charley gasped and dropped to her knees. She put her ear to the door. 'Ella? Oh, God, Ella, are you there?'

'Of course I'm here.'

Charley bit her bottom lip to stop herself from yelling. She had to try and get the upper hand. 'Ella, please, can you let me out and we can chat about things?'

'No.'

'Why not?'

'You've been a bad girl, and bad girls get punished. They get locked in the cupboard until they can behave themselves. Isn't that right, Charley?'

'I haven't been a bad girl, Ella.'

'You've been telling people about me.'

'Have I?'

'Yes! You've been talking about me. I don't like that.'

Charley realised Ella must be referring to Tanya's earlier visit. 'Tanya Smith is a colleague of mine,' she explained. 'She saw me with you in Hanley, when we bumped into each other in TK Maxx.'

'When you were rude and didn't want to know me. I remember.'

'I –'

'Tanya Smith should mind her own business. So should you.'

'But, Ella, we're only trying to help you. I think we –'

'She showed you my notebook, didn't she? DIDN'T SHE?'

Charley jumped when Ella raised her voice. 'Yes, but only because she thought it –'

'Did you read it?'

'Yes.'

'All of it?'

'Yes.'

'Why would you want to do that?'

'Because I want to help you and I thought it would make me understand why you feel sad.'

A snort. 'Yeah, right. I'm not that stupid.'

'I know you're not stupid! I just wanted to help and –'

'You can read from the beginning, if you like,' Ella cut her short again. 'On the shelf above the coats, in the top box. The rest of the pages are in there.'

Charley lifted her eyes, wincing as the swelling caused her to move her head up so that she could see properly. It was an old shoe box, a monochrome picture of a wedge-heel court shoe and a large number 6 on its end. She pulled it down and removed the lid.

Inside, on top of a few pieces of crumpled tissue paper, was a pile of loose pages, lined paper torn from an exercise book. She recognised the writing from the notebook Tanya had shown her. She recognised the paper from when Ella had accused her of snooping the first time she'd visited her flat − were these the ones that had fallen out of the *Kama Sutra* book that evening?

'You want to know what happened to me as a child?' Ella cried. 'It's all there. Read it, then maybe you'll understand why you shouldn't have ignored me.'

'Let me out and I can read it with you,' Charley tried.

'Not bloody likely.'

'Please, Ella, I −'

Don't you fucking dare let her out of there! She needs to suffer!

'Do as you're told.'

'But I −'

Make her read it!

'JUST FUCKING READ IT!'

Wearily, Charley sat down on the floor again.

Chapter Thirty-One

While she left Charley to read the notes, Ella, her wine glass empty now, opened a new bottle of vodka, filled the glass neat, and took it through to the living room. From the window, she could see Jean.

What the fuck is she staring at?

'She's staring at me!' Ella tutted. 'She shouldn't stare at me – no one should stare at me. I don't know why, though. People don't even like me.'

They don't.

'They hate me.'

They do.

'They try to categorise me, put me in a box so they can put a tick against me and then move on to the next lost soul. That's what they do!' She held up her glass in a silent toast. 'I know I'm lost but I don't really want to be found, do I?' She sniggered before taking another large gulp of vodka, wiping her mouth as it spilled over. 'I want to be screwed. And you,' she pointed at Jean, 'you just want to watch, you sleazy cow. Shall I give you something to watch now, huh?'

Ella staggered slightly as she set down the glass on the windowsill with a bang. She was about to pull up her jumper, when she remembered Charley in the cupboard. Barefoot, she raced back to her bedroom and put her ear to the closet door, but she could hear nothing.

'I hope you're enjoying reading that filth,' she said, knocking on the closet door loudly. 'That's my life story. Every last detail. I hate Malcolm, I hate Mark, I hate Brendan – I hate everyone. They all hated me. My life was shit.' Ella began to cry. 'My life has always been shit. What did I do wrong, Charley? What did I do wrong?'

After I'd been at Ravenside for a few months, trying my best to fit in, I started to withdraw from everything. I didn't want to spend time with Billie so I stayed in the common room downstairs. But everyone ignored me in there, too. They said I was strange, a weirdo, a quiet little thing.

Billie hid her mean streak well – that's what I started to do when I changed from Cassie to Ella later. I learned to put on the charm in public and be the real me in private – or when I went out to be screwed.

When I was eleven, I was fostered out for the first time. I went to live with a family in Liverpool. Far away from anyone who knew me. I liked it at first. I could pretend to be someone else and leave my past behind. And now that I was rid of Billie, I could relax. My foster parents, Sally and Phil, were great. I had my own room, my own space to feel safe in. No one ripped my covers off in the middle of the night so I had to sleep on the mattress shivering. No one would wake up, run over to me and thump me, giving me a dead leg while I was asleep. And Sally and Phil bought me books. I read them all.

I started another new school, settled in as much as I could by keeping my head down, getting on with my work and staying quiet. For the first time since my family had died, I felt happy.

Then Sally and Phil's son, Ian, came home from university.

Ian was nineteen; he was someone who should have known better. I could tell he wanted me, with those beady eyes of his that used to look me up and down, follow me around the room when he thought no one was watching. I was eleven, for fuck's sake.

One night, he was babysitting while Sally and Phil were out. I was asleep in my bed but he woke me up as he pulled the duvet from me, grabbed for my hands, and pinned me down. I struggled to get free, kicking out my legs underneath him as he straddled my body. I screamed but no one was there to hear me. Sally and Phil were out and Ian was looking after me – is that what you'd call it? Holding me down by my hands while he forced himself into me, thrusting and grunting like an animal while I screamed, telling me I wanted it and I was going to get it.

I continued to scream but eventually he hit me, told me to shut up or else he'd hit me again. I was so shocked that I let him finish, closing my eyes tightly, hoping it would be over soon.

Afterwards, he squeezed my chin hard. 'You tell anyone and I'll do much worse than that,' he warned. 'No one will believe you, anyway. You're just a damaged kid who tells lies.' And then he left my room.

I curled up in a ball, my thighs bruised, my insides hurting like hell, blood all over the covers. How could you do that to me, you sick bastard? How could you take away my innocence? I was vulnerable and I was so scared.

Sally found me the next morning, afraid to come out of my room. I couldn't hide the bruising, or the blood. She said not to tell anyone what had happened as Ian would get into trouble. And because it had happened, I couldn't stay there any longer. I was sent back to the home. Sally told the authorities that I was unruly and she couldn't handle me. I was labelled again. And it wasn't my fault.

Sally and Phil should have protected me. They all should have looked after me! I was their responsibility. They should have kept me safe from harm. I was put into their care and another piece of my *innocence was taken away. Never to return. Their son saw to that, that piece of lowlife shit.*

Do they know? Do they have a sixth sense that tells them 'this child has been abused so you're welcome to abuse her again?' What was wrong with those people? Or was it my fault?

Charley came to the end of the page, unsure if she could cope with reading any more. This was far more harrowing than the notebook she'd flicked through. What Ella had gone through at such a young and tender age was appalling. Charley couldn't begin to understand, the raw emotion from the words alone putting her on edge.

Ravenside Home was no longer open when she'd worked for the local authority so Charley hadn't been around to visit it. But she had heard the tales of ill-treatment and abuse, the reason why it had been closed down.

Page by page as she read, Charley was able to understand more about why Ella craved attention, her mood swings, her eagerness to be accepted, and to please. Head beginning to pound, she dabbed at her swollen eye with the corner of her sleeve. It kept watering, the effort of reading too much for it, but she had to continue. Because if she was going to talk herself out of this situation, then she needed to know everything about Ella, no matter how unbearable it became.

My worst fears came back when I was returned to Ravenside, the home I'd left before. Billie was still there but there was a new boy called David. He was fifteen and Billie had a soft spot for him. But David started to look at me too.

Billie didn't like it.

I didn't like it!

I knew then that I needed to wise up and start defending myself. I would learn but first things were about to get a lot worse. I thought

Billie had found out that I was raped when I was at my foster home. Yes, I was raped, wasn't I? I didn't realise that at the time. I was torn and ripped apart, violated by a man who should have known better.

But if I'd thought about it, she couldn't have found out, could she? Because no one said anything about what had happened to me. Sally told me to be quiet about it, said no one would believe me and that it would only bring trouble to their door. So Billie was just being her usual vile self.

Billie was fourteen by then. One evening, she came into our room and she brought David with her. I was sitting on my bed reading a book. While some of the boys watched by the door, Billie grabbed my arms and held them over my head. David sat between my legs and pulled up my skirt. I remember him laughing as he played with the elastic on my knickers, enjoying seeing the fear in my eyes as I tried to kick my feet. Billie now had both my wrists tightly held together in one of her hands; her other one was covering my mouth so no one could hear me call out.

My knickers were forced down and I was on display. It was so embarrassing. Then he pushed up my T-shirt. I wasn't developed enough to wear a bra so the whole of me was on display. He circled my small breast with his dirty fingernail. I can still remember praying, Please let this be over soon.

But it wasn't. It was far from over. Billie held me down while David forced himself into me. It hurt, God it hurt. Just writing this I can remember the pain.

The fucking bastard! He was fifteen: he knew it was wrong. I shut my eyes again, so I couldn't see him. But all the time he was inside me, I could still hear Billie. She was laughing at me, egging David on while he grunted and groaned on top of me, just like Ian.

And all the time I screamed, my screams were muffled.

I'm glad it happened, though. I know it won't make sense to anyone who's had a wonderful childhood and upbringing. Raped twice by the age of twelve made me into a better person. It sounds *perverted, I know, like something from* Jeremy Kyle. *But it did. Because from that day forward, I realised that no one was going to look out for me. I realised that I could trust no one, that I could only rely on myself. Age was making me that little bit stronger, taller, harder to manipulate.*

Billie continued with the bullying, enraged that I had David's attention. He didn't like Billie, it was plain to see. Ha ha ha! Stupid bitch. Luckily, he'd had his fill after one go with me so he never touched me again.

When he was sixteen a few weeks later, he had to leave. You're kicked out onto the streets at sixteen, sent to a hostel if you're really unlucky. Most of them were worse than Ravenside. More bullies, just a little bit older.

Billie missed David and took her anger out on me. I let her for a while. Until that day, when I was twelve. You see, she might have had me scared, and she might have controlled me for years, but something inside me snapped.

I heard it go ping.

Billie told me I had to clean our room up. I did as she told me but once I'd finished, she came in and said it was still a mess. The room was *tidy, exactly how I had left it, but then she wiped everything off my chest of drawers with one sweep of her arm; my belongings crashed to the carpet and scattered all over the room. She pulled drawers out, threw socks and knickers to the floor.*

It was when Billie pulled a book from the shelf that I saw red. I was reading more and more: I've always lost myself in a good book, you know? There's nothing better than escaping into someone else's happy life when yours is shit and has no chance of improving.

Billie gathered all my books up and took them down to the communal bathroom. I followed behind her quickly, trying to get them from her arms. She laughed as she dumped them all in the bath and turned on the taps. I tried to stop her, turn the water off, but she hit me, knocking me onto my bottom across the floor.

But I wasn't staying down this time. Those books were my trea-sured possessions – my only possessions.

I had taken three years of abuse and that moment,

that exact *moment,*

I tipped over the edge.

I charged forward and pushed her head into the bath water. I held it underneath as she flailed around. Her head came up and she gasped for breath, crying out before I managed to push her underneath again. One of the younger kids came to the door. I saw his terrified face before he ran away.

I realised that I did have the strength to overpower Billie as she fought against me.

Then Jean, one of the workers, came in. She closed the bathroom door and locked us all in there, away from prying eyes while she assessed the situation. Then she held me in her arms until I was calm. Billy sat panting, gasping for air, but Jean didn't go to her: she comforted me. It was the first time anyone had done that since my parents had died.

I remember Jean glaring at Billie. 'You think you're never going to get a taste of your own medicine, don't you?' she said. 'Well, think again. You can only push people so far. Let this be a lesson to you to change your ways.'

I liked Jean. She hadn't been working there long, yet she could see through Billie. What she said, and what I had done, shocked Billie enough to realise that I could be dangerous if I wanted to.

Billie hardly ever spoke to me after that. She kept her distance, made everyone think she couldn't be bothered to interact with me. But I knew. I had won my first battle to survive. When I tried to drown her, a little bit of doubt had emerged. I stopped her in her tracks, didn't I?

Ella stood in the window again. Rain poured down outside; the wind was getting up too. All in all it looked like a murky night, a night to draw heavy curtains on and curl up on the settee with a mug of hot chocolate and a feel-good movie.

'A night not to go out on the pull,' Ella said with a grin. She could cope with that. She had all she needed here.

Then she thought about Charley and her mood changed again. *She's in there. Reading all that filth about you.*

'I should stop her – drag her out by her hair and kick the fuck out of her. Just like Billie did to me. See how she'd like it. I know she –'

The sounds of Neyo's *Beautiful Monster* filtered into the room. *What the fuck is that?*

Ella glanced around, trying to figure out where it was coming from. Charley's handbag was on the settee: it was her phone! She rummaged around, searching through zipped sections until she found it. It was an incoming call from Aaron.

She let it ring.

When it finally stopped, a text message arrived moments later. *Be 15 mins. Picking up takeaway. xx*

Ella smiled again.

Let the fun begin.

She was going to show Charley just how much it hurt to have someone she cared for taken away for the second time. That would teach her not to interfere.

Yes, that would be perfect. Once she'd dealt with him, there'd be time to come back to sort out Charley. She would keep for now.

Now you're singing in tune.

Ella laughed hysterically. Charley *couldn't* escape anyway. Just like she hadn't been able to when Billie locked her inside the cupboard over the stairs.

She texted Aaron back: *Great. C u soon Cx*

Then she let herself out of the flat.

Charley froze at the sound of Neyo. It had to be her phone! She pulled herself up quickly, unease ripping through her body. It would most likely be Aaron.

But then the music stopped.

She strained to hear. Had Ella answered it? She held her breath, wishing she could slow the beat of her heart down, or at least the noise as it banged out of her chest. But then she heard the beep of an incoming message.

A feeling of helplessness washed over her again. If Aaron had sent a message, it meant he'd be arriving soon. It could be good news because he'd want to know where she was. He had keys now; he was bound to use them to get in. He'd find the flat empty, see her car outside, and start to investigate.

He'd probably look upstairs first, right? Which meant he could be in danger too.

And she couldn't warn him.

'Ella?' She banged on the door, panic back again. 'Ella, are you there? Let me out of here. ELLA!'

Chapter Thirty-Two

I ran away from Ravenside several times when I was thirteen but each time I was found and brought back. Malcolm hated authority – the police or the social. He hated anyone poking their nose into how the home was run. Because there was a lot that they could find if they did dig deep. A FUCKING LOT!

And each time I got back, Malcolm would give me a good thrashing. Luckily for me, Malcolm didn't like little girls or else he would have taken a turn shagging me too, I'm certain. Instead he used me as a punch bag, explaining the bruises away by saying I was fighting with the other kids. Everyone thought I was the troublemaker. I wasn't! I SO wasn't!

The only good thing to come of the running away and the beatings was the trouble I brought back to the home. For punishment when I ran away, I was locked in my room every night. Hilarious, don't you think? Being locked up meant that no one could get to me but it brought demons with it too. Memories of Billie; memories of banging on the door to get out; memories of time passing so slowly that I had no idea whether it was morning or night.

I was so lonely, though. No one to call my friend; no one to talk to. No one at school wanted to know any of us kids from the home. We were doomed, wherever we were.

Billie left when I was thirteen and, now just that much older and stronger, I saw my chance and wised up. It took me a few months of fighting my way to the top of the pile, most of the kids thinking I was still going to be the pushover they had grown up with. But I got there eventually – after banging Melody Johnson's head repeatedly on the floor as I sat astride her and throwing one last punch before being pulled off, I gained respect. It was easy from then. I had everyone wanting to be my friend.

That's the pack mentality of being in an institution. Either join in and survive, no matter what you have to do, or be singled out for being a loner, like I was. Peer pressure. Fitting in. Being a sheep. Better than being on your own.

But I was different to the Davids and the Billies, because woe betide anyone who picked on any of the younger kids then – unless I told them to, obviously. Which wasn't very often, I admit, but if one of the little shits annoyed me, I'd get them back. Or if one of the older kids thought they could recruit to get one up on me? Then the fists started to fly. I surprised myself by how hard I could punch.

This was my home now; until I left I was going to be its lead girl, even if it meant fighting every minute of every day for it. I had done my time as a punch bag. Even Malcolm became wary of me. He was right to be. I began carrying a flick-knife everywhere and I knew I'd use it if I was vulnerable again.

Surprised to see Charley's rooms in darkness when he arrived, Aaron knocked on the door to the flat twice before letting himself in with a key. His pulse quickened with anxiety, as Charley was normally there to greet him at the door when he'd texted her to say he was on his way. Maybe she was going to surprise him, greet him naked or something. Maybe she was lying in the bath, waiting for him to strip off and step in next to her. He felt a stirring in his groin. Stuff the takeaway getting cold: slipping into hot water with Charley would be even more of a treat.

'Anyone home?' he said, switching on the hall light. 'Charley?' He went into the kitchen and put the takeaway down on the worktop.

Weird – no light on in there, either.

'I hope you're where I think you are?'

Still no reply.

He popped his head around the living room door and switched on the light, but the room was empty. The bathroom and bedroom were too.

Disappointment replaced with concern, he went into the living room this time, glancing around in confusion. There was no music on; the television was off too.

He checked his phone; there were no new messages. He rang Charley again but her phone went straight to voicemail. Deciding not to leave a message, he sent another quick text.

His sense of excitement replaced by concern, Aaron felt strange to be there all alone, with no sign of Charley. He wondered if she'd lost track of time and maybe nipped out to the shop without her phone. But no, she wouldn't do that.

His eyes flicked around the room again. Where was her bag? He couldn't see it anywhere. He looked out onto the road, before noticing the paperwork spread around the table. He picked up a file, smiling to himself. Charley was such a conscientious worker, she even brought it home with her, bless.

Bless? He snorted into the silence, and then grinned, embarrassed even though he was alone. Damn that woman taking over his heart.

A handwritten note caught his eye. He knew the writing was Charley's. *Cassandra Thorpe:* The name didn't mean anything to him. He leaned forward to take a closer look.

'What the fuck are you doing?'

Aaron turned to see Ella standing behind him.

'Christ, you gave me a fright then.' He put a hand to his chest. 'I was waiting for Charley – you haven't seen her, have you?'

'Why would I have? She's completely ignored me since *you* came along.'

As the silence became loaded, Aaron stared at Ella. Her hair hung limply; she had nothing on her feet. She wore a grey tracksuit that had seen better years. With no make-up, she seemed no older than a teenager. But the look was of a wild animal, her right eye twitching rapidly.

'Have you seen her?' he repeated.

'Are you deaf? I said no.'

'I'm not sure I believe you, Ella.' Aaron took a step towards her. 'It's a little unusual that she isn't here, considering she told me she was coming home straight from work.'

'She sent you a message, though.'

'She did – how did you know that?'

Ella said nothing.

'Where is she?' He stepped nearer, hoping to keep the alarm from his voice.

'I ask the questions.'

Aaron looked down, spotting the knife in her hand at the same time Ella charged at him. Before he could react, she plunged it into his side.

He gasped, for a moment stunned.

Ella turned the blade, then drew it out so quickly he could almost imagine a whooshing sound. She didn't take her eyes off him for a second.

He dropped to his knees, having no time to cry out further as heat burned through his torso, followed by an icy chill, nauseating him. He pressed a hand to the wound; his palm came away covered in blood.

'Fuck,' he muttered. 'Ella, what have ... have ... you done?'

I was fourteen when a support worker called Peter turned up. Peter was one of the good guys, not wanting to take advantage of the younger girls needing to be loved or the older girls with their raging hormones – or the boys, for that matter. Not there to beat the shit out of us kids, either. He just wanted to help.

He was so gorgeous! I swear my heart went zoom *whenever I saw him. He was in his mid-thirties, fairly tall to a small teenager. He had dark hair and a fringe that flopped into his eyes every time he moved his head. His smile made my insides go a little squishy and he was so pleasant to talk to. I spent a lot of time with him, sitting drinking coffee, daring to dream about my future and plan for a better life. Peter even helped us kids with our homework – yes, of course we had to go to school, even though we tried our best not to. He helped us with our self-esteem, urging us to realise that we could all become someone to look up to someday. The world was our oyster, and all that.*

Malcolm despised Peter because he stuck his nose in where it wasn't wanted. He wasn't one to clean and tidy up the mess, sweep everything under the carpet away from prying eyes when he knew a home inspection was due from Social Services. He wouldn't cover up what was going on at all, so things had to be dealt with rather than put away in a box, never to be mentioned again. He even made a couple of staff members leave because he sorted out their bullying ways – either they left or he would report them. He wasn't scared to whistle-blow. I loved him for that alone.

Malcolm started to watch his every move. Everyone knew he wanted Peter to slip up: Peter didn't give a shit, though. He knew Malcolm was watching him too; thought he knew too much about the place for Malcolm to ever act on anything. Peter didn't care what happened to him as long as us kids were treated right.

It was the best year of my life, when I was fourteen. I felt safe, even with the door to my room unlocked at night now. I was still top dog – no one would mess with me. I didn't even want to run away.

It was totally one-sided, of course. Honest to God, he was a gentleman. One of the best. But Malcolm told my social worker that he'd seen Peter being inappropriate around me.

When I next saw her, she asked me all sorts of questions: was I often alone with Peter, did he touch me, was he ever in my room with me, did he ask me to do things? To. Touch. Him. Noooooooooooo! For God's sake, there was never any of that.

I kept on telling her that he was one of the good guys. But she didn't listen. They didn't listen. Everyone in authority just saw PERVERT stamped across his forehead. Despite his protests that nothing had happened, or ever would happen, between us, in the end Peter was asked to leave.

I knew it had something to do with that bastard, Malcolm. So rather than take it out on his face, I trashed Malcolm's car instead. Who was laughing then, you sick bastard? Hmm? HMMMM?

Yet again, I had found someone to trust and they had been taken away from me. What was wrong with me? Would I always be left to my own devices?

Ella stood quietly in the doorway until she watched Aaron pass out. She wiped the knife on her trousers, cleaning it of his blood, and took it into the kitchen. The smell of takeaway roused her. She picked it up to take back with her.

I hope you've killed him. He deserves to die.

Just about to leave, she checked on Aaron one last time. His eyes were still closed; he hadn't moved. If he wasn't dead now, he would be soon, she was certain. She couldn't wait to tell Charley what she had done for her.

Why not put him in Charley's closet?

Ella grinned – what a great idea! It would be poetic justice to leave him there to die, for Charley to find him.

If she ever let her out of the closet upstairs.

She put down the takeaway, grabbed both of Aaron's hands, and dragged him across the room. Christ, he was heavy. It took over a minute to get him a few feet towards the door. She decided to give up on that idea.

Sensing someone, her eyes were drawn upwards, across the road. She glared into the darkness at the upstairs light of number thirty-eight, seeing only an empty chair in the window.

Had nosy Jean been watching her?

She saw what you did!

Ella slapped at her face. That stupid bitch. She'd ruin everything.

———⌣———

Jean had moved away from the window as soon as she'd witnessed the attack. She couldn't believe her eyes. Ella had put a knife into Charley's young man! She had, hadn't she?

And she would know she'd been watching her, wouldn't she?

She held onto her chest, hurting as she struggled to breathe. She had seen some things in her time of snooping on people but she had never witnessed anything sinister until today. First the attack on Jake from next door when Ella had hit out at him. And now, she'd assaulted someone else – or even murdered him! Jean didn't know whether the man was dead or alive, but she didn't want to look again. She'd seen how quickly he'd dropped to the floor.

People-watching, that's all she did; she didn't mean anyone any harm.

Jean needed to call the police. There was no time to write anything down in her notepad. She looked around the room for the phone. The handset was here somewhere: where had Ruby put it so that she would remember where it was?

Still unable to accept as true what she'd seen, she moved forward slowly to check again. She had to! She didn't want to be witness to something so terrible but she had to know.

In the darkness, the light beamed out from Charley's living room windows, allowing Jean a clear view of an empty room. She looked up and down the avenue; no signs of life there, either. But why would there be? It was a dark and cold November evening. Other neighbours would be in their warm houses now, engrossed in *The One Show* or *Sky News*, no doubt, eating their evening meal, or catching up with the kids' day. Normal stuff that people do. Not this!

Jean looked down again. Wait a minute, what was that? She bent her head a little lower, thus lowering her vision too. The man was flat out on the floor now, near to the door. She gulped: he didn't seem to be moving.

A shadow crossed the window and Jean screamed. It was Ella.

There was no mistaking whether or not she had been seen this time because she was looking straight up at her.

And not only was she looking at her, she was pointing up at her too.

Chapter Thirty-Three

Once Peter had gone, I felt abandoned again. There was no one to talk to, no one to have a laugh with, and certainly no one who treated me like an adult. Malcolm tried to take control of me, make me scared of him. But it was too late for that. If he couldn't do it when I was running away, he sure as hell wouldn't be able to do it now.

And as always in these types of homes, staff came and went. With Peter gone, I was alone for ages until Brendan came along when I was fifteen. Brendan was young, an average-looking guy, so once I got to know him, I let him screw me. It's not something I'm ashamed of. I'd learned by then that sex was a powerful tool and I could use it to my advantage.

I reckon it was about that time that I learned if I screwed around with my body, no one screwed around with my mind. I could take control – use someone rather than be used.

I tried to enjoy sex but I couldn't. For me, it was a means to an end. It still is. It always will be. That's why I have one-night stands. That's enough, sometimes.

Until the guilt takes over – the humiliation, the rejection, the hurt. No one has ever loved me. I fucking hate that, you know. Why didn't anyone love me? I had so much to give.

Me and Brendan screwed lots of times. I'd let him screw me for a fiver, a few fags, a drink; whatever I could get my hands on. We'd been sleeping together for a few months when Malcolm caught him in my bed one night. Brendan was often on nights, so he'd creep into my room and sleep on the job. We'd never come close to being caught as he'd always screw me and leave, but this night the silly idiot fell asleep.

I woke up to find Malcolm laying into him before dragging him out of my room by the hair, naked and bleeding where he had punched him. Brendan fought back; they continued outside in the corridor. I screamed for them to stop, I ran out of my room naked too. I didn't care who saw me. I was wild and trying to pull Malcolm off Brendan, calling him names and digging my nails into his face. But it didn't work.

Apparently one of the other staff had reported him to Malcolm a week earlier. He hadn't wanted to get involved at first but knew he'd get into trouble if anything came out. So when he caught Brendan in my room, he was sent packing then.

I was alone again when he left. I didn't love him, knew he was using me, but I needed him. He said he would take care of me. I wanted someone to trust, to look up to, to be with.

I was chucked out of Ravenside on my sixteenth birthday and moved to a home for young teenage girls. It was hideous – another place I had to fight to survive. I lasted a week before someone nicked all my belongings, but I got wise and stole them back. No one was having my stuff. I might not have had much to call my own but it was mine.

And then I met up with Brendan again. He screwed my life up good and proper for nearly two years after that.

Would I ever fucking learn?

Charley paused when she came to the last page and read the name *Brendan* again. It had to be Brendan Furnival that Ella was referring to. She knew first-hand that Ella was capable of violence, and it also would explain the blood on the banister. That had been Friday, and the day that she'd spoken to Tanya, which was the morning after the attack.

Was it meeting up with Brendan that had tipped Ella over the edge? If it was, she must have been enraged to see Tanya turn up. Charley's stomach flipped over.

She stood up again, knocked on the door. 'Ella, are you there?'

She listened for a moment but there was no reply. She listened again but couldn't hear any signs of movement either. She glanced upwards to the shelf, looking for anything she could use as a weapon.

Come hell or high water, she was getting out of this room.

———

Jean almost cried with relief when she remembered the door system: Ella wouldn't be able to get in. She dared to look again. The window was empty. She took the time to search round for her phone. Where on earth had she put it? She searched in her knitting bag, removing the parts she'd completed. Had the phone dropped inside the bag?

The buzzer on the door went. Jean banged her head on the arm of the chair as she heard it. Rubbing at it, she stood up slowly. Fearful of what she would see, she looked down onto the avenue.

Ella stood back on the pavement. In her arms was Tom. She held on to him firmly by the scruff of his neck.

Jean let out a sob, her hand to her mouth. No, not Tom. If she could injure that man, she could kill Tom with her bare hands.

The buzzer went again.

'Let me in, Jean!' Ella shouted through the letter box. 'I know you've seen what I'm capable of.'

What could she do? With Ella unstable, Jean knew she could easily kill her too if she let her in.

She heard a strangled meow.

Tom!

Maybe if she stayed calm, pretended she hadn't seen anything, then Ella would calm down enough to leave.

A loud screech.

Tom!

'Let me in!'

Another screech, this time louder and more distraught. Jean couldn't bear it any longer. She pressed the release button.

Charley reached a hand up to the shelf above the coats, feeling around unable to see it all from her level. There must be something she could use as a weapon – something to knock Ella off balance if she could talk her way out of the closet.

The shoe boxes were empty. She took down the coats and scarf, searched the pockets to find nothing in those either, threw them to the floor in a temper.

The hooks: could she get them out of the wall? There were four of them on a plinth of wood – they would make a pretty good weapon if she could get them down. With all her body weight behind her, she held on to the outer two hooks and pulled. The wood gave out a creak. Charley held her breath but there was no sign of movement from outside the door; no sign of noise from the flat at all.

Putting all her body weight behind it this time, she lifted her feet from the floor and pulled again.

'Come off the wall. Come off the wall. Come off the fucking wall!' she cried out in frustration, but to no avail. Shoulders sagging, she slumped to the floor.

Her eyes fell on a patch of light that hadn't been there earlier. She crawled towards it on her knees. In the far corner of the room was a hole in the floorboards, no larger than a ten pence coin. The light was brighter there.

She pushed her eye to it and looked through. In dismay, she realised she was looking through another floorboard a couple of inches lower and then down at the floor of her bedroom. It was right in the corner of the room.

Charley couldn't see anything more than a few inches all the way around it, a patch of the carpet and a part of the skirting board. But she could see a black wire. She tugged at it, but it was stuck. She pulled once more: it wouldn't come loose. She peered down into the room again. Whatever it was had been tied to old central heating pipes that ran up the corner of the wall in her room. No wonder she hadn't noticed anything untoward. Surely, it couldn't be ...

Was it a camera? Had Ella been into her flat, set up it up, and been watching her? Watching her and Aaron, in bed, making love? No ... that was sick.

She shook her head to rid it of the images she was seeing, herself and Aaron on the bed, Ella sitting here. The calculating cow!

The conniving, devious, fucking bitch!

What the hell was she up against?

Chapter Thirty-Four

Ella plopped the cat down onto the step and went into the house. The downstairs area was in darkness; she looked around for a light, switched it on. The hallway felt aged but stately, wooden panelling halfway up the walls, deep red tiles on the floor. A few winter coats and a hat were draped over a mahogany coat stand in the corner; a large mirror hung next to it.

The carpet on the stairs was old, threadbare, and hard to the feet. Ella moved around the stair lift and crept upstairs. She knew the layout: it would be the same as her house, before it was converted into flats.

Keeping her back to the wall, she took one step at a time. She didn't trust the nosy cow – she could easily throw something at her. Jean would want to hurt her. She hated Ella just as much as everyone else. That's why she'd been spying on her, telling everyone what she was doing. That's why that social worker had come after her.

You're right. It was Jean's fault.

'I know you saw what I did,' Ella spoke loudly, her voice echoing on the stairs as she inched her way up. 'So now is the time that your neighbourhood watching ends, do you hear me?'

She trod carefully along the landing, creaking floorboards underneath the carpet betraying her every step; she moved forward to the front room, where she always saw Jean sitting. Slowly, she pushed open the door.

Jean was sitting on the edge of the bed. 'Hello, Ella,' she said softly.

'So this is where you do your thing?' Ella pointed a finger and made a circling notion. 'Where you nosy at us from the window. Do you get your kicks out of it?'

'I don't watch. I just ...' Jean faltered.

She's a freak.

'She is!' Ella clapped her hands like an excited child. 'You're a freak! Watching people is perverted.' She stepped into the room. 'I suppose you think what I do is perverted too.'

'No, I don't.'

'But you've been sent to spy on me, haven't you? Who do you work for?'

Jean shook her head. 'I don't work for anyone. I retired a few years back now.'

She must work for someone. She's a spy.

Ella walked around the room, touching the chair, inspecting a painting on the wall, all the time keeping an eye out for Jean to move. She noted Jean's empty mug, the dregs of a drink still inside it; a knitting pattern, the circles of blue ink where she'd marked out the stitches that corresponded with her size.

Then her eyes fell upon a notepad ledged on the windowsill.

'What's that?' She turned to Jean quickly.

'Nothing,' Jean replied.

Ella picked it up, flicked through it, taking time to read each page that had been filled so far. When she got to the last entry, she began to read aloud.

'*19:33: Charley's man arrived.*

'*17:35: Charley home from work.*

'*11:55: woman in red car RB 59 DUC arrived and went into the house with Ella. But I'm sure I heard the woman refer to Ella as Cassie.*'

Ella closed her eyes for a moment and pinched the bridge of her nose. There was that name again.

I told you she was a spy.

'You've been writing everything down.' Ella spoke matter-of-factly.

'Yes. I've been so lonely since my husband died. It's a hobby, something I do to while away the time. I don't mean any harm by it, but I'm housebound, you see. I have osteoporosis and it's hard to move around. I'd love to get out in the garden more often but I –'

'Since when?' Ella interrupted.

'Oh, a few years now. I was diagnosed –'

'Not the fucking osteo – how long have you been writing things UP?'

Jean paused, her eyes momentarily flicking to the rest of the notepads, stacked up neatly in the corner of the room. She averted them quickly, but it was too late. Ella stepped towards them.

'I'll be in every one of these, won't I?'

'No, they go back a lot longer than that!'

Ella snorted. 'You sound as if you're proud of the fact.'

'I meant that I don't just note down what you do. I note down what everyone does.'

She's mad too!

'Why?' said Ella.

Jean sighed. 'For no other reason than for something to do. My life is so monotonous now.'

Ella felt as if her head was ready to explode. Her eyes hurt from staring but she couldn't believe what she saw. If she went into as much detail here as in the last three entries she'd read, Jean would have recorded her every move. If the police were to get hold of the notebooks, there could be evidence of her coming back from attacking Brendan. She wouldn't have an alibi. It could ruin everything, unless she was quick.

Get rid of the evidence.

'No one needs to see them,' Jean added.

Ella nodded, remaining silent. Then she picked up the top notepad and tore out a few pages. She screwed them up and slung them to the floor; ripped out a few more.

'Wait!' Jean protested, slowly getting to her feet, her arms outstretched. 'I promise you I won't show anyone anything but please, don't rip them up. They're all I have.'

Ella turned quickly and brought the back of her hand across Jean's face. The force of it caused Jean to lose her balance and she fell to the floor, landing awkwardly on her knee. Her foot slipped underneath her as she tried to get up again, struggling to take any weight. Reaching up to the mattress, she strained to hoist herself up but it was no use. Jean's knee gave way once more and she cried out in pain.

Ella moved closer to Jean, placing her hands on her knees and bending to her level.

Cry baby.

'Jean,' she spoke softly. 'Why are you spying on me?'

Disorientated, Jean didn't reply.

'Come on, let's get you up to your feet.' Ella held out her hand. 'You can't stay down there all night.'

Jean clasped onto it but before Ella could react, she had pushed up the sleeve of her jumper. Ella let go of Jean's hand and pulled it down again quickly, but not before catching the look of recognition on her face.

'It is you,' Jean cried. 'Oh, Cassie, what did they do to you?'

Ella stepped away, slapping at her cheeks.

Cassie, Cassie, Cassie. She's saying your name again. How does she know you?

She pointed at Jean. 'How do you know my name? Has someone been talking about me? I knew it. All the neighbours know who I am, don't they? You're all in this together. Every one of you – you, and Jake and Charley. You're all out to get me, aren't you? HOW DO YOU KNOW MY NAME?'

'Because I tended to that burn!' Jean shouted. 'I held you in my arms as you cried afterwards. I tried to comfort you. Those little bastards got away with it. I couldn't do anything to protect you.'

Ella roared like an animal in pain at the sound of Jean's words, flicking back in time, recalling a woman at the home who was kind to her, who always told the other kids to back away. The woman who stopped her from drowning Billie when she was twelve years old.

'You!' she whispered loudly.

She left you there.

Jean nodded, tears welling in her eyes. 'I – I looked after you while you were in Ravenside Children's Home.'

'You didn't look after me. You left me there to rot!'

'No, I didn't! You have to believe me. I tried to tell Malcolm, make him understand what was happening, but he told me to keep my mouth shut. And when I threatened to expose him and his staff, he ... he fired me.'

At the mention of Malcolm, Ella flinched. She dragged an image from the back of her mind of a man who used children as punch bags to rid himself of his own demons. A man who took his frustration out on youngsters who couldn't defend themselves. A man who she knew took immense pleasure from the power of his position.

'Have you ANY idea what happened to me after you left me in the hands of that ... that fucking monster?' she screamed.

'No one would listen to me when I was there! I was sacked because I was interfering.' Jean was crying now. 'I wouldn't let it rest so Malcolm had to silence me some way. He said if I continued with my complaint that he would see to it that I was tarnished – say that *I* had been found abusing one of the children.' A sob caught in her throat. 'I've never hurt a child in my life. You remember that, don't you? I wouldn't. I couldn't.'

'You still left me to rot.'

She left you there!

'There was nothing I could do. I reported him while I worked there but they finished me. I reported him again, to the local council. There was an investigation but everything was covered up. I never saw you again until you moved in across the road.'

'Why didn't you tell me that you knew me?'

'Because I didn't know!'

She's lying.

'Liar!'

'Until I heard that woman shouting *Cassie*, I hadn't thought of you in a long time.'

'That's rather nice of you!'

Jean screwed up her face in anguish. 'It doesn't mean that I never think of you. I often wondered how you were.'

'How fucked up they had made me?'

'No ... I don't know.'

'Ah, but you do know,' Ella put her hands on her hips and glared, 'because you see everything that goes on in this street.'

'From a distance! You had blonde hair as a child ... and I last saw you when you were fifteen. We've both changed in that time. And I've never been able to see your scar. I would have known then. I would have remembered the little girl who needed my help. The beautiful little girl that I let down.' Jean's shoulders dropped and she began to cry. 'I couldn't help you. I should have fought more for you, and the other children. It was a terrible place for a child to be, especially one who was torn by grief like you. I'm so sorry.'

It's all her fault.

Ella shook her head fervently. Somewhere in the past minute or so, Jean's face had morphed into Billie's. All she could think about was how that bitch had tortured her, beaten her, bullied her. She pictured her sitting here at her feet, a young girl kneeling by the side of the bed almost as if in prayer, begging for forgiveness.

She hates you.

'You never liked me!' she shouted.

'That's not true!' said Jean.

'I could pull your teeth out with pliers, rip out your nails one by one, and it wouldn't be half as much agony as you caused me. You made my life hell!'

'No, I didn't. Ella, you have me mixed up with someone else. I –'

'Shut up.' Ella drew back her fist and punched Jean. She pushed her backwards so that she was flat on the floor, straddled her chest and punched her again.

'Please!' Jean coughed, spitting out blood. 'Stop.'

Do it!

Ella's hands slipped around Jean's throat. All the time, she could see Billie, knew that the only way she could get rid of her resentment was to squeeze the breath out of the bitch. Yes, she was in control and it felt good, knowing that Billie would never hurt her again.

'I hate you,' she whispered, before squeezing harder.

Jean's arms flailed as she fought with the pressure applied to her neck. All she could see was Ella's face, her demonic eyes, her angry expression. She couldn't get her breath; it hurt to even try. The blood rushed to her head, almost making her oblivious to the pain in her knee. Her eyes began to water, her vision becoming dim around the outside as it slowly ebbed away. When she could struggle no more, her arms dropped to her sides. She took one last look across the room, over at the window, the chair, her knitting.

She would never be able to finish her snazzy purple cardigan now.

I was ten when the accident happened. That's what I was told to say. By the adults. Malcolm told me if I said any different, he'd lock me in the room with Billie and leave her to her own means. He knew that Billie bullied me. I supposed it saved him a job – one child less to thump.

Us kids were playing in the garden after school. It was a September day and I was sitting under the tree at the bottom of the garden, away from the others. I had my nose in a book, as usual. So I didn't hear anyone coming near. When I did look up, Billie was in front of me with Mikey, one of the younger boys. He had a yellow canister in his hands.

'Go on, do it,' said Billie, pushing Mikey forward.

He stepped back. I could see the fear in his eyes. He was pleading with me to run away but I was too scared to move.

Billy pushed him forward again. 'Do it, or I'll kick your head in.'

Mikey looked at me with dismay. Then he squirted the liquid over my arm. At the time, I didn't know that it was gas. How would I? I was ten years old. Before I could move away, Billie lit a match and threw it at me.

The liquid lit up and in seconds, the shiny polyester material of my cheap tracksuit top was a ball of flames. My arm was on fire!

Mikey yelled and ran away but Billie stood and stared. If it wasn't for the quick reaction of a new lady assistant, I'm not sure what would have happened to me. She came running over, pulled off her coat, and doused out the flame. Then she picked me up in her arms, took me back into the house, and called an ambulance before anyone could stop her.

I can still recall the smell of my skin singeing as the material stuck to it.

I can still remember my screams.

I can still remember the pain.

I had to have five operations to repair it, and skin taken from my thigh to put over it, the wound was so deep. It left most of my *wrist and forearm burned and shrivelled away, twisted and bumpy, like the material of the jacket had seeped into my skin. The redness has faded over the years, changed to candy-floss pink, but I keep it covered anyway. I hate having it on show. It reminds me of a time when I was vulnerable.*

I'm not vulnerable anymore.

Chapter Thirty-Five

Charley hadn't heard a sound from the flat for a while. She wondered where Ella was, what she was doing, all the time trying not to think that anything terrible had happened to Aaron. She wasn't sure how long she'd been trapped but she did know he would have arrived by now. An hour must have passed, probably more.

Once Ella came back, she was going to try and talk to her again. Persuading: she did it all the time for her job. Coercing frightened women to stand up for themselves was part of her role, even when she knew that if she'd been in their situation she would never press charges either.

Maybe if she could get Ella to offload, make her feel empathized with, she might let her out. Then she could make a run for it.

Feeling calmer for now, she sat still. If it took her all night, hell, what did she have to lose?

She would get out of this closet.

———

Ella stood in the middle of Jean's room, clenching and unclenching her fists.

How the hell did she find you? She couldn't have known about you. It's too much of a coincidence. And who else knows? Does everyone know about you?

She stopped for a moment and looked across at her house, the front door left wide open in her hurry to get across to Jean.

It's all her fault – that Charley.

Ella nodded slowly. 'If she hadn't come along and poked her nose in my business, none of this would have happened. She deserves to be locked in that closet. Until she can be a good girl, she's going nowhere. I won't feed her and I won't let her out. No one knows she's there. I can do this as long as I want. I can keep this game up forever.'

She stepped over Jean's body, glancing at it briefly.

'Why did you have to fuck my life up? What did I do? I wasn't naughty yet I was punished every day. And now look what you made me do. I hurt Aaron and I killed Billie. It's your fault.'

But just as quickly, her jumbled thoughts changed direction. Dropping to her knees, seeing not Billie but Jean's face again, distorted by fear, eyes staring widely ahead, she froze. Had she killed her?

She touched her face, gently. She was warm.

She's dead!

'No.'

Was she still breathing? Ella wasn't sure.

'I'm in so much trouble.' Then she frowned, looked around the room. Where the fuck was Billie?

She turned to the door quickly. 'I have to get out of here.'

———

In the quiet of the closet, Charley's heart began to boom when a door slammed shut. Then, footsteps. There was someone inside the flat. She stood up, pressed her ear to the door, praying it wasn't her imagination.

'Ella?' She knocked on the door. 'Aaron! Who's there? Please let me out.'

'You're not going anywhere.'

Charley's eyes welled with tears at the sound of Ella's voice. She didn't want it to be Ella. She wanted it to be Aaron. Why hadn't he come to get her out?

She knocked on the door again. 'Ella, please. I need to pee.'

'Piss in the closet.'

'I can't do that. Please let me out and then we can talk again. You'd like that, wouldn't you?'

'You never wanted to talk to me after you started seeing lover boy.'

Charley held in a sob as she thought of Aaron again. *Keep cool*, she told herself.

'I know,' she said. 'I'm sorry. But we can talk now.'

'Like we have all the time in the world?'

'Exactly.'

'Sorry, I'm busy.'

'Two minutes! You can spare me that much time, surely.'

'Okay.'

She gave in far too quickly for Charley's liking but, now she had her attention, she didn't know what to say, or even where to start. But Ella filled in her silence.

'You're a support worker, right?'

'Yes, I am.'

'What exactly do you do for your job?'

'I help people, talk to them and listen to their problems. If I can get someone else to assist them, I do that too. Otherwise, I encourage them to help themselves.'

'Maybe I could have got better if you had been my support worker, like you rallied round that woman, that Margaret Owen.'

Charley's brow furrowed. How did she know one of her clients?

'I followed you there. I saw you talking on her doorstep.'

Charley shuddered, goose-bumps rising over her skin. The last time she had seen Margaret Owen was just before she was due in court as a witness. That had been eight weeks ago, not long after she had moved in. Christ, had Ella been following her all that time?

No, she couldn't have. She must be bluffing.

But the Ella she was dealing with wasn't rational; she was quite capable of doing something like that.

'If you were a proper support worker, you would have helped me anyway,' Ella continued. 'You would have listened to me, and not gone off at the first sniff of a man. You should have been there for me too.'

'I know. I'm sorry. I –'

'Fuck you, Charley!'

'But I care about you, Ella. Please, I can help you, if you let me out of the closet.'

'Piss off. I'm not that stupid.'

Charley ran a hand through her hair and stepped back from the door. Then she tried a different tack. 'Ella, did you assault Brendan Furnival the other night?'

'No.'

'It doesn't matter if you did because –'

'It was Cassie. She just hit him and hit him and hit him.'

'I would have!' she cried excitedly, realising she was getting somewhere. Ella had never mentioned the name Cassie before. 'I know of him and what he's done in the past. He's an evil man.'

'He was the father of my baby.'

'Is that Amy?'

'Yes.'

'She died.'

Charley put her fist in her mouth to stop herself from crying out. She didn't want to feel sorry for Ella but she could feel her anguish. The pain of losing their daughter two weeks after Dan had died came flooding back, grief ripping through her as if it were yesterday. It had torn her apart. She squeezed shut her eyes to stop the tears, trying to regain control of her breathing, stay calm. She had to keep it together.

Pushing away her sorrow, she tried to use the information to her advantage.

'Ella, I'm so sorry,' she replied, her voice now even and authoritative.

'No one else was. They took her from me.'

'Who took her?'

'The angels. Amy was my little angel.'

'How old was she?'

'I don't know. I can't remember.'

'You would have been a good mother, I'm sure,' she told her.

'I know.'

A sniff: was Ella crying now? She tried to get her to open up some more.

'Brendan Furnival wasn't a nice man, Ella. If he hurt you, it wasn't your fault.'

'All men are nasty. I hate them all. Especially Aaron; he took you away from me.'

Charley had to ask, she had to know what she was up against. 'Have you seen him this evening?'

'Yes.'

'Has he been into your flat?'

'No. He's been into your flat, though. And so have I.'

'Have –'

'He won't come to your rescue. I made sure of that.'

'What do you mean?'

Silence.

Charley banged on the door. 'Ella, what do you mean? What have you done?'

'I stuck a knife in him.'

'NO!'

———⌣———

As Charley banged on the door, Ella rushed to her feet. What was she doing sitting on the floor having a conversation as if she had all the time in the world? Everyone would be coming after her soon.

You have to leave.

'Yes, I'll do that.' Ignoring Charley's protests, she reached under the bed for a suitcase and unzipped it quickly. Opening a drawer, she scooped up everything inside and shoved it in. Then she looked around. Was there anything else she should take?

You can't come back.

Her books! She couldn't leave behind her beloved treasures. But she wouldn't be able to carry too many. There wouldn't be room.

You know that, don't you?

She would take three and that would be her limit.

You can't come back. Ever.

Ella headed off to choose.

———⌣———

Charley sobbed as her hand slapped on the door again and again. The thought of Aaron lying wounded downstairs when she was locked up brought out the claustrophobia she had been battling to contain. What if he was bleeding, and there was no one there to tend to him? He might bleed out and die! He might even be … no, she couldn't bear it.

With her breathing rapidly ascending into panic, the tips of her fingers started to tingle. She closed her eyes, trying to think of nothing. Keeping her mind blank was the only way she could calm herself down. She concentrated on conjuring up the colour purple. She'd read online somewhere that this helped focus the mind and return the breathing to normal. But all she could see was black.

Suddenly she heard a noise. She listened carefully. It sounded like a zip – then a drawer opening and closing a moment later. A thump as something dropped to the floor. Her breathing took on a life of its own again. Was Ella leaving? She'd be left in the closet. No one would know where she was. She could die in here and no one would know!

'Ella?' She knocked on the door this time. 'Please let me out and we can talk!' She listened for the front door to open but nothing. 'Ella? Ella, are you there? ELLA! Where the fuck are you?'

'I'm here, for goodness sake. Chill out.'

Tears of relief fell. Charley wasn't sure if she could keep it together for much longer.

'I don't understand what's going on,' she said. 'Why would you lock me in here?'

'Are you stupid? You've just read my notes!'

'I know, I understand that, but –'

'How can you understand with your perfect life and your perfect house and your perfect job and your perfect new boyfriend? Just because your husband died, you think you've endured grief? You don't know anything.'

Charley closed her eyes, rubbed at them for a moment. How could Ella think her life was perfect when she had lost the man she thought she would spend the rest of her days with? She might be with Aaron now, and yes, it was a new beginning for her, but that would never take away the loss that she'd felt. She couldn't even use that to talk to Ella about. In her mental state, Ella wouldn't understand.

Knowing she couldn't reason with her anymore, Charley tried a different tack.

'This is ridiculous,' she said, her tone of voice dismissive. 'I can't do this through a door. Open up, Ella, or I won't talk to you anymore.'

Ella slid the books into a bag and then sat on the bed. She stayed quiet for a while to see. Would Charley really not talk to her anymore?

She's bluffing. She just wants to get out of the closet. Ignore her.

But minutes later, she couldn't bear it.

'Charley?' she spoke into the silence.

'Oh, so now you want to talk.'

'Are you mad at me?'

'Of course not. I just want to talk to you face to face. That's what friends do, Ella.'

'I don't need a friend.'

'Yes, you do. Everyone needs friends.'

You need to get away!

Ella slapped at her face, knowing that Charley was right. She would be much better if she had someone to help her get through the bad times. Then, perhaps she would feel better soon and the dark days would be replaced with sunshine.

She'll leave you.

She shook her head, trying to rid it of the uncertainty.

They all leave you eventually.

'Stop!' she sobbed. 'I don't want to listen to you anymore!'

'Who are you talking to, Ella?'

'I'm a bad person, Charley.'

'No, you're not!'

'I don't know what to do.'

'Let me out and we can talk things through.'

'It's too late. I'm all fucked up again.'

———⁀———

Charley could sense victory and her voice rose with excitement. 'Let me out, Ella, and we can have fun together. I can help you. You'd like that, wouldn't you?'

'I'm beyond help. I told you.'

'I don't give up on people. I'll help you. Would you like that, Ella?'

A pause. 'You're trying to trick me!'

'No, I'm not. I just want to get out of this closet.' Charley laughed half-heartedly. 'It's not much fun in here, is it?'

'It's not supposed to be fun.'

'I know.'

Silence again.

Charley wanted to bang and kick at the door but she held in her frustration for one last time.

'Let me out, Ella, please,' she begged. 'I'd like to be your friend.'

'You promise you won't hurt me?'

'I promise.'

Chapter Thirty-Six

The second Charley heard the key turn in the lock and the door open a smidgeon, she held onto the side of the frame and kicked out with all the strength she could muster. The door caught Ella straight in the face, knocking her to the floor. Charley blocked it as it flew back at her. Then she ran.

Behind her, she heard a scream but was out of the bedroom and into the hallway before Ella yanked her back by the hair.

'Come here, you lying bitch!'

Charley grabbed for the door lock, fingers reaching to open it. But the more Ella pulled, the more she couldn't grasp it. Turning slightly, she slapped out at her face. Ella punched her on the side of her head and she cried out in pain. Adrenalin pumping through her, Charley bunched up her fists and hit out like she'd never thought possible. After a few blows had landed, she finally gained enough breathing space to make a run through the door.

Ella followed, pouncing on her back and wrapping her arms around her neck. They fell to the floor. Charley kicked back as she tried to crawl away. She could see the entrance door in her sight, out onto Warwick Avenue. If she could get to the street and run, she could summon help.

'No!' cried Ella.

In desperation, Charley kicked out again. She was not going to let Ella get the upper hand.

But Ella managed to scramble in front of her. She blocked her exit at the top of the stairs.

'You had no intentions of helping me, had you?' she said, eyes narrowed in anger, bloodied fists formed, ready to pounce again.

Charley shook her head. 'All I wanted was to get out of that closet and as far away as possible from you!'

'Back to your precious Aaron?'

Charley's heart sank as Ella held up her bloodied hands. There was blood on her trousers too.

'Were you not listening back there, you silly bitch?' Ella taunted. 'I told you, I stabbed him! He was unconscious when I left but I doubt he'll be alive now. There was blood pouring from his stomach. I think he –'

Charley felt a sob bubble in her throat but it released itself as a roar of fury. Arms outstretched, she charged at Ella, knocking them both down the stairs. They tumbled over; for a moment, she was disorientated until they reached a stop. Charley landed two steps above Ella, who fell further, smashing her forehead on the tiles as she clattered to the floor.

Dazed, Charley glanced at Ella; saw she wasn't moving. She sat a moment longer, enough to catch her breath. Still, Ella was motionless. Realising she would have to step over her to get past, she tried to stay calm.

To her left, through the balustrades, she could see the door to her flat. It stood ajar, streaks of blood on the handle. She sobbed again. All along, she'd thought Ella was bluffing. Had she really killed Aaron?

Her natural instinct was to make a run for it, out of the entrance door and into the night, to get the hell out of the house. But seeing the blood there, as well as on Ella's hands, she knew it was likely that she *had* hurt Aaron.

She looked at the entrance door. Would Ella have locked it so that she couldn't get out? After all, she'd been sneaky enough to remove her phone and shoes.

She glanced over at the door to her flat again. Could it be Ella's blood on the handle and not Aaron's?

With a resigned feeling, she knew what she had to do.

She got up slowly, moving down onto the next step and then onto the floor. Taking a deep breath, she stepped over Ella, half expecting a hand to shoot up and grab her ankle. But all she heard was a groan. Then she ran to the entrance door.

She heard a scream behind her as she reached it.

'Don't leave me!' Ella cried.

Startled, Charley turned back, noting the demented expression in Ella's eyes. She knew this was her only chance. It was either her or Ella, and she wanted out. She wanted to get on with her life without some mad bitch stalking her, watching her every move.

'Nobody leaves me,' Ella seethed. 'Nobody fucking leaves me!'

Charley glared at her for a moment. 'Don't count on it.'

She opened the door and ran, flying down the steps, praying she wouldn't stumble. Wanting to put as much space as she could between them, she headed across the green and over to the busier roads up above. The rain hindering her view, the earth slippery beneath her bare feet, she kept on running. There was no one around. What the hell was the time? She had no idea.

If she could see someone – anyone – in the distance, she could run to them. But she didn't dare shout out until she was farther away.

She reached the road and, oblivious to the cuts on her feet, the discomfort from the fall, she ran straight ahead. It was a few seconds before a car came into sight. She waved her arms in the air, praying she wouldn't be ignored. As it drew nearer, she stepped into the road in front of it, causing it to halt with a screech. In the dark, she could make out a man and woman sitting in the front, the man gesticulating wildly at her.

'Please!' She ran to the woman in the passenger seat. 'Please, I need your phone. My neighbour has attacked me. My boyfriend … I don't know where he is. I don't know what she's done.'

'Don't give her your phone, Maggie,' the man told her. 'It could be a trick. She might car-jack us or something.'

'Please!' Charley reached across to him. 'Give me your PHONE!'

'Look at the state of her, Charles!' Sensing her distress, the woman rummaged in her bag and gave Charley hers. 'Can I help?'

Charley held on to her chest. It hurt to inhale, thinking of Aaron. But, before she could reply, she heard the noise of a car screeching along the road towards them. Its engine roared as the accelerator was floored. And she knew.

She knew it would be Ella.

As the car came into view, panic engulfed her again. She was in the middle of the road. In her frame of mind, she knew Ella would drive straight at her.

She turned back to the couple. 'Call the police,' she pleaded. 'Thirty-seven, Warwick Avenue. Please!'

Quickly, she ran back to the pavement. There was nowhere to go but farther into the grassed area. The sound of her cries ringing in her ears, she tore across the wet ground. Her feet slipped on the muddy grass and she scrambled to stay upright. Glancing over her shoulder, fear mounting inside her, she saw Ella clip the wing of the car that had stopped. Then she watched in terror as she mounted the kerb and drove straight at her.

Charley ran until she feared her lungs would explode, gaining momentum as she heard the noise of the engine getting closer. She looked ahead in the dark, hoping that a shadow would loom up in the distance, revealing itself slowly as somewhere she could hide. But she knew there were only one or two benches ahead, the odd bin perhaps. If she stooped down behind one, it wouldn't stop the car from injuring her, but it might slow down the imminent impact.

Where the hell were they?

Ella was nearly behind her now. Charley knew the game was over. In a moment, she would be ploughed down. Looking over her shoulder for one final time, she realised the car was so close that she could see Ella's face now. A look of pure determination was set upon it, not a hint of panic. A sob caught in Charley's throat. Oh, God, Ella really wanted to hurt her.

Charley held her stare for a moment. It was as if time stood still for them to acknowledge each other one last time. From somewhere deep within, she found enough breath to scream.

Rearing out of control, the car sailed past her, tearing across the grass. Head on, it crashed into a tree a few feet ahead. A thunderous bang woke up the quiet night, reverberating through the ground. Charley covered her ears; the noise was deafening but over in seconds.

Steam rose from the bonnet where the radiator had been crushed; the front of the car was embedded in the tree. Ella hadn't been wearing a seatbelt; the force of the crash had thrown her through the windscreen, half in and out of the car.

Unable to stop herself, Charley ran towards it but, as she drew close, she could see Ella's eyes were dead, still. Blood seeped from the side of her open lips. Her arms stayed where they had fallen.

The sense of déjà vu overwhelmed Charley as she stood barefoot in the rain. In her mind once again, she could hear the sirens of the emergency services. She could see the flashing lights of the vehicles coming into view. Except this time, it wouldn't be in her imagination. This time it would all be real.

The couple in the car came running towards her. The man reached her first.

'Are you okay?' he asked. 'I'm sorry I didn't believe you but you can't be too careful nowadays. But when I saw that... that maniac run up the pavement and head towards you, well, I –'

'Did you call for help?' Charley interrupted, holding onto his arm as she felt her knees wobbling.

'Yes, love, they're on their way.' He took off his coat, wrapped it around Charley's shoulders.

His wife came up beside them with a puff. 'I can't believe my eyes,' she said, before looking over at the car. 'Is she … is she …?'

Charley nodded. It was all she felt able to do. Soon more assistance would arrive. No one could help Ella but for now, the images Charley had carried of Dan in the car had been erased.

The nightmare really was over.

But there was still one thing she needed to know. She turned back towards Warwick Avenue and ran.

Epilogue

The next two weeks went by in a blur of police statements, hospital visits, and packing. As soon as Charley had all her belongings in boxes, she was never setting foot inside thirty-seven, Warwick Avenue again.

The incident had been front page headlines in *The Sentinel* for three nights, news on the local television channels the following evening. No one could understand how a young woman living in a quiet and respectful street could have been so violent. Some of the neighbours had been interviewed. Only Jake Carter, from number thirty-six, refused to speak to the journalist when asked.

Ella had left Jean's door open in her rush to get back to Charley. The police had gone across to find Jean's body alongside several notebooks thrown to the floor around her. On reading their contents, they came to the conclusion that Ella, in her warped state of mind, thought she had motive to kill the elderly neighbour. Jean's home help, Ruby, had been devastated and had insisted on adopting Tom rather than let him be re-homed. It was the least she could do.

Brendan Furnival was out of hospital and recovering from his injuries. Charley had mentioned to the police that Ella had confessed to her but on further questioning, Furnival had refused to say he knew who his attacker was. And, although he'd always have the mental, and some physical, scars after the attack, Charley still couldn't help coming out on the side of Ella over that. Some things must have been hard for her to bear.

Later, once all the forensic evidence had been gathered, Charley was told by the police that a man found dead in his bath the day before, in the north of the city, had also been linked to Ella. Even now, it was hard for her to imagine she had once shared a house with a killer. She'd read Ella's notebook again, plus the loose pages she'd seen in the closet, but was no nearer to understanding whether it was all true, partly true, or completely fictional – another thing that would remain unsolved. Charley had her suspicions, but it wasn't her place to speculate.

The worst thing on the night in question had been not knowing about Aaron. Had she left him dead at the house? She'd raced back across the muddy field, hoping that the ambulance wouldn't be too far behind.

She'd found him slouched against the back of the settee, eyes closed, head lolling to one side. Blood had soaked through his jumper and his jacket, pooled at his jeans. She'd lifted his head to feel for a pulse, crying with relief when she had found one. Moments later, the ambulance had arrived and he'd gone to hospital and straight into surgery. It had been a long and tense evening but thankfully, he'd pulled through. Seeing him the next day, sitting up in a hospital bed with colour in his cheeks and that smile she knew so well, was the moment that she realised everything was going to be okay.

'Come on, you,' she smiled at her passenger. 'Are you sure you can manage to walk that far?'

'Of course, I can,' Aaron replied. 'I can survive anything.'

'So all those ouches, ows, oohs, and ahs – they're all for show, then?'

'It's my equivalent to man-flu and I'm using it as long as I can get sympathy.' Aaron looked at her with the expression of a puppy who wanted a cuddle. 'She nearly took my spleen!'

Charley indulged him with a tickle under his chin. 'You're such a wimp.'

'I know.'

They'd parked up in a new development of apartments and houses along Wedgwood Terrace, a couple of miles away in Meir Heath. It was another beautiful area of the city. But this time, Charley was going to view a flat with an intercom and a camera and, she hoped, some friendly neighbours.

Aaron released his seatbelt, wincing as it caught across his stomach. 'Are you sure you don't want to take me up on my offer?'

Charley placed her hand on his thigh and leaned across to kiss him.

'I'm really grateful, but this is another short-term lease. Six months.' She smiled at him shyly. 'And then, who knows after that?'

'If we get that far, maybe we should start afresh with a new pad? I could sell my house too.'

Charley nodded her reply and smiled.

The estate agent was waiting for them at the entrance and let them into the two-storey building. 'Service charges are in with the rent. There's a fully fitted kitchen with all appliances,' she said, going into practiced sales mode. 'And wait until you see the view from the lounge area.'

Aaron followed the two women up to the first floor. 'If it has a walk-in closet, we're not moving in,' he said.

'Sorry?' the estate agent turned back to him.

Charley giggled. 'He wants to know if it has lots of storage space.'

'Yes. And it has ample-sized bedrooms, too.'

Charley turned to give Aaron a warning look. As they drew level to the landing, a face appeared over the banister of the upper floor.

'Hi there,' a voice shouted down to them.

They all looked up to see a man, mid-thirties.

'Are you moving in?'

'Yes, I might be,' said Charley.

'Great.' He came down the stairs to them. 'It's a nice place to live. Not much goes on. We keep ourselves to ourselves, you know. It's quiet too.'

'Sounds just how I like it!' Charley enthused.

'Marvellous. I'll probably see you around.' He continued on past them. At the top of the stairs towards the ground floor, he gave a friendly smile. 'I'm sure we'll get on like a house on fire.'

Charley shuddered as if someone had walked through her. Those were the exact words that Ella had said to her on the first day they'd met. Memories of the last few months came flooding into her mind. How lucky she had been to escape from Ella's clutches. To get out of that closet, to find Aaron and to find him alive. She couldn't bear the thought of losing him too.

'You okay?' Aaron touched her arm, a look of concern on his face. 'You've gone a little pale.'

Charley took a deep breath as she pushed her thoughts to one side. Then she nodded at him.

It was all about the future now. There was no need to dwell on the past.

Acknowledgments

My dream has always been to have a traditional deal with a publisher. So I'm often asked what it was like to go from self-publishing and being in complete control of everything to now having a team of people behind me. I can tell you it has been amazing. So these thanks have to be about everyone who is in Team Mel right now.

Firstly, thanks must go to Maddy Milburn, who never ceases to fill me with confidence when I have none left. Who gets my writing for what it is, who encourages me at every opportunity, guides me and above all treats me as an equal. I'm not often lost for words but, well, thank you so much.

Thank you to Emilie Marneur for her friendship, wisdom and patience. Also to the gang at Amazon Publishing, to Sana and Ben, the Thomas & Mercer design team, Paul for his patience and skills creating the interior.

My editor, Charlotte Herscher who added something to my words that I never thought was possible. I've learned so much from you and it was a wonderful process to go through. Also my copy editor, Jennifer, who added even more sparkle and glitter.

My biggest confidantes, Talli Roland, Alison Niebieszczanski and my new recruit, Sharon Sant. Ladies, you keep my rocky world steady! For the many authors and writers I now have the pleasure of calling friends. Thank you for all your support.

For all my readers, many of whom I now call friends too. Thank you for the emails and messages and continued support. I love that you enjoy my smutty grit-lit just as much as I love to write it. Also a special mention to Tracy Shayler who sent me my first reader email and made me cry because she liked my writing so much.

Thank you to David Jackson, Matt Hilton, Emlyn Rees, Will Carver, Mandasue Heller, Niamh O Connor and David Mark for offering to give me quotes when they had read *Taunting the Dead*. You'll never know how much that meant.

Finally, to Chris. What can I say, fella. You are the man and always will be. I know you have so much to put up with and I thank you for your patience and support too. I got there!

About the Author

Mel Sherratt has been a self-described "meddler of words" ever since she can remember. After winning her first writing competition at the age of 11, she has rarely been without a pen in her hand or her nose in a book.

Since successfully self-publishing *Taunting the Dead* and seeing it soar to the rank of number one best-selling police procedural in the Amazon Kindle store in 2012, Mel has gone on to publish three more books in the critically acclaimed *The Estate* Series.

Mel has written feature articles for *The Guardian*, the Writers and Artists website, and *Writers Forum Magazine*, to name just a few, and regularly speaks at conferences, event and talks.

She lives in Stoke-on-Trent, Staffordshire, with her husband and her terrier, Dexter (named after the TV serial killer, with some help from her Twitter fans), and makes liberal use of her hometown as a backdrop for her writing.

Her website is www.melsherratt.co.uk and you can find her on Twitter at @writermels.